Reflections

Reflections

Richard Paul Junghans

Copyright © 2015 Richard Paul Junghans

All rights reserved.

ISBN-13: 9781508477044
ISBN-10: 1508477043
Library of Congress Control Number: 2015903247
CreateSpace Independent Publishing Platform
North Charleston, South Carolina

Dedication

This Book is dedicated to and salutes, our National Emblem Flag, the men and women who have served our country, as well as all people that are true to the United States of America and believe in its Constitution.

Table of Contents

Prologue ix
Chapter One 1
Chapter Two 9
Chapter Three 17
Chapter Four 23
Chapter Five 26
Chapter Six 31
Chapter Seven 38
Chapter Eight 44
Chapter Nine 54
Chapter Ten 62
Chapter Eleven 65
Chapter Twelve 67
Chapter Thirteen 72
Chapter Fourteen 77
Chapter Fifteen 83
Chapter Sixteen 87
Chapter Seventeen 96
Chapter Eighteen 101
Chapter Nineteen 109
Chapter Twenty 125

Chapter Twenty-One 149
Chapter Twenty-Two.. 155
Chapter Twenty-Three.. 158
Chapter Twenty-Four.. 166
Chapter Twenty-Five... 176
Chapter Twenty-Six... 199
Chapter Twenty-Seven 208
Chapter Twenty-Eight..209
Chapter Twenty-Nine 214
Chapter Thirty... 217
Chapter Thirty-One 221
Chapter Thirty-Two... 223
Chapter Thirty-Three... 236
Chapter Thirty-Four.. 242
Chapter Thirty-Five... 254
Chapter Thirty-Six... 268
Chapter Thirty-Seven 269
Chapter Thirty-Eight... 276
Chapter Thirty-Nine 285
Chapter Forty 292
Chapter Forty-One..298
Chapter Forty-Two..306
Chapter Forty-Three... 311
Chapter Forty-Four.. 324
Chapter Forty-Five... 328
Chapter Forty-Six... 331
Chapter Forty-Seven 337
   Epilogue
Chapter Forty-Eight... 342
Chapter Forty-Nine 348

Prologue

Sky-splitting lighting! crashing thunder! near Cyclone Winds! Driving, Blinding Rain! Nothing even remotely close had ever descended upon their mountain and cabin before. Nothing!

They had ventured out on the wrap-around deck to see if its roof was still holding, and as they drew back from the raging storm to the best protection they could find on the mountain cabin deck they continued to watch the incredible increase in the torrential rains and the water cascading down the mountain from above and on down their drive. As they watched by the light of the lightning they could see the lanes and roads washing out below them. They agreed that the alert that they had received from the Mountain Emergency Patrol and the National Guard to be prepared for total evacuation on a two-hour or less notice was completely within reason.

In all of the near twenty-five years since Harry had retired and lived in this high mountain, forested sanctuary he had never seen a storm to remotely approach this one. They would be lucky if their home survived the water and probable tree and mudslides, if not the rain-loosened rockslides, and if they could get out with their lives and their German Shepard, Breeze.

They were situated where a helicopter could not "bucket" them out because of the tall pine and aspen trees and the severe slope of the mountain, so they would have to wait for a military large-wheel or treaded ATV to try to get up to them over the washed out terrain.

Unknown to them, what had been the main service road along the base of the mountain was now a twenty-foot wide by ten-to-fifteen foot deep panoptic, churning ditch, nearly three miles long, all the way down to the already overflowing dam threatened Estes Park lake below.

Their heavy-duty Chevy SUV at this point was useless; their basement garage and storage area, its wall already breached, was rapidly flooding, but fortunately the backup electric power generator still had twenty or more hours of reserve and was holding so that he could still partially open the garage door and periodically let the flooding waters rush out.

But, somehow or another, reflecting on all of the ups and downs in their lives, he felt little concern that they would not overcome this too. He had always 'made it' before. Against all and greater odds; he had even 'found her'.

As he drew her closer into the crook of his arm, and looked down at her it came to him that it was high time to begin to think through and put down on paper the unbelievable narrative of their lives. One way or another, it had spanned three-quarters of a century, and it still continued to be as unpredictable, unexpected, and as exciting as ever.

And then as they huddled together, true to their expectations, a treaded ATV crawled across the adjoining property and pulling up to the side of the deck unloaded four National Guard Men who quickly loaded each of them and their essential luggage up the access ladder into the vehicle. The burliest of the four gathered up their eighty pound German Shepard, 'Breeze' in his arms and tossed her up with them. 'My God, what a conclusion!' he thought.

Taking one more brief look out onto the Colorado snow covered mountain peaks that she had brought him 'home' to some nearly twenty five years ago, its contrasting normal tranquility further brought him to the realization that the time had finally arrived to think through it all and let loose the story and the facts of it; to set the record straight. To tell the entire story.

By now that all were gone save for the two of them and the children and grandchildren scattered about. It was time to drop the wall; to open the pages to the past and set forth the facts of the extraordinary life and chronicle of 'Harry Morgan.'

As they rode down the mountain his thoughts were drawn to when his now relaxed life style was very much different; to a time when his sustained life-long sense of a need for control as well as privacy had encouraged a wall of silence to be thrown up about it all; to a time of tension some fifty years before, where this story begins.

CHAPTER ONE

Harry Morgan mashed together the production report that he had been trying to make some sense out of, and angrily wadding it into a grapefruit-sized ball, slammed it into his wastebasket. "Damn it all!!! Can't anyone around here ever get anything right?"

It was not unusual for him to berate what he viewed as the senseless lack of useful information that he found in these reports, but today he had been restive when he arrived at work and the carelessness of the report was more than he felt he could forgive.

Unable to ignore his restlessness and growing aggravation, but seeking some diversion, he gathered together the other papers and reports on his desk and stacking them on a large side-table in the corner, turned to see what he could find to look at through the one-way office window that overlooked the manufacturing area.

Shortly after his appointment as the Executive Vice President and General Manager of Manufacturing at The W. D. Bender Company, Harry commandeered the company founder's old executive office suite, unoccupied since his untimely death.

Harry immediately ordered extensive remodeling including the one-way window, a private entrance, un-listed private telephone lines, and the complete soundproofing of the room. These precautions against eavesdroppers and his rigid attitude of administering the company on a strictly disciplined and need-to-know basis reinforced his feeling of security. These restrictions also served to insulate him from all but the most infrequent voluntary communications and relationships with the work force.

To deal with this isolation, Harry had established a very select company-wide network of "friends and cronies". It was their mission to circulate; to serve as Harry's eyes and ears, and to get the word around that he was always available for off-the-record consultations, and that his door was always open to any employee. The success of this campaign was best spelled out by the various names that in a very short time had been assigned to Harry's office. The 'Spider's Web', the 'Boar's Nest', or the 'Kennel'-- depending on whom was speaking.

Despite his intuition, Harry seemed quite ignorant of these characterizations and believed that the workers endorsed his slogan posted above the time clock: **"We can all reach any level of success if we all work as though we have but one mind and purpose."** Of course, the **"one mind and purpose"** was unquestionably Harry's.

Discovering nothing of interest, Harry drew away from the window, still bothered by the continued uneasiness that told him that there were forces somewhere at work that could disrupt if not weaken his empirical system. However, for most of his working years he had handled threatening people. Those that he could not control or win over, he disposed of with suggestions of planned greater opportunities elsewhere, a farewell party, and a hearty slap on the back. Harry caught himself smiling at the thought that there really wasn't much difference between a hearty slap on the back and a swift kick in the rump to accelerate the departure. Remarkably few people realized what happened or the difference.

Harry finally decided that his self-esteem was on the mend. He would get back to work and start developing his own report. After all, he reflected, 'Why should I worry, I am still in charge. It's only a matter of days and I'll totally control this company; its people; everything. I'll make my move at tomorrow afternoon's board of directors meeting. After all, I vote and control fifty-one percent of the voting stock and proxies. Hell's fires! Tomorrow I'll vote myself in as the company's Chairman of the Board and Chief Executive Officer, and not one person can do one damn thing about it!' Harry settled himself into his expensive leather chair and smiled. It was going to be a good day after all! He was feeling great! Harry swiveled his chair around and surveyed the room that he had considered his life objective since his first trip here when he was just seven years old.

Harry's mother, Mr. Bender's office cleaning lady, had come to ask Mr. Bender for some time off and seven year old Harry had delightedly tagged along. Harry's older sister was featured in a Chautauqua assembly scheduled for the following Saturday evening, and Arvilla Morgan hoped that she could get off work to see her daughter perform.

Despite Harry's delight in and awe of Mr. Bender's office, from the moment he saw him it never occurred to Harry to like Mr. Bender. Sitting behind that immense and ornately topped desk Mr. Bender appeared ruthless to Harry, and to own and manipulate all of the riches and power in the world. Harry instantly disliked everything he saw. Harry never forgot that his first reaction to the man was to want to cry and to strike out at him.

"Of course, Mrs. Morgan, you can have the time off. As a matter of fact, Mrs. Bender and I noticed in The Weekly that Miriam has a leading part. That was a fine photograph of her in the paper. She is an unusually attractive young lady. We agreed that we should attend the program. In fact, as I think of it, we would very much enjoy your attending with us as our guest. Yes, it will be quite nice, just the three of us, and of course later with your daughter. I suppose she will have a beau? So, it will make five of us. Yes, we can take an evening drive down along the lake road and over the new concrete bridge by the willows in our elegant new Franklin touring car. We can even stop at Brown's Ice Cream Parlor for a treat on Mrs. Bender and me before returning home. He rubbed his hands together enthusiastically as he continued in his non-stop manner. "By the way, this Saturday evening is all on Mrs. Bender and me. You will still receive your regular pay, just as though you had cleaned the offices. I will have someone else do that for you. Yes, that will be just right! Well, Mrs. Bender and I will call for you punctually at five-fifteen on Saturday evening."

As Harry lingered over these reflections, it came to him again, as it had that afternoon in the late spring of 1927, how even his mother had been taken in by that Mr. Bender. How Mr. Bender and his non-stop talking, and his mother, occupied with her own interests, had failed to see how Harry had been ignored and then injured by that autocratic man. Harry still remembered as if it was yesterday, how Mr. Bender had ignored him and then finally herded him and his mother to the door. He had watched the man slide open a drawer in a big table over against the wall and carefully cull out the most worn copper coin Harry remembered ever seeing. He had not forgotten how the cruel man had finally noticed him; how he had turned to him--his breath reeking of tobacco--and bent down into his face and then patronizingly said, "And here's a fine reward for the little man who was so obedient and mannerly when he came with his nice mother to Mr. Bender's office. I am sure you must be very proud to be able to say that you have been in such a fine office." Turning to Harry's mother, he said, "You must be very proud of your little man, Mrs. Morgan".

Returning his attention to the boy, he beamed, "Someday, when you've grown, Master Morgan, we must see if there is something that you can learn to do here. Then your mother can be proud of you for following in her footsteps and becoming one of our great families of hard working employees."

Pressing the coin into Harry's palm and folded Harry's fingers shut over it, he went on while roughly squeezing Harry's hand ever tighter, "Now, if this is your first penny, put it away and save it. Surely, you will earn more. Save them and put them with this coin, and someday you will be able to say, 'Mr.

Bender gave me my first money and started me on my way to saving and success.' You must always mind your mother, Master Morgan, and never forget to respect and obey all of your elders and superiors. Do as you are told, follow instructions and you will be well taken care of".

He squeezed Harry's hand ever tighter but Harry refused to cry, although the coin felt as though it had cut clear through. Then he let go and roughly steered Harry out of his office. At the same time, it seemed to Harry that Mr. Bender rather covertly slid his arm around his mother's waist as he guided her out of the door.

Over the years, Harry never saw fit to erase that meeting from his memory. He relived and embellished it time and again, always recalling it as one of the most difficult occurrences of his life. He never forgot how he had fought not to cry in pain and for self-control. He wanted to root that old man out of his own office. Harry knew that he had to hurt Mr. Bender as much as Mr. Bender had injured him. No, more! He had to get to him, one way or another, or he felt he would incinerate in the fires of his own anguish. Somehow, he had to show this old man that he or no one else could ever overlook Harry Morgan! Harry's anger and hostility so filled and consumed him that for most of the next fifty or more years he would be driven by these recollections--along with one other.

Life had never been easy for Harry and his sister, Miriam. She was 12 years older than he, and had fled the household as soon as she could find respectable employment. The family had been poor and miserable in their poverty. Hard words and treatment came easy from Harry's father, and his mother, while a kind and devoted woman to her two children, had come to find herself at a loss as to why she had ever married Harry's father. Even-though Harry lived in terror of his father's wrath, he yearned for his father acceptance and friendship, neither of which he would ever enjoy. His early emptiness which grew into a bitterness was only increased by the realization that he had never been able to erase from his memory how less than a year after his experience in Mr. Bender's office, he had hidden behind his bed in fear of the shouted accusations and tearful protestations that had raged through the shabby, paper-thin walled house all night long. He had cried out in terror as he heard the repeated sounds that even a small boy could recognize as flesh and bone striking flesh and bone in anger.

Finally, as the light began to break through the window of his room the night of terror came to an end, and his mother, face deeply bruised, blood trickling from the corner of her mouth, stumbled into the bedroom and fell across the bed where she lay long into the day.

Harry heard his father moving about in the other room that served as kitchen and parlor. He was glad that his sister was not at home. After a while, he heard his father leave. Harry looked out of the window and saw him, his face strained in anger, stride across the back yard and down the alley. Harry wanted to run after him. To call him back. Then he was gone, around the corner on his way to his job at the car factory. Mysteriously, Harry's father never returned. It was as though he had walked from the face of the earth. Along with that and the likes of Mr. Bender, the shaping of the matrix began that only served to cleave deeper, to distort, and to further harden the young Harry Morgan.

As the years passed Harry found life to be lonely. All he could foresee in his future was a continuation of people like his father and Mr. Bender. Wherever he turned, he found the world about him either ignored or rebuffed him. However, his anguish and anger served his newfound inner purpose; the promise he made to himself as he left Mr. Bender's office so many years ago. And such so that these irritations served to become the flint from which he drew his spark of life and purpose. He knew that time would be on his side. The time would come when 'all of them' would come to know and feel the determination and impact of Harry Morgan. God would need to help those that might try to stand in his way. They would gravely wish that they instead had come to his side while they could. And as his thoughts came around to the time at hand, he realized that nearly all of his lifetime had been dedicated to the preparation for this moment. The reward that he had so covertly, patiently and single-mindedly worked and planned for all these many years would be his in but a matter of hours. Indeed, the time was at hand.

CHAPTER TWO

Harry glanced at his desk clock. It was too late for him to go to the company commissary for lunch. He decided instead to have his secretary get a snack for him. She could bring him some milk and Oreo cookies.

As he reached across his desk to press Ann's intercom button, he noticed that one of the telephone signal lights had begun to blink, followed shortly thereafter by the tiny "ping" of his office call announcing that Ann was holding an incoming call for him. He pushed down on the button and growled into the phone, "Who wants me? Did you say if I was in or not? I want you to get to the commissary for me, so when I get off this call, come in here. Who'd you say it was, anyway?"

If Ann had been in a more empathetic mood, she might have recalled that after nearly fifteen years of guarding the 'kennel door', most of the time she got the same cheerless response to any call she made to the "inside". Most of the time she didn't know whether Mr. Morgan was in his office because he often left by his private exit, much of the time without telling her. Later he would abruptly appear in her outer office from the general office and manufacturing's entrance.

In her present mood, about all Ann was up to was setting one foot in front of the other. Her husband, Charlie Harris, had come home after bowling Friday night and had proceeded to finish what he had started in the bar--all through Saturday and part of the way through Sunday. Mercifully, he had run out of spirits by Sunday afternoon, and there was no place open for him to re-stock. She had been up all Sunday night pouring black coffee into him so that he would be able to make it to his job in the company's maintenance department on Monday at seven am.

By now, she was just trying to hang on until the end of the day. About all she had left for Harry's blast was a defensive, "Please don't yell at me, Mr. Morgan. It's your wife on line two.

"I told her you said she was supposed to come in on the private line and not through the switchboard, but she told me to mind my own business. She said she'd have me fired if I didn't remember whom I was talking to, and . . . well, I'm sorry, Mr. Morgan. I'll come in when your line clears. Is that all?"

Harry had long since grunted at the phone and switched over to line two. Feigning weariness, he grumbled, "What in the hell is it now, Irene? Why are you on the switchboard line instead of the private line? How in the hell do you expect me to keep some decorum and respect around here if every time anybody down here turns around they get an earful of speculation over whether our lousy cat made it out the back door to the sandbox? Now, what's so damn important that it can't wait until I get home tonight?"

Harry reflected that if those switchboard girls were listening they would certainly recognize that he ran his household with the same authority that he ran the company. Not only that, they'd know that they'd better do what they were supposed to do around Harry Morgan if they thought anything about their jobs!

As he now listened for Irene's responses, Harry began to feel uneasy again. It had become embarrassingly apparent that he had been carrying on his heated conversation with an abandoned phone. Then Harry heard the phone being picked up, and he knew that he had lost whatever initiative he had had.

"Hello? Is anybody there? I had to let Pansy out to her sandbox. Ann? Is Mr. Morgan going to answer this phone? Harry? Is that you, Harry?"

"Yes, Irene, it's me. What do you want?"

"Oh, Harry, we got a wedding announcement in the mail today, but we can't go!"

Good! Harry thought, but to Irene said, "Why can't we go, Irene? Where is it at, and who is it, anyhow? And was it so damn important that you couldn't keep it until tonight? Why bother me over something like that at this time of day . . . ? And . . . .Oh well . . ."

Harry trailed off in utter resignation to his wife's concern over something as insignificant as a wedding invitation. It was probably from someone he had never heard of or never wanted to hear of again.

Taking strength from these reflections, Harry swiveled his chair around and wearily began to re-inspect the contents of his wastebasket.

"Well, Harry, you'll never guess, so I'll have to tell you. Cyd is getting married! I mean the invitation is for a wedding that was two days ago. I guess that means it's over with now, and we won't get to go. I don't know what to do."

Who was this guy named Sid? Harry wondered. He'd sure never known anyone of importance named Sid. And then it dawned on him.

"Irene! Did you mean Sidney somebody, or Cyd, like your niece, for instance?"

Irene's niece, Cyd, the daughter of her brother, Bob, the Air Force Colonel, always impressed Harry as being hard-nosed, but being the only sensible one of the lot. But after her husband had been killed in a crop-dusting plane crash just a few months after completing his tour of duty over Vietnam, Cyd had been left with two small children and a bitter flamethrower disposition that would have blistered a saint from a block away. Harry was sure that she was not the Cyd who was the source of Irene's concern. No one could get along with her. That Cyd was a closed issue. Harry was sure of that!

"Harry, I don't mean like Sid like Sidney, I mean Cyd, our niece! She just up and got married again. Mother was at the wedding and Bob and Jean flew down from California. Nobody missed Joe because they all knew he was in his seventh heaven at some pro-am golf outing. We could have been there if you didn't have our phones so screwed up with all of your idiotic neurotic security!"

Harry inwardly squirmed because this was not the first time Irene had thrown up to him about his scanning of all of the personal mail at his office and the unlisted phone numbers at their home and the private line at the office. Many times this had thrown off the delivery of mail and messages to their home by as much as a week.

"And another thing, Harry, we should have been at the wedding. I thought Cyd's new husband's name sounded familiar." Harry sat up a little straighter in his chair and began to pay attention.

"And then, right after I got the mail, Mama called on the private line, and boy, did she tell me about it! She said she was at the wedding, and everybody wanted to know where we were, and Cyd had to say that they couldn't get through to us because our number was unlisted and you had it changed again, and they had to wait until Mama got there with her private phone numbers. So, with the invitation being so late, we missed out, as usual, and . . . Harry, are you listening to me?"

"Yes, I'm listening!"

"After Mama got through telling me about that, your old 'ace-in-the-hole' said she is on the way up to help Cyd and her new grandson-in-law gets settled in the lake house until they can find a place for themselves. Cyd's kids are in boarding school for the winter so they are taken care of. Mama says she wants to have a talk with you, Harry, about getting young Mac properly placed in the company."

Now attentive, sweaty, and breathless, Harry leaning into the phone and almost devouring the mouthpiece, croaked, "Irene, who in hell is young Mac? Not that damn fool Palmer McNeil! Jesus, Irene, not him!"

"No, Harry, not Palmer McNeil. You don't like anybody with money, do you? It's McIntyre! Alan McIntyre! Remember? He was that nice young man from Ohio State University that worked with the company during summers. Wasn't he part of that Personnel-Employee Relations loan program you got started in the plant? Then, after he graduated he was here for a while, and I thought you said he was doing so well and was going to be your assistant, and then he wasn't here anymore, and you said he left you flat for some other job--and after all you did for him, too.

"Remember, you were so nice to him, even though you said it hurt you? You had a nice office party for him, and I remember because when I picked you up that night after work he was leaving too, and you sent him on his way with a nice smile and a real solid slap on the back. You remember, Harry!"

Harry remembered all right! He also remembered, but this time without any trace of a grin, that this slap had really been one of those never-come-back ones. As a matter of fact, Alan McIntyre had been one that Harry especially hoped he had recommended so highly that McIntyre would never find his way back. It never ceased to bother him that that young man had the most unnerving way of turning over rocks and snooping around things that Harry in his paranoia sensed would lead to other occurrences that he wanted hidden forever. But this was not the most alarming or disturbing element of the conversation. Far from it!

"Irene, that's nice", Harry hastily answered. "So when did Gladys say she was coming up? I'll have to get the company wagon and pick her up at the airport."

"You won't have to worry about that, Harry. Mother is on the way up. She's having Cyd and Alan drive her up in her limo. She said she wants to trade it in on a newer and more functional model. She said that it's time she quit sitting on the beach, vegetating and having others do for her what she should be doing for herself.

"Mama said that she wants to come back into the living world for a little while before she 'cuts away for good.' Can you imagine my mother saying something like that? She must have been on the beach at Fort Lauderdale during the college breaks. I wonder if she has taken up beer drinking, too?

"Oh, she said she'll be here in time for the board meeting tomorrow afternoon, and she's going to preside as chairman. I am supposed to turn over my stock proxies from you to her, and she is going to vote her own stock, too. She says she is revoking her proxies you have been voting along with mine."

Harry began to wonder if there was anything more to further convulse his world that this gentle, empty-headed woman could possibly come up with in her babbling, unconcerned manner.

Irene went on, "Mama said that when she gets back she wants to sit down with you. You have done a good job of taking care of the company. She couldn't have found a better caretaker . . . ."

Caretaker? Caretaker? Harry could feel himself cringe and stiffen. He recalled once before hearing that word used in reference to him, and it took him back to when he was ten years old, and old Mr. Bender had given him an extra five cents after he had pushed that old lawn mower all over the front lawn of the factory for twenty cents. The old man had told him that if he continued to show improved care and persistence, he could someday become an adequate yardman and lawn boy or "caretaker".

"She said I was a what?"

"Caretaker, Harry. Caretaker! And she said she knew and appreciated what a good job you had done all these years. Now she needs to see to the new direction of the company because with Bob getting his Star and he and Jean making a career of the military, and Joe being more interested in golf balls, birdies and such, than in widgets, we have to make provisions for the future and the succession within the company.

"Mama said that it is most important that the company be led by a man of proper formal education, and with Alan being a graduate Of Ohio State University with a degree in Industrial Engineering, and having added a Master's Degree in Personnel and Business Administration from Princeton, along with more graduate work and study in something new she called Systems Adaptation and Plant Computerization, he is just the shot in the arm we need to renew the company and to make us formidable again."

By now Harry was a smoldering mass of raw nerves. Outside of the years he had spent in the Army, Harry had devoted his life and soul to this company. Now just a damn caretaker!

CHAPTER THREE
———

When Harry married Irene Bender in 1949, he had only his high school education and military service and training. Irene had already completed her formal education and finishing school at Smith College and Radcliffe in Massachusetts.

In high school, Irene had been prom queen and was popular in everything. She even had her own car, a Chrysler convertible.

Harry was two years ahead of her in school, so while they knew and spoke to each other when they met, they had no classes together, nor did they sit near each other in the assembly halls. They had never gone out together, not even on a double date. About the only thing that they had in common was that they both were members of the mixed glee club for two years.

Harry seemed content with a small circle of friends that he intentionally kept clipped to a minimum. He was uncomfortable in large groups where he was unable to keep an eye on the general goings-on. His athletic endeavors were largely as a spectator, because, while he possessed more than average ability, he was unable to relax his reserve. He simply wasn't a good team player. Nonetheless, his recollections of his high school years were relatively satisfying.

He was a good student and made outstanding grades in courses which permitted him to go at his own fast pace. He constantly compared his results with those of other students, and he invariably stood well above them. Yet, in spite of his generally favorable status throughout his years in the community's schools, as Harry moved from grade to grade and school to school, an aura of tension arrived with him and moved on when he did.

Like nearly all of the other young men of Troy, when Harry graduated from high school he put in his application at the Bender Company. It was not that he, like the others, was anxious to work there. In his view, it was the only opportunity to find a way not to have to end up there.

He was called in for an interview and was told that because his mother was such a good employee, he would be given an unusual opportunity to learn a fundamental part of the business. He would be assigned as an apprentice in the press department. He would be allowed to work ten hours, five days a week, and four hours on Saturday morning. His starting wage would be twenty-six cents an hour and his wage would not increase until he had been in the department for six months, and if he were to be retained. There were no other benefits.

Two of Harry's high school friends were also hired. Leo Hagen was assigned to the press department along with Harry, and Frank Lange was assigned to the receiving department. By the following spring, all three were still on the job and had been accepted as regular employees. Though still apprentices, they had been raised to thirty cents an hour. All of the boys were hard workers. Their foremen pushed them hard, and they responded just as hard. All in all, they were liked by their co-workers and found their jobs adequate, if not interesting.

All three of the boys saved or shared their money. Harry took a small part of his check, with the larger portion going to help his mother. Leo saved his money to buy a used car because he had to walk over two miles to work. Frank was saving his paychecks, giving practically all of them to his girlfriend, Margie, so that they could have something to get married on.

Then, one Saturday afternoon Margie ran off, got married with Frank's money, but neglected to include Frank in the ceremony. Margie's unexpected behavior was quite a blow to the three close friends and made a further negative impression on the already cynical Harry.

As the futures of Asia and Europe were darkening more each day with the war between China and Japan and the pending war between Germany and anybody, it was not hard to find an exciting topic to divert the now disillusioned Frank, and take his mind off Margie and what his two cronies were by then convinced was a fortunately averted disaster.

The local weekly newspaper did not devote much copy to the war news, but whenever the boys came across a paper from a larger town, such as Fort Wayne, they combed the columns with all the fervor of seasoned war correspondents.

The Saturday after Armistice Day in 1940, the three decided to go to Indianapolis to watch the military day parade. After the parade, they came across some recruiting literature. This led to the three being swept up by the rationale and excitement of a military career of their choice through enlisting.

Frank signed up for the Tank Corps, went through Officer's Candidate School, and was commissioned as a second Lieutenant. Ultimately, a Captain and three times decorated for gallantry in the face of the enemy, Frank left part of his left hand and the sight of his right eye, along with his command in the defense of Bastogne on Christmas Eve of 1944.

Leo enlisted in the Air Corps, got his wings, and flew fighters over North Africa and Southern Europe. He shot down fourteen Italian and German planes and finished the war a double ace and a Major.

Harry, for what he held as a more practical reason, enlisted in the Military Police. He, too, went through Officer's Candidate School and became a Second Lieutenant. He was then assigned to Fort Belvoir, Virginia. After completing his secondary training, he was sent to a special Air Corps topographical map school. He retained his commission in the Military Police.

By the time Harry came home on his first leave in the late summer of 1941, he was a twenty-one year old second Lieutenant and, never lacking in good looks, a beguiling sight for any girl. While on that leave Harry discovered that Irene Bender was home from Smith College.

Irene was sort of promised to Bob Harkness who was a Pilot and Lieutenant in the Navy, but he was somewhere in the distant South Pacific. Wondering how he would fare with her against the rest of the boys, Harry asked her for a date. There was no contest at all. There just weren't any other boys around, and Harry had Irene all to himself.

Between Harry's curiosity and Irene's inclinations, things developed rather fast. Harry finally returned to camp, minus one wristwatch that he pawned for the down payment on an engagement ring, and Irene returned to Smith College, minus one virginity, her down payment--on Mr. Bender's back porch--on the same engagement. After a few weeks of considerable uncertainty and meager correspondence on both parts, Harry invested in a phone call from his new station at Fort Jackson, South Carolina, to North Hampton, Massachusetts.

From Harry's end, the conversation consisted of:

> "Well . . . ? Anything happen yet . . . . ? Well, tell me, what do you think. .? Gee, I sure hope so . . . ! Well, let me know if you do."

And from Irene's end, the cryptic response went pretty much like this:

> "What-well . . . ? No, not yet . . . . It's too soon to tell, I think, but I'm sure everything will be okay . . . . Okay, I'll let you know, but why would you worry?"

Then, about a week or ten days later, Harry got a very short and terse letter from Massachusetts, which said:

> I'm okay now. I told you it would be okay. I know you don't want any more to do with me now, so I will send your ring back as soon as I know that this is a good address, and you will get it for sure. Please be good enough to confirm your address. Sincerely...

The following weekend, Harry, ever one to recognize when fate had smiled on him, managed to wangle a special order to proceed from Fort Jackson to Fort Devons, Massachusetts, for seven days for the purpose of learning new systems of map reading and interrogation under study by the Air Force and Signal Corps. To finance his mission he took time to clean out two barrack's crap games. What was really in back of all of this activity were the nightly appearances on the nearby Smith College campus for the purpose of locking up whatever advantage he had gained while on leave back home in Troy.

CHAPTER FOUR

―――――――

Harry shook himself back to awareness. Irene was still prattling on about what Gladys had said and what Cyd and Alan had worn for the wedding--which was of no concern to him. It was time for him to come to grips with the facts. There was no question in Harry's mind as to his course in respect to his future and that of the company.

"Irene, tell me all that stuff later on. I need facts now--if you can sort it out from all of that gaggle. I get from you that Bob and Jean's daughter, Cyd, got married again. She married this kid Alan McIntyre, who worked here for a couple of years, on and off, and then went to work out East. Now that they're married, they are coming to Troy, and he is supposed to come into the company, or so Gladys thinks. By the way, did she call herself my 'ace-in-the-hole,' or was that your bright idea?"

"No, Harry, she called herself that; in fact, she made some sort of a point of it. I told her that sounded strange coming from her, but she said you'd know what she was talking about. I'm just repeating it to you the way she said it to me. Other than that, you got it all right, so far."

Harry winced at this disclosure. He was not sure he understood Gladys' reference, but he was absolutely certain that he should have and that Gladys would fully expect him to dig back into his memory to recall why she had gone back to a portion of a conversation that had started before he and Irene were married. Harry knew that he would have to clarify this for himself before Gladys' return. If there was any negotiating to be done--and for all her years, Gladys was as formidable an opponent at the bargaining table as there was anywhere on the face of the earth--he would have to know exactly what she meant and what she was leading up to.

"Did Gladys give you any sort of idea of when she would get here? You said she is coming up with Cyd and her new husband. What about the twins? Are they coming too?"

"I thought I told you that the kids were in boarding school! Aren't you paying attention? Cyd and Alan were going to Jamaica for their honeymoon, but Mama talked them into putting it off and they are on the way up with her. They should be here in the morning. At any rate, you'd better get that smart-aleck secretary of yours to get her lazy husband out to the lake house and get it aired out. As a matter of fact, tell her to get out there and clean it up herself. You can give her an extra five dollars in her check. It'll probably be the first good work she's done in years.

"Oh, Harry! I enjoyed that! I just hope she was listening in and got a good earful!"

Harry was already starting to sort out the danger signals that he had clearly heard, and was searching his memory for related ideas and observations that he felt should be emerging.

He felt he had cause for concern, but there was no reason for panic. He needed to carefully evaluate the facts. But, before that, he had to finish with Irene.

"Irene, is there anything else? Are you going to be home this afternoon so I can get in touch with you, if something comes up? Can you get in touch with Gladys if you have to?"

"Yes, Harry, I think I've covered it all. The cleaning lady is here, so I'll be around home all day, but I don't see any way I can get ahold of Gladys. She's somewhere on the highway between here and Fort Lauderdale."

"Oh! Irene. Do you think Joe knows about the wedding, and about Gladys wanting all of these meetings?"

"Harry, Joe is probably still out at some nineteenth hole in California or Arizona at a pro-am outing. I doubt by this time that Joe has the slightest idea what she wants, or who married who, or for that matter who Gladys is."

Harry had to agree with Irene. Joe was a nothing. But Joe, as titular president of the Bender Company, did hold twenty-four and one-half percent of the outstanding voting stock in the company.

CHAPTER FIVE

MANY YEARS EARLIER, HARRY HAD mentioned the voting stock to Gladys during one of her visits to Troy. She had looked sharply at Harry and, smoothing imaginary wrinkles out of her lap, evenly said, "Joe owns stock in the Company, Harry, and so does Irene . . . and so does Bob, but their three sets of twenty-four and one half percent of the voting stock still can't do a thing unless they vote it all together.

"Fortunately, Harry, before their father passed on, he and I sat down one evening and took a long look at the future.

"When we built this business all of the kids were little, and we didn't think much about what would happen as we got older. But with the war coming on and Bob going into service and Irene getting to the age where she would be getting married someday, we thought we had better make some plans for the future.

"Mr. Bender visualized that a day might come when there would be a need for a steadying hand other than his. He wanted a reserve control, sort of a super trump card. At that point he owned this company in his own name, lock, stock and barrel, but for-seeing a possible future, while he willed each of our children twenty-four and one-half percent of the stock, he left me twenty-six and one-half percent of the stock. So, you see, no matter what direction I really feel this company should go in, all I need is for one of my children to give me his or her stock proxies to go along with mine. Without me, they have to go it together. With their diverse views of life, that seems rather unlikely.

"So, my dear Harry, I really am still very much in control of this company. You could even say that I am the super trump card—'the old ace-in-the-hole'."

Harry saw that Gladys was leading up to something and tried to conceal his mounting interest, as she, closely watching him, went on, "Now, if you want to grow in this company; to play a hand in this with me, I'll be your ace-in-the-hole. I'll even see to it that someday you can run the company--if I think you're good enough.

"Someday, as long as it looks good to me, you can vote Irene's proxies. I'll even let you vote my stock. Bob and Joe will go along with it because all Bob wants is the stockholder's checks at the end of the year, so that he can keep taking those Pentagon-style vacations with the generals in hopes that someday someone will pin a star on him before they retire him. And Joe? All he wants is a gold-plated golf cart, a million golf balls, a twenty-four- hour-a-day caddy, and wall-to-wall golf courses.

"Harry, I sometimes wonder about that boy of mine. All he has ever chased, as far back as I can remember, are little white balls down those things with that funny grass on them--fairways! I can't even remember his having ever chased a girl since he knew what they were! I once hired a detective to find out, and he hasn't been chasing boys either. He's just in neutral! It's a good thing he has his company president job's income to fall back on because his only real gear for Go is Golf!

"So that leaves Irene, Harry, and she's a good girl. A little dumb, otherwise she wouldn't have settled for living here in Troy and what she got."

The recollection of that remark always cut into Harry, and he was pretty sure that Gladys knew and enjoyed his discomfort.

"I always wanted Irene to have as much out of life as she wanted," Gladys continued. "It's too bad she can never have any children. I still want to blame that little 'excursion' you two had before you were married, but Irene told me that's the way it is these days and that had nothing to do with it. I talked to a specialist at the Mayo Clinic about it and he said that Irene was probably right. But all the same, I still think it could have been a punishment for not waiting. Oh, I'm probably old-fashioned. Certainly, when I look around I know that I wouldn't be able to cope with and keep up with the young girls around today!

"No, Harry, it just doesn't look good. With no children for Irene to raise and you not willing to adopt--which I have to agree with in some ways because you never know what you're bringing into your home that way--I'm not pleased with what we have to work with.

"Bob's wife, Jean, is all right if you want to live on army posts. That's what she was brought up to do, her dad being a general. And that leaves Joe with no wife at all and little prospects of any in the future.

"Like I said, with Irene having nothing to show for her married life, it looks like for now the future fortunes of the Bender company are going to be in the hands of an old woman and the possibility of a daughter's husband as a manager because there is just no other future in sight.

"You have a great war record, Harry, and maybe you can develop into something here. I'm inclined to give you a chance because I'm going to move you up to Production Manager, and if that works out, Mr. Breitweizer is not getting any younger and the day will come when he will want to retire, and I may make you General Manufacturing Manager if I see fit. You do a good job there, and you'll be a vice president someday. Harry, you take care of the company and I'll take care of you. I'll be 'your ace-in-the-hole'. As long as you do it my way, I'll be there in the background, and as long as I think you're going about it right, you won't even know I'm alive. But remember; don't try to play around with the 'ace' without being sure that it is there for you. Don't take me for granted. There may come a day when I will want to call in my cards, so don't force me to make a fool out of both of us because in the final analysis I will come out on top."

As Harry pieced together the bits and pieces of a conversation that had taken nearly two decades to run its course, he returned to stand unseeing before his one-way window. The difference was that when he had last been there, he was congratulating himself on the successes that he soon expected to celebrate. Now, he was faced with the realization that he was about to be confronted with the greatest crisis of his life. Evidently, Gladys had decided to write a new ending to a scenario that Harry had considered a closed book.

CHAPTER SIX

When Ann Harris came into his office, she found Harry deeply lost in his thoughts. She spoke to him several times and finally found it necessary to get his attention by tugging at his sleeve and saying, "Mr. Morgan, you asked me to come into the office after the phone call. Is there anything I can do? Is there anything wrong?"

Harry, finally realizing that Ann was trying to get his attention, savagely snapped, "Tell your Charlie I want him at my house tonight at eight-thirty, sharp! I want him to open the lake house and get it cleaned up to be lived in. You tell him that he had better damn well be sober, too! Go to the commissary and get me a big glass of milk and a bag of Oreo cookies. Sign a charge ticket for me. You got that?"

"Yes, Mr. Morgan," Ann replied. "I'll take care of it." Ann silently hoped that her husband would be sober enough by evening to make it through Mr. Morgan's back gate.

Charlie hadn't shown up at the office that noon, and that generally meant that he was out trying to find the last drink that he hadn't been able to manage the night before. Fortunately, most of the bars in town knew that Mr. Morgan would have them boarded up by the next morning if he caught them giving Charlie anything besides black coffee to drink. All things considered, Charlie was pretty safe and would probably give up by mid-afternoon and call her to see if it was all right for him to come home.

Charlie's calls still puzzled Ann. From the very first night, some twenty years ago, when he had come home with a deep bruise all down his left side, and reeking from alcohol and vomit, crying and mumbling about killing or being the cause of the death of someone out on the lake road, he had always called whenever he had gotten drunk. That night, so many years ago, his face and head had been covered with blood, his scalp had been cut by what appeared to be gravel, and there was a deep bruise on his left hip and down the backside of his left leg. Ann had to fight him to let her clean him up, and as soon as that was done, he had taken the fifty dollars that they had been saving toward a new refrigerator, stuffed some clothes in a bag, along with some cheese, bread, and sausage, and painfully limped out the back door. He told her that he would call her to see if and when it would be all right for him to come home. She never knew where he had gone, but he had called her a number of times.

Then, three weeks later, he came home on Friday night and quietly slipped into bed with her. She took him in her arms and tried to comfort him and ease his anxiety. He lay close to her but was still and breathlessly tense as though listening for something before he finally fell asleep. When she awoke the next morning, he was in the kitchen making coffee, and by the time she got into a robe and was downstairs, he had left for the day. That night when he came home, he told her, "Ann, I don't work for the garage no more".

She looked up. "What happened? Did you get fired because you were gone those three weeks? Don't worry, Charlie, I saved some other money this past year. We'll do fine until you find something else. Don't worry, Charlie. Have a nice cup of coffee."

"No, I got another job. I quit the garage. I work down at the company, now."

"Bender's?"

"Yeah, starting Monday morning."

"Doing what? You don't know anything about what they do, do you?"

"They hired me 'cause I'm a good mechanic, and I'm going to work in the maintenance. I'm going to learn how to take care of the presses. I'm goin' to the Press Company school next week. You don't have to know nothing about making widgets if you know about the machines that make 'em."

"Funny, I didn't figure they'd be hiring anybody so soon after old Mr. Bender's killing himself in that car wreck. Did you ever . . . ."

Charlie quickly got up from the table, moved to the window, and intently watched the paperboy cut through the back yard. He continued to show only his back to her as he interrupted, "Annie, pour me a cup of coffee. I got to go out tonight, and I need some."

Ten minutes later Charlie looked back at Ann as he nervously let himself out of the back door. His voice breaking with emotion, he said, "Annie, if I can do it, I ain't gonna drink no more. I'm trying, honey, honest I am." And for a while it seemed to be working just that way.

Two years later when Ann left her job at the phone company and took the job on the new switchboard at the Bender Company, Charlie still had not taken a drink. Their lives looked full. Charlie had been sent to special schools and was doing all the pressroom maintenance. Ann found time to go to night school and brush up on her typing and shorthand skills. When she heard that there would be an opening as executive secretary to the new production manager she was ready. She applied for the job, and after a three-month probationary period, was told that she was permanent in the position.

She had not told Charlie that she had tried out for the job and had kept it her secret for the entire three-month trial period. It had not been too hard because she still spent part of each day on the switchboard and Charlie rarely came over to the administrative offices. She was so excited and certain that Charlie would share in her happiness. He had frequently gone back to the plant for Mr. Morgan on some special night project, so she assumed that he had been working with and liked Mr. Morgan.

That evening, Charlie had left word at the switchboard that he would be working late and that she should not wait for him in the parking lot. He would be home for supper about six-thirty. Ann hurried home and tidied up the house. She decided that she would prepare Charlie's favorite light meal and whipped up a Denver omelet. By the time she had the table set and the coffee and toast ready, Charlie had walked up the back sidewalk and was cleaning up in the little half-bath just off the kitchen.

After supper, Ann began to clear the table, and as she did, she said, "Charlie, I've got a surprise for you. I think you're going to like it and be proud of me."

"Yeah? They give you some help on the switchboard, I know. I heard there was another girl there today. One of the salesmen that comes in told me. Wanted to know if you was sick or something. You got made head of switchboard!"

"Nope, I did my last day on the switchboard yesterday. I got moved up, and it's not part-time any more. It's permanent, and I'm going to get a nice raise next month, too!"

"Geese! What'd you get, mail room?"

"Nope, wrong again. Oh Charlie, I'm so excited! I'm the new executive secretary to the Production Manager, and I've got a private office of my own, right outside of Mr. Morgan's own office! I'm supposed to do all his personal, important letters, and I'll get to help him with all of the confidential things he does.

"He says he expects great things of me. He says he knows you real well, and he says you do important work around the plant for him. He told me that I can be part of his special team, and we can all work real close together. He helped me keep it a secret that I was trying out for the job. He agreed right away with me that it would be a wonderful surprise for you when he said I would have the job for sure."

Ann had been so carried away with her good fortune that she hadn't noticed that as she mentioned that the new job was with the production manager, Charlie had gotten up from his chair and walked over to the window and stood staring out into the darkness. She had not noticed that he had begun to rub his face and eyes as she continued, and when she came over, put her arms around him, and pressed her cheek against his stiffened back, she did not detect the tightness and tension about him.

"I'm so happy, Charlie. This job, along with your job, will give us a chance to have some independence. With both of us working so close with Mr. Morgan, we ought to be able to get somewhere. Aren't you proud of me, Charlie?"

"Yeah, it's real nice. It's a real surprise. I'm glad for you. It's a big promotion, I guess." Reaching around and patting Ann's hand, Charlie went on, "Annie, I got to go back to work tonight. I got to go now, too. One press ain't working just right and the night shift guys will get on me if I don't straighten it out. I might be late, but if I am, don't wait up for me. We'll talk about your job tomorrow." And giving her a brush of a kiss, he almost ran out of the door and through the back yard.

When Charlie finally came home it was well past three. It was also the first time in nearly five years that he was drunk. It was a good thing that it was Saturday morning because he was drunker yet by Saturday night, and while he did sober up by Monday work-time, he gave Ann no clue as to why he had returned to the bottle. As the years went by he became more and more morose and irritable, with never a word to explain his change.

Ann soon learned that Charlie's deep trouble involved Mr. Morgan because as time went by, the messages to have Charlie do this and do that around the plant and the orders for after-work meetings at Mr. Morgan's back gate were passed on from Mr. Morgan to Charlie, through Ann.

With the passage of time, the noose of absolute obedience and bondage that Ann passed on to Charlie and in which she came to feel enmeshed grew unbearably tighter. What had once appeared to be the rainbow on the horizon had become the storm that seemed without end. Ann found herself wishing with all her heart that she and Charlie could break free and find other jobs where she did not have to be the instrument of what she ultimately came to recognize as Mr. Morgan's humiliating and degrading orders to Charlie. She knew there just had to be a more honorable way of making a living for both of them than being part of Mr. Morgan's dirty work and being one of his 'cronies'.

CHAPTER SEVEN

Ann quietly opened the door and brought the milk and cookies into Harry's office. He had been staring out the one-way window again but he wheeled about as he heard her enter. His voice, heavy with hostility, crashed down on her. "Mrs. Harris, gimme that stuff and get out! I changed my mind about Charlie. I'll get hold of him myself. He'd better be home where I can find him, I'll tell you that! Another thing! I don't want any more phone calls in here! I don't care or give a damn who it is. I'm out of touch until I tell you otherwise!"

Harry snatched the lunch tray from Ann, slamming it down on his desk, and ominously shook his finger in her face, as he shouted, "You damn well make sure you hear me good because I mean what I'm saying. Nobody gets by that door! Nobody! If my phone rings or if that door opens or if anybody knows where I am or what I'm doing today, you are out of here and out of any job. And that goes for your Charlie, too! And he can start to worry about himself all over again, and a lot of other things, too."

Ann had never heard anyone speak with such dripping rage and torment as Harry snarled, "Get out! You want to breathe one free breath the rest of your life; you do what I tell you. Get out! Make sure my door is locked! You don't let nobody in!"

Assuring himself that she had left and locked the door as he had ordered her to, Harry swung his attention back to the window. He saw nothing at all. He might as well have been blind. The panic that he told himself he would not permit had begun to creep into his consciousness. He could not recall that he had ever felt so totally challenged and suddenly so inadequate in coming to grips with a situation since he had been in the Army.

Over the years since his return from service to his job at the company, Harry had experienced critical times and there had been obstacles along the way, but his person and actions had never before been in question. Harry's quickness to remove dissenters had taken care of most of the predicaments, and if anyone had doubted his judgment, much less his honor and valor, all they had to do was to look closer inside the locked glass case that hung on the wall behind his desk.

As the thought came to Harry's mind, he moved behind his desk and looked into the case. There were a pair of mint-condition pistols--an American Colt .45 and a German 9 mm. Luger--each carefully nestled into a red velvet background.

Across the top in the case were seven decorations and medals for valor and bravery: The Purple Heart with two Oak Leaf Clusters, the French Croix de Guerre, the British Order of Merit, the American Bronze Star, the American Silver Star, the American Legion of Merit, and American Distinguished Service Cross, and an eighth--a most unusual golden medal in the shape of a great and expensively ornate key that hung from a red, white and blue ribbon. Its clasp read:

To our most famous son in service
Colonel Harry William Morgan
A Hoosier Welcome Home
and
The Key to the City and Hearts of Troy

Below that there was a row of campaign ribbons: the Pre-Pearl Harbor Citation, the American Defense Citation, The North-African Campaign Citation with one invasion arrowhead and one battle star, and the European Theater of Operations Citation with two invasion arrowheads and four battle stars.

Across the bottom portion of the case was a row of the insignia of the commissions that he had held while in service. There was a gold Second Lieutenant's bar, a silver First Lieutenant's bar; a well-used Captain's bar, a Major's oak leaf cluster, and a Lieutenant Colonel's silver oak leaf cluster, and a Full Colonel's silver eagle. Two .45 caliber and two 9 mm. cartridges were cushioned in the lower left hand corner of the case. In the lower right hand corner was a single, curiously forlorn, badly battered, burned, and scarred silver Captain's bar.

Harry unlocked the lower left hand drawer of his desk and took out a small metal box with ornamental lithographing emblazoned across the lid that told the merits of British Potter's Sweets. Taking out a small key, he turned to the glass case on the wall, unlocked it, and took out two cartridges and loaded the chambers of both guns. He started to lock the case when his attention was drawn to the decorations, the well-used Captain's bar, and finally to the battered and burned Captain's bar.

For a moment he stood in indecision. Then he reached into the case and gingerly touched each of the emblems of office.

Reflections

After another moment's consideration, he unpinned the two Captain's bars that had commanded his attention and returned to his desk. He unconsciously pushed the two loaded guns aside and returned to his chair with the two Captain's bars-- one in the palm of each hand. He sat without expression or movement. He simply stared at them.

Harry slowly closed each hand around the bars until the pain from their sharp edges and the clasps and pins reminded him again, of how Mr. Bender had, so many years ago, hurt his hand with his old penny. He gripped tighter.

As the pain in his heart grew, he no longer felt the pain in his hands; he did not see the blood begin to seep between his knuckles.

Harry sat without awareness or feeling. He felt no presence of time. There was only the terrible ache in his heart and head that seemed to be coming from his whole life, from as far back as he could permit, and then, finally, there were the tears.

The tears that as a boy he had never been able to shed because there was no one who had the time or cared enough to share them with him. The same tears that as he grew older he had so fiercely fought. From the time when his father, after confronting his mother in a towering rage, stormed out of the house to a job that he was never to return from, Harry had always had to be a boy and later a man without joy. But now there was something else. He suddenly felt very old.

At forty-eight, he was the equal of any man regardless of age. But once again, he felt the anguish of fear. He felt that he was once again fighting for his very life and was on the brink of a more titanic struggle than he had ever experienced while he wore those bars and other emblems of military office, and during the years since his return to the company. He felt drained of the capability and strength to meet the challenge.

As his tears slackened Harry became more aware of his surroundings. He saw the two loaded guns on the desk with full recognition of why he had put them there. He calmly regarded the stained silver bars in his bloodied hands, now shakily opening.

"My God! I thought this was all behind me! I never meant anything to happen to anyone, not to Mr. Bender, not to anyone, even during the war. Wherever I went, people got hurt. They died, and it was my fault. If I share anything with them, it turned out that it killed them. If I need them, even when I try to be good to them they die. And now there's nothing I can do about that young McIntyre. If we both stay, something will happen just like it always has. There is only one way to keep it from happening. I just don't know any other way!"

Harry turned in his chair and looked up at the case on the wall. "All I know is that one way or another; I see my whole life as a lie. That whole case, the medals, the decorations, the key to the city, all the promotions and citations, are one monstrous lie!"

Harry turned back to the desk and dropped the bars in front of him. "I didn't have the guts to tell the truth. I let them believe anything they wanted to." Picking up the German Luger, Harry went on, "I was the one who you should have killed! It should have been my place."

Sliding back the bolt, Harry put the loaded Luger in the ready-fire position and, holding the gun up, but inches from his face where he could clearly see the rifling in the barrel and the Swastika marking, said, "That night in Holland, you fired shots that were meant to kill me. Why didn't you kill me? No! You couldn't hit me! You hit the man behind me, and you killed him. All you did to me was make a mark on my helmet. Just a little mark, but it was enough to turn the shot into another man's face. If I had moved quicker or even called a warning, you would have missed him. I helped you kill him, too!"

Harry unloaded and put the Luger down and said, "No, You won't get me this time either. You had your chance."

As Harry reached for the U S Army Colt 45, he noticed the blood on his hands and the bars for the first time. Where it had run down and dried on his left wrist, it looked grisly.

Shaken, he instead tried to pick up the bars and as quickly dropped them. "Oh, My God! After all of these years...blood to my hands again! Why now? It's been over for too long! It's like its starting all over again. Like I was back on that boat to England again!"

Harry slumped into the chair and then at a loss as what to do next, again, grasping the Captain's bars in each hand, slumped forward across his desk as his mind drifted off into the story of it all. The somber reflection of what he expected might have been, and what little expectation he now saw before him.

CHAPTER EIGHT

IMPATIENT TO GET ON WITH the evening, young Harry Morgan hurriedly put on his new First Lieutenant's bars. His shoes glistened as though they had been lacquered, and his trousers and shirt appeared freshly cleaned and pressed. He hung up his extra uniforms and fatigues and reminded himself to write to Irene about his promotion.

The unfamiliar movement of the floor reminded him that his present quarters were somewhat close to the water line of the ATT-340, light-armed military transport which in peacetime had been the flagship of the Western-Hemisphere's Luxury Lines: the 45,000 ton U.S.S. Brazil. While she was called a "banana boat" because her peacetime routes were to the South American ports, she and her sister ship, the U.S.S. Argentina, had been equal in luxury and nearly in speed to all but two or three liners on the Atlantic.

Harry wondered where he would be going but decided that he had benefited in the Army by not questioning the orders that he had received. He had discovered that recognition and now promotion and other considerations came from conscientiously and unquestioningly following and enforcing orders, and that now was not the time to change his attitude.

Reflections

His area cleaned to his satisfaction, Harry put on his heavy field jacket, stepped out into the passageway, checked his I.D. with the enlisted guard on duty, and made his way up to the exercise and relaxation deck assigned to junior officers. Blackout regulations were at a minimum as the ship was still moored in the New York harbor, and Harry could see the cigarette glows of groups of fellow officers. Not a smoker in any form or wanting to join the conversation, Harry went to the darker side of the deck that was next to the interned French luxury liner, Normandie. In the two days and a night that he had been on board, Harry found this to be a rather isolated area that he had not been obliged to share with anyone.

Silently making his way through the darkness, he slid his hands along the guide ropes that had been strung around the ship's decks. As he neared his destination, Harry became aware of a puzzling but pleasant odor. Shrugging it off as some strange doings of the winds that continually swept in and out on the piers and jetties, he continued on.

His hand suddenly found that the rough, damp rope had become warm and soft. He instinctively drew back, and as he did, he sensed a nearby faint rustling and movement. For a split second Harry felt alarmed, and then his months of intensive and specialized training and conditioning took over. He froze in breathless silence--listening. No sound! No sight! Nothing! But by now Harry knew where to find what he could not see or hear.

One hand still clutching the guide rope, he carefully reached out again and felt a warm softness. As he became aware that what he was touching had the familiar feel and shape of a face, he found his hand suddenly grasped and his fingers wrenched so that they seemed to be torn from their roots. He was further tortured by teeth being sunk into his already tormented flesh. Roaring in pain, he tried to wrench his hand free, but his unseen assailant twisted, tore, and bit deeper. Harry let go of the rope with his free hand and, half lunging, swung his fist at where he judged his foe to be. His deduction had been correct and he felt the shock of the solid contact of his fist and the relaxing of the grip and teeth on his hand.

Following his advantage, Harry smashed his adversary against the nearby bulkhead and then onto the deck. Harry quickly rolled his assailant over and drove his knee into its back while his undamaged hand clawed for a handful of hair. He was about to deliver a judo chop to the back of the neck when he realized that the strange but pleasant odor was coming from the fistful of near-shoulder-length hair that he was clutching. "What in the name of hell is a woman doing on the deck of an all-male military transport? What have I gotten myself into now?" he thought? He suddenly wished that he could just evaporate.

All of the resistance and fight was gone from the woman. Harry frantically dragged her across the darkened deck and through the blackout curtain into a low-lighted, but empty passageway. After securing the curtain and glancing around to be sure that no one was coming, he returned his attention to his still unconscious tormentor.

Harry propped her up against the passageway wall. He brushed aside her soft auburn hair that had fallen forward, covering most of her face and discovered a rapidly rising red lump next to her right eye. What really caught Harry's attention, though, was a military raincoat with bright, gleaming, silver, First Lieutenant's bars on each shoulder.

"Good God, Harry groaned, "I've clobbered a female Lieutenant! They'll hang my butt for sure!" Harry jumped up and fidgeted about wondering what he should do. He decided to run. As he started to pull the curtain back to leave, he wondered if she might really be badly hurt. Deciding that he'd better take a closer look, he returned to see if he could check her pulse or something. Harry listened, but he couldn't hear her breathing over the vibrations and humming of the ship. He tried to feel for her pulse, but could not find it. Harry found that if he was going to listen for a heartbeat, he was going to have to get down on his hands and knees and put his ear to her chest. He momentarily thought he could reach inside the trench coat to see if he could feel a heartbeat, but he also realized that if someone should come along or if she should regain consciousness about that time, he'd never be able to explain why his hand was fumbling inside her blouse.

He propped her up in a corner and carefully positioned her head so that it was properly balanced. He noticed that her color was returning and that she was quite young, and even in this condition very beautiful. Harry retreated to the wall across the narrow passageway and hunched down to inspect the damage to his throbbing and bleeding hand and to consider what to do while he watched the woman for further evidence of recovery. As he sat wondering what he should do, he noticed that she had moved and that her eyelids fluttered. Her lips parted ever so slightly, and she even seemed to be taking regular, though painful, breaths.

He looked at the girl's face. One of her eyes was swollen shut; the other was trying to focus on him.

"Where am I?" she sobbed. "Who did this to me, who tried to kill me?"

Harry remained frozen as her undamaged eye finally came to rest on him and then on his bloodied, throbbing, and now swelling hand. She took it in hers and examined it in the dim light. Harry watched helplessly as she first felt and then recognized the deep scratches and marks left by her nails and teeth. She dropped his hand and shaking her bent head, sobbed,

"Oh my God! It was you! You attacked me! I hurt so badly--I hurt all over!"

Harry didn't know what to say. He didn't know what to do. He felt that time had stopped and that he was guilty of causing that too. He became aware that the girl had stopped talking and, though she was still sobbing, was less convulsive. He realized that both of his hands were wet from where her tears had fallen as well as the blood. He felt ashamed but remained silent. After a few moments the girl got her breathing under control and pulling away from his clumsy efforts to help her, dragged herself to her feet, and staggered toward the curtained doorway.

Harry finally found his voice and huskily croaked, "Hey! You can't go out there in the dark the way you are! Wait!" But without so much as a look his way, the girl brushed his words aside with a wave of her arm and plunged through the curtains and staggered out into the night.

Harry scrambled to his feet and followed, but she was gone. The darkness made searching futile. "I can't believe this really happened! You'd a thought it was my fault. Dammit, if she would have said something when I walked up, or acted like a person, none of this would have happened. It sure as hell wasn't my fault!"

The next day Harry discovered that an army field hospital nursing unit commanded by Colonel Fern Hawthorne had moved onto the "B" Deck of the ship for the crossing. As if as by magic, all of the class "A" officer's uniforms leaped out of the bottom of the barracks bags, and permission to go unshaven during the voyage was forgotten. The ship's commissary was cleaned out in one afternoon. No troop transport ever smelled better.

That afternoon Harry met his compartment mates. First Lieutenant Walter Abher, a coastal geodetic surveyor for the Army Corps of Engineers, and First Lieutenant Alvin Keesling, an Infantry heavy weapons specialist. Neither officer seemed to offer any real idea why he had been ordered on the ship, and both shared Harry's ignorance as to where they were going.

By the time Abher had explained how everything was bigger and better in Texas and Keesling had waxed on about the girls and cows of his Wisconsin, the sun had moved to somewhere west of both locations, and Harry along with each of them had decided to turn in.

The three men awoke the next morning to unprecedented activity. Hurrying out on the officer's deck, they found that the ship was gorging itself with soldiers in full battle dress and equipment marching in a steady stream up the six gangplanks.

Booms and cranes were struggling to fill the open hatches with trucks, artillery pieces, bags, crates, barrels, aircraft parts, and cases of uncountable numbers that were untranslatably stenciled. Trucks were backed up to conveyors sending carton after carton of foodstuff into the lower refrigerated compartments. Messengers and orderlies were streaking to all parts of the ship.

Harry was called to "A" deck and informed that from sixteen hundred to twenty-four hundred hours for the voyage, in keeping with his Military Police training, he would be Provost Officer of the ship. He would be responsible for the security of the ship, a section of the military police detachment, and the posting of the guard. Harry was impressed beyond expression by the assignment and in later life would refer to this as one of the early positive influences on his career.

By the time darkness began to creep across the eastern horizon, the loading had been completed, and within another two hours the ship was certified secured for sailing. The Merchant Marine hands and the Navy gun crew were fed, and then came the first try at feeding the troops--14,500 advance party and special services officers and enlisted men and women nurses--as well as the stowed away passenger list consisting of seven dogs, two cats (one pregnant), a "matched" pair of snakes, a profane crow, and a nervous skunk of questionable origin, disposition, and medical history. The combined feedings took slightly over five hours, which tried the patience of some but exceeded the expectations of others. In two days, the time would be cut to less than three hours, and that acceptable schedule was held throughout the passage.

After all personnel were fed, they were ordered to remain in quarters, with the exception of the people assigned to Mess and K. P. duty, runners, orderlies, and, of course, the guards.

Early the next morning, while the general restrictions were still in effect, the ocean liner was 'warped' from her moorings by the tugboats and eased out into the Hudson River and into the holding area. Because he had been assigned to the 'Bridge Deck' as a result of his Provost Officer duties, Harry had the good fortune to witness all of this precise maneuvering. During the rest of the day, all of the 'Decks' were brought up for exercise and relaxation in the sun. The following night, the tugs took the great ship down the river through the 'Narrows' and past the Statue of Liberty, out into the lower New York Bay, and cast her loose.

When the sun burned the fog and surface clouds away the following morning the soldiers who were on deck discovered that they were alone on the ocean. This caused considerable alarm for many since it had not occurred to them that the ship, able to make well over thirty-five knots, could easily outrun any submarine in the Atlantic and nearly all of the surface vessels. Once the word was passed around from the Merchant Marines and the Navy gun crew, the uneasiness was replaced by casual lolling about the decks, 'crap' and card games, and spitting over the sides--which was quickly curtailed by the Ship Master's prompt order: "No Spitting!"

On the second day at sea, the 'men' learned that their destination was Southampton, England. A short while later the puzzle that arose with this announcement was solved when the 'tropical equipment' labels on the prominent cartons on the after-deck were stripped off, revealing orders for the European Theater of Operations. The false labeling was part of a successful deception intended to mislead the suspected informants of the offshore German submarine pack into lying in wait along a route to the Panama Canal for a 'leaked' troop movement to the South Pacific, while in reality the ship was running at flank speed on a northerly route for Southampton.

For a short time during the voyage, the ship was accompanied by two destroyers. She passed through a convoy late one afternoon, and, unknown to all but a few of the bridge and signal personnel, relayed information to the British Atlantic fleet Rescue Service on the sighting of debris and the lifeboats of a torpedoed merchantman. Her own orders were to stop for nothing. It was expected that the British navy would affect the rescue that could not be expected of the great ship. The crossing was probably logged as routine, although the Captain's log did show that she had outrun a roving 'wolf-pack' of four-to-eight submarines off the coast of Greenland and lost them after the third day. It further noted that she had been sighted, and supposedly reported, by two German reconnaissance planes about one hundred miles out of Southampton. While a German bomber searching for her could be heard in the clouds above, she had masterfully used the cloud cover and gathering darkness to cloak her final dash for the port. Without further incident, she docked in nine days and six hours--one hour and forty-five minutes later than her proposed arrival time.

Even though Harry was busy for the entire crossing, he did wonder what had happened to 'his' lady First Lieutenant. He did not see her during the crossing and would have missed her at the debarkation had not a young sailor from the Navy Gun Crew discovered that there had been women on board.

In his excitement the sailor leaned far over the rail, yelling wildly, "Hey! We had women on here, and I missed it all! Look, there's hundreds of 'em comin' out!" Harry looked over the side just in time to see a First Lieutenant with soft auburn hair, now cut in a boyish bob, and take one last look at the ship that had brought her to England. Harry felt sure that it was she as he absently rubbed his still-tender hand. He was filled with mixed feelings and regrets, but decided that he should be glad that his involvement with her was over. He reflected that even from this distance she sure was darn good-looking! "Too-bad" he mumbled and got ready to go.

CHAPTER NINE

Because of his shipboard duties, Harry was one of the last to leave the ship. He did manage to return to his quarters in time to say goodbye to Abher and Keesling. While they had not had a great deal of time together on the trip, they all agreed that they had established a common bond. They exchanged home addresses and promised that when they got their assignments, they would try to get together in London sometime. Each had been shipped unattached to England. None appeared to know what to expect or where he would be assigned.

As he was getting his things together, Harry was called to come to the compartment that served as Colonel Middleton's Provost Office. Harry entered and saluted his superior officer. His salute was returned, and he was told to stand at ease.

"Lieutenant Morgan," the Colonel said. "I wish to commend you for the manner in which you handled your portion of the security and guard duties on this voyage. While the whole voyage was for the most part without incident, your's were the most difficult hours. Oh, there was that one incident where an army nurse was assaulted during your watch time before the ship put to sea. However, since it was before you were assigned we can't hold you accountable for that."

The Colonel opened a file folder and went on, "It is my intention to make notes in your file of your fine efforts. As I was reading the file, I noticed that you have military police training. Give me a rundown on your background. Are you graduated from a college yet, Lieutenant Morgan?"

"No Sir, not yet." Harry replied.

How much college do you have, Lieutenant?" The Colonel pressed on in what now seemed to Harry to be a mocking tone.

"None, Sir." Harry responded.

"None? Do you think that's good?

Harry was startled and began to boil inside. He was sure he had become the object of the Colonel's scorn, and he began to lose his self-control. He felt that he was locked into another old man Bender. He started to burst out in anger, "I . . . , I sure as . . ." Harry stopped short and held his temper as he sensed that the Colonel was up to something and was watching his reactions very closely. He knew that the next minutes, even seconds, were critical.

The Colonel leaned back in his chair and folded his arms across his chest and, with what Harry took to be a taunt, repeated, "Lieutenant! Do you think you're as good as college people are? After all, you only got through high school. Tell me something. How did you get to be a First Lieutenant at your age? What are you, twenty-two, or so?"

"Yes, sir." Harry tightly responded.

"You could just be another '90 day wonder, OCS second Lieutenant, but that's not what I see on these papers before me. You must have had powerful friends along the way who looked out for you!" He glanced down at the paper he held in his hand. "I see where you got your promotion just two days before you came on this vessel. Furthermore, that promotion was ordered from Fort Meyers, Virginia. You know, Lieutenant, that is very unusual. According to your records, you have never even been at Fort Meyers!" Leaning forward in his chair and irritably punching his finger at the folder, the Colonel went on, "How do you explain all of this to me, Lieutenant? . . . Hmmmm? . . . I'm waiting, Lieutenant! And--return to attention!"

Harry realized that the Colonel was not only mocking him, he was daring him, and, having placed him at attention, was making the meeting a matter of military record. To further complicate matters, Harry realized that the Colonel and he had been joined by two other people who were sitting behind him, just out of Harry's line of vision. He felt that he needed to get a clear look at them, but, being at attention, he could not face other than forward. Why hadn't the Colonel shown this side of his nature during the nine days of the crossing? Harry had reported to the Colonel numerous times, and the relationship had been either pleasant or, at the least, uneventful and militarily correct.

"Lieutenant! I am still waiting for an answer! Are you, too, along with me, wondering about you, Lieutenant? Or, can't you think of an answer to give me?"

"Colonel, Harry began, "I didn't go to college at all. I didn't go because there was no money to go with. I went to work for twenty-six cents an hour when I got out of high school. My mother scrubbed offices for people that I mowed lawns for, for money so that I could even finish high school. I went to work because I had to be the man in the family. I had a father, but he left for work one day and just kept on going. After that, I had to help out.

"I had a job, and when it looked like war, I found that if volunteered for the service, and if I could become an officer I could send my mother an allotment check bigger than what I was able to give her from my regular job, and if I enlisted I could get a chance at the service I wanted.

"I always wanted to be a policeman, but there was no chance at home. I wanted a job with responsibility and a future, but there was no chance for that either. Then the Army gave me a chance at both, and I could still help my mother. I enlisted and went through Officer's Candidate School, and they commissioned me a Second Lieutenant. I got sent to the Military Police School at Fort Belvoir, then I went on to Fort Devons to learn military map reading, and then to Maryland where I learned Code. S-2 Army Intelligence training came next. From there I went to Fort Benning for parachute training and then to Fort Bragg for more jump and glider training. You have my record, Colonel. Whatever there is, it's all there. I can't tell you how I got to be a First Lieutenant! I thought that somebody upstairs thought it was time. I didn't know that my orders came from Fort Meyers or why they came from anywhere. I can only tell you that I have been on detached service ever since I got out of O.C.S. About college; if I could have gone, I would have, but I couldn't! I had to make the most out of what I had, and this is the best I could come up with!"

As Harry finished, he continued to himself, "Why do people with power have to act like old man Bender? Someday, Colonel, you are going to get yours!"

The Colonel leaned forward and glanced through the folder one more time, and then looking up at Harry, with a trace of a smile, said, "Yes, Lieutenant, I have your record here. You covered it pretty well; however, I didn't expect that we would become so involved in your personal life. However, while that adds interest it is beside the point.

"What you did fail to tell me, and which you may or may not know, was that you graduated from every military class either first or second. You also seem to be unaware that throughout your military life the same notes appear again and again. 'Very high achiever--' 'Has a strong must-have complex--' 'Makes no close friends, only acquaintances--' 'Displays no deep trust in others, only in self--' 'Highly capable--' 'A loner--.' Now, Lieutenant, all of this, combined with your present attitude, can add up to a very big plus or an equally large minus for your military career. By the way, you may stand at ease again.

"About the matter of the college education, I could not care less, but Lieutenant; I do care what you think about it. I pounded a beat as a Detroit cop for ten years. I studied at night school for my College and Law degrees and I spent five years as a revenue agent during prohibition. I know what I think about an education. It's what you think about it that I am concerned about. Your answers came off most satisfactory.

"Now, what I also want to know is WHY you think you are here, and WHAT you think you can do about what I am about to further explain to you. Take a chair, Lieutenant."

Harry, confused by the twisting and turning of the events, moved to a chair. As he turned, he discovered that the two people who had earlier sat down in the back of the room were Abher and Keesling, but they were no longer First Lieutenants.

Abher had become a Lieutenant Colonel wearing the wings of the Army Air Corps and Keesling had been transformed into a Major wearing Marine Corps insignia.

Colonel Middleton smiled and motioning toward Abher and Keesling, said, "Lieutenant, did you know that on the way over you were the subject of an exercise in surveillance and counter spying for these two officers? Until just thirty minutes ago, neither knew that you were the officer you said you were, or that each of them said they were. We wanted these two officers to observe you, but at the same time to observe each other. Both of them thought you and the other were suspected of being subverted, and they were each to submit a report on their conclusions. Both of them were told to watch the other for signs of weakness and the possibility that you might try to subvert the other. They were ordered not to confide in one another, as you might have broken through the other, and in any case, their cover would have been lost and with it their usefulness in the future. We found this to be a most interesting exercise, and the results, along with this interview, conclusively tell me that it is time to bring you in on why you have been ordered to England.

"In the first place, Lieutenant, I have been your Commanding Officer for the over the past year. I became aware of your record shortly after your graduation from O.C.S. You appeared to be rather young, and for that reason we decided to have you continue with Military Police training. We allowed, and sent you through the Air Corps map reading program and then on to the tactical jump schools at Benning and Bragg. Beyond that, we have been watching your progress, and we now feel that you are ready for the next stage of your training, which, very frankly, sorts the boys from the men and then beyond that, the men from the men.

"You must realize that if there is any boy left in you, you are too dangerous to yourself and this program and we can't afford to endanger these critical activities with immaturity. The odds are that you will not make it through the training. Only two out of every five do. We want you to be aware of these odds because what I am getting to is to offer you the opportunity to volunteer for a very unusual and exclusive branch of your country's military; the Foreign Intelligence Forces, also known as the Office of Strategic Services, or more cryptically; O.S.S.

"You seem to show an unusual capacity to learn languages rapidly, and we will be sending you through a high speed course to learn Dutch, French, German and Arabic. After you have acquired a satisfactory knowledge and use of the languages, you will continue your training with Ranger-Commando orientation in Scotland. Beyond that, I cannot tell you any more at this time. You will have twenty-four hours to make your decision, during which time you will be confined to this ship. If you decide to reject this opportunity, you will be reassigned somewhere over here as a Military Police officer.

"If you decide to join our team, you will be given a five-day leave in the London area followed by a short orientation period. Following that, you will be forwarded to the First stage training school and language schools, and then on for further preparation until you are, as our British friends say, 'Posted, Service

Ready.' If you have any further questions, Major Keesling and Colonel Abher will be able to help you."

Harry stood at attention as the Colonel left the room. Then he slouched back into his chair, only to jump up again with the realization that the remaining officers now substantially out-ranked him.

Keesling said, "Okay, Morgan, be at ease. Get the load off your feet. Let's finish talking this out as far as we can. Abher and I have been playing private spy for the past ten days, and you just about wore both of us out. I'll tell you, when we found out he and I were both in the same business, it really broke us up. It turned out that we were both a hell of a lot more suspicious of each other than we were of you."

Chiming in, an amused Abher suggested, "Go bring your gear up here and stow it in the cabin across the passageway. The Colonel is gone and that leaves this whole side of the ship to us. Get going and we'll see you later.

CHAPTER TEN

Harry lay stretched out on the bunk with his hands folded behind his head, staring at the ceiling. Nothing seemed to register from the conversation of the past hour. Still puzzled, he got up and went to the cabin next door looking for Keesling or Abher. Peering through the partially open door to Abher's compartment Harry saw that he was asleep on his bunk, but, in looking into Keesling's room, he found him reading a tour guide of England. Harry knocked.

Looking up, Keesling waved Harry into the room, "Need something, Harry?"

"Well, I have some questions."

"Try me."

"If I decide to go in with you guys, can I change my mind along down the line? And if I can, do you have any idea when it gets to the point that I can't?"

Keesling folded the tour guide and put it in his pocket. Making himself comfortable on his bunk, he motioned Harry to the chair in the corner. "Hell of a fine question, he said. "Don't know the whole answer for sure, but I'd say for a while you can change your mind. I do think that after you get into the Ranger-Commando training 'you are committed'. Time-wise, that's about six months down the line, but it could be six weeks, too. Nobody really knows what the timetable is around here.

"You still have to make up your own mind about this business, but it can't hurt to take the language courses which come first. If nothing else, think about the jump you'll have on the rest of the guys when it comes to picking up bimbos in North Africa, Italy, or France and then Germany--if that's the direction, you're headed. I've been through these language courses. They're great! They stick with you, too, I took them in '40, and when I got in for the refresher a year later, I was back in the swing of things in a couple of days. They say Abher, here, is a language wiz, particularly in French. With his dark complexion, he passes for whatever he wants to. When he's in Africa, the French think he's an Arab with bad French, and the Arabs think he's a Frenchy with bad Arabic. He's really got it made! Now, my red hair kind'a makes it hard to explain what Arab tribe I came from, but I can still manage to know what's going on. You gotta suit yourself, though, Harry."

Harry nodded and thanked Al for his help.

The next morning he told Abher and Keesling that they could count him in. Within an hour, he was on a train headed for London with a tour guide in one hand, a five-day pass in the other, and a redheaded, grinning Keesling for a companion. Harry supposed that Lieutenant Colonel Abher was still catching up on his sleep back on the ship.

The trip to from Southampton to London was uneventful. Major Keesling, who preferred to be called "Al," spent most of his time either quietly admiring the countryside that rushed past the high speed train or spreading maps all over the compartment which they shared with other military personnel.

Keesling finally folded the maps and put them away and, hunching down in the corner of the seat, fell asleep. In looking about, Harry discovered that he was the only person still awake in the compartment.

Playing soldier-cop in the swamps and simulated towns in Tennessee, the Carolinas, and Georgia was one thing; becoming a soldier-spy somewhere in Africa or Europe seemed to be another. Harry spent most of the next half-hour wondering what he had gotten himself into, and when no answers came, he finally gave up and went to sleep.

Had he remained awake for only a few more minutes, he might have seen an Army Nurse with soft auburn hair dragging an oversized duffel bag past his compartment

CHAPTER ELEVEN

FIRST LIEUTENANT SALLY ANN ARCHER had had just about all she wanted of the United States Army Nurse Corps! Being an Army Nurse was a lot of tough work--although she'd volunteered. But this dragging everything a girl owned around in a green canvas bag just didn't help make life any better. After being assaulted and then seasick on that 'boat' she had just about no esprit de corps left in her.

Her luck was running true to form. She had been late getting away from the ship because of her interview with Colonel Hawthorne, and now she had been run out of the civilian section of this silly train and left to fend for herself. "Please God; just let me find a corner to sit in. Just for five minutes."

Finding herself in the military section of the segregated train, she thought she saw an empty seat, but then in dismay realized that the space was really taken by a hunched down, soundly sleeping, marine officer. Sally wrestled her load past two more compartments before she found one with an empty three-seat bench that she promptly threw herself upon. Punching her duffel bag into a crude pillow, she fell into an exhausted sleep. As she drifted into sleep, it occurred to her that the soldier sleeping across from the marine officer looked a little like the idiot who had beat her up while the boat was in New York. She'd go back and take a better look at him if she weren't so darn exhausted.

CHAPTER TWELVE

When the London section of the train pulled into Waterloo Station on that twenty eighth day of May 1942, all hell was breaking loose. The newspapers were reporting that Rommel had broken through in the Bir Hacheim sector of Tunisia and was driving for Tobruk. Should he become successful in this move—and there seemed to be nothing that could stop him--Rommel would be in a favorable position to consolidate his advances and drive on to take Alexandria and Cairo. From there, he could easily cut the vital Suez Canal shipping route and drive for the Arabian and Persian oil fields. With this decisive wedge in the Allied side, it would be a matter of weeks before England was cut off from her needed colonies and eastern allies. A British defeat in Egypt would set the stage for the final link-up between von Schulls' Panzer Divisions that were steadily advancing toward the Ural-Caspian lowlands of Russia and the victorious Desert Legions of Rommel. Hitler's dreams of encircling and holding control of all of the oil of the Balkans, the Carpathians, and the Arabian States would be realized. Without question, oil would tip the balance of power in this war. Without oil, the English bulldog would be chained to his island. Without oil, the Russian bear would starve in his mountains.

In addition to the ominous news in the papers, German Luftwaffe's night bombers were causing immense destruction in London, Guilford, and as far north as Leicester. London's damage was particularly devastating in the Waterloo Station vicinity.

When Harry and Keesling came out of the station, they were greeted by their first taste of the cruel and savage struggle. Until now, the war had been a headline in a newspaper, a radio commentary by Edward R. Murrow, or a letter from a relative or friend. But now the war was all around them. They could feel it and smell it. As they emerged from the station, they could feel the fear that crept into everyone. Neither of them ever forgot that early morning in London.

Half a block away, a fire brigade and home guard unit was loading its equipment in preparation for pulling out from a bombed building, when a delayed action bomb leveled what was left of five stories of the building and ruptured a large gas line under the street. The flames blew into the sewers and out through the drain and manhole grate sending lethal showers of bricks, mortar, metal, and other debris in all directions, driving the brave and foolhardy alike toward the shelters.

Sirens screamed in advance of the returning fire vehicles and ambulances. As Harry and Al fled wildly from the station's portico they blindly ran out into the street and into the path of an on-coming ambulance. The bleating of the horn was completely lost in the plethora of sound that engulfed them. The wetness of the street from the fire hoses of the past night turned the tires of the vehicle into gliders. Then without warning, the unsuspecting pair was tumbled off of their feet and onto a nearby pile of sandbags.

The ambulance, nearly out of control in its efforts to avoid the two bewildered Yanks, careened by as its totally unnerved driver yelled out, cursing their stupidity, blindness, and animal forbearers. As the dazed pair scrambled to right themselves, they found their path blocked by a squat little lady who was calmly pinning her hat back onto her graying hair. Still clenching a couple of bobby pins in her teeth as she finished the job, she reproached them,

"Yanks! If you do not take better care of yourselves, you'll be of no use whatsoever in helping our lads to turn back the Jerry. Whatever did you rush into the street for? And then to turn your backsides to the lorry! Mercy, the bombs and the fires are bad enough, but we just can't have everyone--and especially gentlemen of service--popping about and panicking! It's a bad example for our children, you know."

Harry and Al looked at one another in utter disbelief, and then back at this English 'Nanny'. It was Al who finally found his voice, saying, "Ma'am, it looks like you saved our hides for us. I sure didn't see that truck, and with all the other noise, I couldn't tell where the siren was coming from. Isn't that right, Harry?"

"Uh-huh", mumbled Harry, still captivated by this unflappable benefactor, who, having looked to her purse to see that it was properly closed, calmly began to brush the sand and dirt from her cloak. Harry was convinced that he was watching a real live Dickens character.

"Harry, help me get this lady's stuff together. We'd better move out of here before something else goes up. What's your name, lady? The Marine Corps owes you a debt for saving me, and the Army owes you something for him."

"Oh yes, I'm Mrs. Worsham. Mrs. Stanley Worsham, but my dear Stanley is gone now."

"Sorry to hear that, Ma'am. I'm Alvin Keesling. I'm a Major in the American Marine Corps. That one that's staring at you is Harry Morgan. He's a First Lieutenant in our Army. Can we help you with anything, Ma'am?"

"No, not a'tall. I have just arrived at the station from Harrow and was walking out here when all of this came about. I was going to the linen shop down the way to see if I could find some material to make new napkins for the tables at our Inn."

Harry finally emerged from his trance; "Do you work at an Inn, Ma'am?"

"Oh, my now. I do and I don't. The Inn is my dear departed Stanley's and mine. But with all the war shortages and rationing, there really isn't much left of it. I keep it together in memory of my dear departed husband because it was in his family for over two hundred years, and it is so nice to have guests from time to time when there is a holiday. It's not really very much, but it's nice for me to have something, you know."

By now Mrs. Worsham was moving down the street toward the linen shop with the two Yanks tagging along. Harry again found his voice, "Mrs. Worsham, is Harrow far from here?"

"Oh, about a one-hour ride on the express, and a little longer on the commuter. It's a nice trip through the countryside."

"That's not bad. Harry replied, "I have a five-day pass, and I haven't the slightest idea what to do or where to go. If I can afford it, I would like to go to your Inn at Harrow for a couple of days. I have a lot of things to think about, and I would appreciate being your guest if you could find a room for me."

"I was going to look for some of the night and entertainment places around London, Al said, "but that sounds like a great idea! I'd like to spend a day or two out there, too. How about it, Ma'am?"

Measuring the two young men, Mrs. Worsham smiled and said, "I'll strike up a bargain with the two of you. Meet me in two hours at the station platform that reads Harrow with your tickets bought, and I'll put together a pair of rooms for you when we get to the Inn. Rest assured that the cost will not endanger your pocketbooks. I am not sure that the modest bill of fare will suit your lavish American taste fancies, but that will be your chance to take. Now, off with you while I go about my shopping."

Feeling sunnier than she had since her dear Stanley had died some fifteen years earlier, she toddled off to see about her linen.

CHAPTER THIRTEEN

Dusk was beginning to descend on Harrow as Harry, Al, and Mrs. Worsham, stepped from the train to the platform. During their ride, they talked of many things. They learned that while her given name was Dorothy-Daphne, she preferred to be called Mrs. Worsham in memory of her dear Stanley. They discovered that England really was backed to the wall, and, while there were plenty of people along the sidelines cheering England on, only England's people had been suffering and dying. The boys began to realize that there was a vast difference because England had been at war for nearly three torturous years, while America, as far as Europe was concerned, had only been *going* to war for a little over six months.

The passengers on the train seemed to enjoy the young Americans. Mrs. Worsham told Harry and Al that while there were still English who remembered with discomfort some of the Yanks of the American Expeditionary Forces of 1918, most everyone else shared a readiness to open their homes and their hearts to the Yank sons and daughters who were now coming to their aid.

Mrs. Worsham was childless. Her husband had died years before his time because of gassing and wounds received in

Flanders during World War I. She was brave and she was a hard worker. But she was alone and starved for friendship. All of the young people whom she could have mothered had long since left for the war or the factories in the west, beyond the reach of the German bombers. She had resigned herself to living out her days in keeping the memory of her cherished husband alive by doggedly keeping the two-century-old Spotted Dog Inn open, to which her Stanley had brought her home to as a new bride in 1910.

She felt a warm glow as she watched the two young men visiting with the passengers on the train, and took pride in the fine impression that they made. As she thought about it, she decided that their coming into her life was a reward from above, and she was determined that this benefaction would not go unnoticed. God had been good to her in the past, and now He had shown his care for her again. She would pass on His gifts in her treatment of these two fine boys.

She could tell that Mr. Keesling--Alvin--was a young man who liked to live life to its fullest. She could not be too matronly with him. He might say and do some things that would startle her Victorian nature, but he had been so pleasant and kind to her that she would look the other way if that became necessary. She instinctively knew that young women would be drawn to him, but that he would not be unkind or abusive. He would be no problem.

She had watched Mr. Morgan--Harry--from the start. How she wished he could have been the son she had never had. He was a fine figure of a man. He stood as tall as Mr. Barlow, the conductor on the train, and she knew him to be six feet and two inches because he took pride in his height and spoke of it from time to time. Harry's shoulders were square and broad and his chest filled out his well-tailored military uniform. Judging from the look of the rest of him, she thought he must weigh well over fifteen stones. Her curiosity getting the better of her, she quietly inquired, "Mr. Morgan, how many stones do you carry?"

"I beg your pardon?" Harry answered in surprise.

"I asked you how many stones you are. Your weight."

"Oh. According to the army, I weigh about one hundred ninety-six pounds. But what's that got to do with stones?"

"You don't take the measure of your weight in stones?"

"Nope, I'm afraid not."

"And you gauge your weight by currency? My stars but you Yanks must be a wealthy lot."

"Currency? What's money got to do with it?"

"Pounds, lad. Good English Sovereigns of gold. Do you mean to say that you Yanks balance your measure with gold?"

"That's not at all what he means to say to you, Widow Worsham," a deep rumbling voice announced.

Twisting around to face the speaker who was lightly leaning on the back of her seat, Mrs. Worsham said, "But you heard him, yourself, Mr. Barlow. He said that he measured his weight in pounds, and . . ."

"It's not that kind of pounds. See here. In my new railroad handbook for managing servicemen from, ahem, foreign lands, it says that Americans have attempted to carry on some fine old English traditions, but in their coming from their wilderness, they have confused their money with their drinking habits. It takes fourteen of their pounds to make one of our stones.

My calculations make his proper weight to be exactly fourteen stones."

"Oh. Well then, what has drink to do with it?" Mrs. Worsham asked.

"My book says that Yanks will ask you for a place when they can become 'stoned'. We are not to weigh them, nor are we to pelt them in any way."

"Then what does your book say we are to do?"

"We are to direct them to the nearest pub, where they can, as my new handbook says, become 'stoned', which in their confusion means to have multiple 'pints.' Oh, yes, then we are to inform the constable and stand clear out of the way."

Dorothy Worsham shook her head. Such strange customs these Yanks have. But hadn't they always been known to be a strange lot?

As the train left them on the deserted Harrow platform, Al wondered aloud if there were a taxi or some other means of transportation. However, Mrs. Worsham made it clear that there was but one form of transportation available to them, and that was the two legs they stood on. So they trudged the near mile to her old Inn.

Through the fading light, they could see the Inn in the distance beyond a small park with a well-manicured English garden and a pond with two graceful black swans. An old abbey, part of which was in ruins, nestled close by the pond. In the distance, a quiet little stream scrambled out of the pond, and ran its way to the horizon where it appeared to pause pensively and then slip out of sight. As they reached the gates of the

Inn, the early spring sun slid from cloud to cloud and finally dropped from sight into the darkness.

For a time there was silence, and then, as the night moved in, there came from the southwest the snarling of the German airplanes. They brought with them their whomping messages, the angry glow of the fires they had set which clawed the darkness, and the ethereal feeling that reached to no sense, but which left a solemn awareness of the anguish and suffering of the hurt, the wounded, and the dying.

Harry and Al stood on the Inn's veranda. Sharing their concern for what they saw in the sky and their realization that this was just the beginning of their turn at war, they tried to conceal the fear that they found intermingling with the excitement that had crept into their awareness. Somehow the remoteness of the bombing let them experience the excitement of death, yet they each knew that the war had found them, and they were somehow both eager to engage it.

CHAPTER FOURTEEN

THE ROOM WAS COMFORTABLY COOL, and for the first time in many weeks Harry slept without care or concern. It was after ten o'clock when Mrs. Worsham called through the door to tell him that Mr. Keesling appeared to be returning for lunch from a walk he had taken around the lake. She felt sure that Mr. Morgan should get up to share the fare with him. After a bath, a hasty shave, and a change of uniform, Harry hurried into the Inn's breakfast room, just in time to hear Al happily boom through the door, "God, but England is beautiful in the spring! It's just like Wisconsin out there! If only they had a Wisconsin Ger___, er, I mean, if they had a Polish polka band here, I'd think I was in heaven!"

Harry and Mrs. Worsham exchanged wry grins as the humor of Al broke on each of them in separate ways. "Al," Harry said, "I think you had better explain to Mrs. Worsham that with you, Wisconsin is a state of sublimity and not a geographic location. I don't think she is up to the advertising campaign I got on the boat, but she does need something."

"Ok, Harry, you tell her for me . . . But, I guess you just did, didn't you?"

As Mrs. Worsham left to bring the lunch, Al leaned over and said in a low voice, "Harry, you ought to see the women around here. There must be seven or eight of 'em to every man in the town, and the guys are all over seventy-five from the looks of them. You gotta see the one I think I got lined up for tonight. There ain't one brick out of place, and on top of that she's got bricks in places like you just wouldn't believe. This looks like one heck of a place to go hunting. I think if the season ain't open, I just opened it. I sure expect to know by morning! Oops, watch it; here she comes!"

"Here's your luncheon, boys. I am so pleased to have you both here. Did you rest well last night?"

"Oh yes, Mrs. Worsham."

"Sure thing, Mrs. Worsham."

The two young men pitched in, and, after the initial collision of American taste buds and British kidney pie, dined heartily, not only on the fare upon the table, but on the hovering attention of the beaming Mrs. Worsham.

"Mrs. Worsham?"

"Yes, Mr. Keesling."

"You know, you have been treating the two of us like we were part of your family. I know Harry likes it, and for my part, I'm just eating it up. I think it's really great of you, but I feel awkward. You call me Mr. Keesling. I'd feel a lot better if you were to call me Al, or even Alvin like my ma did when she was alive. Her and my pa both died about six, seven winters back from pneumonia. Just my kid sister and I pulled through. Would that be okay with you?"

Mrs. Worsham, beaming, sang out, "I'll strike another bargain with you Mr. Keesling. I, too, have given the matter some thought, and I will be honored to call you Al or Alvin--whichever you like--provided you no longer continue to so formally address me as Mrs. Worsham."

"Okay, what'll it be? Auntie?"

"That doesn't seem much better, does it?"

"No, it sure don't. How about Mom--or Mum?"

"It's a bargain, Mr. Keesling. Mum it is, Alvin!"

"Great. Mum and Alvin. What a pair! How about you, Harry? You want in? Ground floor opportunity!"

"Sure, if it's okay with Mum."

"Harry, you and Alvin are my Yank sons. I thank God for you and ask him to look after the both of you." With that she wiped the corners of her eyes with her apron and, giving each of the boys a peck on the cheek, hurried out into the pantry where she could be heard blowing her nose. Moments later, they heard a slightly off-key chorus of Gracie Fields' latest hit war song, "One for All and All for One".

After they had finished their luncheon, Al and Harry went out on the old veranda. 'Mum' soon joined them and settled herself in a rocker with her ever-present knitting.

"I was talking to an old geezer down the street this morning, Al began. "He tells me that there is a new training camp going up about twenty miles from here. He said that his younger brother had been hired as a carpenter to help put up temporary barracks in an old World-War I camp near here. We could be near home. He says everybody is looking for the Yanks to start coming over, but he also heard that this time they are going to keep them all over in Ireland. According to him, when the Yanks do come, all the guys at the pub are going to lock up their daughters this time for sure. Now this old geezer, he ain't got no daughter, so he's just going to lock *out* his old lady. The boys say they had too much hanky-panky around these parts in the last war and they're going to head it off before it starts this time. But the Yanks are welcome to his old lady."

Mum kept on with her knitting, but began to smile as she quietly nodded with each of Al's reports as he went on.

"He says the Yanks ain't ready for nothing like her anyway. He says he offered her to Churchill to send to Hitler instead of Chamberlain the next time. He thinks his old lady would get back Poland, the Czech country, and all the rest of it in just a couple of days. Hitler would be so damn glad to get her out of his hair he'd send all them countries back. He wants Hitler to keep France because it ain't worth getting back. All they do is make wine, get drunk and then make more lousy wine and trouble. He says Hitler deserves the French."

Harry laughed and began to ask Al about his new friend, but Al stopped him short.

"Wait, Harry, there's more. He wanted to know what a Marine was doing here. He knows that the Yanks use Marines for invasions, and he figures we must be invading England somewhere. He says that Mr. Churchill is a fine and a great man, and outside of his not giving the old geezer's wife to Hitler and getting her off his hands, he runs the war better than anybody, so if the Marines are invading England, he figures Mr. Churchill's got something else up his sleeve.

"And, then, after all of that, this old geezer reaches out and grabs the door knob of the house we happen to be passing, jerks the door open, jumps inside, and slams the door shut leaving me alone in the street, without as much as a twitch of an eye or a word of goodbye. You sure have some funny people around here, Mum."

Mrs. Worsham had continued to smile and punctuate each of Al's sentences with a nod of her head. As he finished she looked up at him and said, "You have had the pleasure of Old Ned this morning. I should have warned you about him. Consider yourself to have had good fortune to have made any sense whatever out of his ramblings."

"He's the darndest character I have ever seen. If you'll pardon my opinion, I think he's a little bit nuts."

Mrs. Worsham smiled. "He's harmless, but yes, he is also quite daft. Twenty and more years ago, he came home to his Rosie, the wife that he would have Mr. Churchill send off to Mr. Hitler, with a friend from the pub that he proposed to have share their bed with them that night.

"The problem, as Rosie saw it, was that she was not about to have either herself or Ned share their bed with anyone, particularly one named Muriel, who, the very first thing, asked to borrow Rosie's best night dress. Rosie made her point clear to this trollop of a Muriel with the poke in the front and then the wallop across the backside with her new hearth broom. When Muriel fled for her life, and poor old Ned protested the treatment of his newfound bosom friend with too great a zeal, Rosie closed the issue with him with a well-thrown, partially used chamber pot. It was well for the both of them that the pot missed old Ned and carried out through the windowpane where it harmlessly broke and ran into the street.

"What was not so well was that in old Ned's haste to scramble out of the path of the flying pot, he fell into the vegetable cellar. Yes, my lads, I'm obliged and sorry to say that he fell in a drunk and crawled back out a daft fool. They say he hit his head on a cask and it near finished him. One good thing came of it. He never tried to bring that Muriel home with him again.

"Now, off with the both of you, while an old woman makes up your beds and tidies her dirty house. The Inn is no place for you, what with the sun shining and the pretty girls about to air out their linens on the fences along the way. Scat, now!"

Needing no more encouragement, the two hastily excused themselves. Within minutes they were walking through Harrow's streets and looking into the shop windows, forgetting everything else in the world but this quiet, misplaced bit of heaven.

CHAPTER FIFTEEN

FIRST LIEUTENANT SALLY ANN ARCHER glanced out of the window of the railway coach for one last look at the countryside of Essex and the village of Great Wakening in particular. Getting away from Great Wakening, the forlorn and God-forsaken little collection of old houses and people and the dilapidated old World-War I hospital, was a guarantee of an improved future. It seemed that she had been at that spot in Essex for a lot longer than six months. But now she finally was shipping out for her next post, with a seventy-two hour leave to spend in London.

So far, being in England was nothing at all like she had hoped for. The exciting and romantic interludes she had looked forward to hadn't materialized, but for that matter, neither had the walks with someone through London's St. James or Hyde Parks. She had been so excited when Colonel Fern Hawthorne had told her that she had been assigned on temporary duty with the Seventh British Rehabilitation Hospital facility at Great Wakening. The Colonel had enthusiastically spoken of the surgery experience she would receive, and of the value it would be to the unit she would return to when the American casualties began to come in. The casualties of the

British North African campaign were already being transferred to Great Wakering from the overloaded hospitals in Cairo and Alexandria.

She suggested that even though Sally was only twenty-two she would be well on her way to Captain's bars within the next year.

Although she had specialized in psychiatric care, she had received advanced training in the administration of anesthesia at Johns Hopkins Hospital. This experience qualified her to help fill the breach caused by the gross lack of trained anesthetists, and near total absence of Anesthesiologists.

At Great Wakering she had assisted in uncountable hours of surgery and had put hundreds of men to sleep. She was very proud that every one of them had survived the anesthetic and at least had gotten as far as post-operative care. Indeed, she had done her job to the total satisfaction and delight of all concerned.

As her train sped closer to London, Sally thought about the free time ahead of her before she had to report to the new American hospital unit near Harrow. She checked to be sure that she still had the letter of introduction that her nerosurgical chief, Major Avery Martin, had given to her for his sister, Gwen.

Major Martin told her that he had not seen his sister for over a year but that he was sure that she still worked at Westminster Hospital. There would be a bedroom in Gwen's family flat that he was sure she could use. At the Westminster Hospital, she found that Gwen Martin was on duty. Sending in an identifying message, Sally sat down to wait.

"Lieutenant Archer?"

"Yes, are you Miss Martin?"

"I say, I can't believe my brother would know someone quite as lovely as you. You have to be a professional acquaintance of his. Avery is simply too stuffy to know anyone other than a doctor or a nurse. Sally got the letter out and, handing it to Gwen, replying, "This will explain everything."

As Gwen read the letter, she smiled. Returning the letter she said, "You may wish to keep this. Avery speaks most highly of you. I find it incredible that he wants me to show you a good time while you are in London. In the past it has always been, 'Gwen, try to bridle your pleasures!' He certainly is changing from the prig I have always known."

Sally smiled.

"It seems that this war has been good for my dear brother. Gwen went on. "He appears to be changing from an accomplished ass to somewhat of a human being. He may be discovering some of what he has been missing--and has been accusing me of enjoying and wallowing in these many years! Regardless, you are going to have the time of your life. I can promise you that!'

Gwen picked up Sally's uniform case and motioned for her to follow along with her duffel bag.

"Is Avery well? I suppose he is still working too hard?"

"Yes, on both counts. Your brother is a most dedicated man, Miss Martin."

"Gwen."

"Okay, my name is Sally Ann; call me Sally. That's what my friends do."

"Sally! I like that. Come along now, Sally. My flat is only a few minutes' walk from here. We'll be settled in before you know it. We'll get you a nice soothing bath, have a bit of tea and dinner, and then an evening on the town."

As they walked along, Sally noticed that the skies had cleared for what seemed to be the first time since she had arrived in England. Even the setting sun, nestling into the bosom of the horizon, seemed as spectacular as it had ever been in the mountains of her native Colorado. She felt a warm glow of happiness that told her things were finally looking up.

CHAPTER SIXTEEN

———

AFTER THE MONTHS OF ISOLATION and denial, Sally knew she would be grateful to Major Avery Martin for the rest of her life. She could only view the way she felt as a complete submission to the most delightful pleasures she had ever experienced. Never before had she felt so drained of energy, yet so sensually sparked. She had long since surrendered to the rapture of this enveloping and searching embrace.

She could feel a comforting caress wherever there was a sensitivity to signal. Wherever and whenever she willed, there was satisfaction. Each movement was accompanied by a countering, caressing pleasure. She had hardly expected that anyone or anything on earth could have provided her with such earthy stimulation.

Ever so slowly she began to stir, seeking the comfort of the jet sources beneath the bubbling white mounds of bubbles. Finally, she discovering the immensity of this great marble bathing pool, she languished for what seemed to her to be an eternity of sensuality. She regretfully found herself being obliged to return from her mental meanderings, and a short time later she stood beside the sunken tub, briskly drying herself with one of the large towels.

When Gwen had ushered her into the room, Sally's mind had been only on getting into a comfortable bath, and she probably would have been happy with a laundry tub as long as it was hot and private. Privacy was one thing that she had found that the Army wasn't long on. Every time she went to the bathroom, for anything, a dozen other people seemed to come along for the trip. In the six-woman shower stall, she could always count on at least eight other girls being there before she turned on the water. Even now, while she was undressing and filling the tub, she had halfway expected someone to pop, unannounced, from under the water!

In all of her life, Sally had never seen anything like Gwen's flat. The bubbling tub would easily accommodate two people at a time. And then the room! The bathroom walls, ceiling and doors were made entirely of mirrors. Even the floors were textured mirrors! There had been full length mirrors back home, but all of them had been at old Mrs. Gerkie's department store and she doubted that anyone had ever stood before one of them naked as she now was.

Looking around, Sally wasn't quite sure how to take advantage of this extraordinary room. Everywhere she looked she was greeted from another angle of another part of her anatomy, which she had never really paid attention to before. She glanced down to the mirrored floor and giggled. She had never before seen herself from that angle, either.

Her moods became more whimsical and capricious as she looked into the corners where the mirrors converged. It was possible to make herself into Siamese twins and accomplish the joining in some rather remarkable and interesting manners and places. In the case of a couple of them she was glad that all of this was being done with mirrors as the thought of such attachment and subsequent detachment being done in a surgical manner made her shudder.

As she continued to enjoy the novelty of the room, she began to tabulate her physical self. She weighed about 125 pounds. She had dazzling white teeth, auburn hair that simply glowed with its sheen.

A shade over five-feet-five-inches tall, she had silky-smooth skin that seemed to glow with her youthful vitality. She was remarkably free of body hair or blemishes except for a tiny beauty mark on her left thigh and a small mole on the back of her right forearm. The blemishes were insignificant in nature, although they did appear on her military medical record.

Glancing down, she was reminded of one thing that did not appear on her record. The second and third toes of each foot were webbed to the second joint. The old Irish doctor who had delivered her had told her father that the joining was a Hibernian omen of outstanding good fortune, never to be tampered with, since the webbing bore great evidence of her future good nature and hardiness for the bearing of great numbers of stout and gifted children. Nonetheless, it was good that her feet were strong, as were her smoothly curved calves and thighs. Her nursing profession required that she spend many tiring hours of walking and standing.

As she searched among her mirrored selves, she slowly swayed her weight from side to side, amused by the discovery of the dimples that seemed to wink merrily at her from the reflections of her backside. She was beginning to understand why she had been hearing throaty male mutterings behind her back for the past few years. Not half bad, she thought, once you got the right things moving at the right angle and in the right direction.

Her inventory continued as she further searched for an interesting profile. Her breasts satisfied her vanity with their firm and erect roundness and well-developed nipples. Moving back slightly so that the seam between the mirrors did not appear to nip off what nature had provided in such generous and provocative measures, she confirmed that her attention to diet and exercise had paid dividends. Her stomach lay flat and firm. Her smooth shoulders flowed into gracefully muscled arms. Her hands bore evidence of strength, yet a sensitivity and capacity for caring and tenderness.

Slipping into the cotton robe Gwen had laid out for her, she sat down before the dressing table. She pressed a switch, and the mirrors and the glass dressing table came alive with the soft glow of concealed lighting. It was almost too much to believe, but everything that had happened to her since she had met Gwen had been unbelievable.

Looking at herself in the mirror, Sally decided that, on the whole, the face that looked back at her from the mirror was attractive, even though she felt that her nose, while straight, was just a trifle small. She wondered how her hair would look in full bangs, and after trying and discarding the idea, drew her hair back to softly shield one eye, and parted and brushed it into place, much in the fashion she had been accustomed to wearing it. Further evaluating herself, she was satisfied that the arrangement best complimented her clear-skinned, healthy looks.

As Sally lingered in her inspection, she was reminded of her father's parting words as she boarded the Denver train for New York.

"Sally, I never really told you much. I don't know if I know how to now. But, I am so proud of you. There may not be another time to tell you that . . . besides, that . . . I love you very much.

Victor Archer cupped her face as gently as his calloused rancher's hands would allow and mustered up all of his years of silent love for his daughter. He cleared his throat. He haltingly continued, as if not wanting to show his awkwardness but knowing that he must have the courage to make this one last effort to express what was in his heart. "You can't never tell what will happen--these mountains ain't easy. You know that. Runnin' cattle back in these canyons, what with the wild critters and the bad back-country, it ain't the surest or safest way to make a livin'. But, it's all I ever know'd. And you know for yourself, it's the only place I know and the only place when your mother was living that we was happy.

"Every once in a while them mountains want something back in return for what we take out. You can never know when that might be. Your mother and me both know'd that, and when she got took from us with that pneumonia flue when you was a little tyke, I was thankful for what she and I did have together.

However, it was hard on you. That's why I'm so dang proud of you earning all them honors and chances to go to them schools. I never had the words to say so, so I just set back and was always just plain proud of you. So damn proud as a man could ever be...

"What I'm trying to say, girl, is that there may not be no other time for us. This is a hell of a time to try to make up for a lifetime of not saying what I should have been saying all along. But, I feel like I gotta try now because it could be all the time I ever got to say it. You got that same wonderful look about you that your mother had.

"She had that beauty--to me--that come from the way she could warm my heart with her way of caring for other folks and that special kindness that showed through her eyes. Sally, you got them same crystal-clear blue eyes. You got a love in them eyes like nothing I ever seen nowhere else 'cept in your mother. I never seen any blue in the world like them 'cept on you and your mother-- and the blue skies out here over our Rockies. I felt like I could always see clean into your mother's soul, and it was just like looking into that blue sky and seeing my own private piece of heaven. I always thanked my Maker that you got that same wonderful things about you."

Sally tried to speak, but her father had touched his work-roughened fingers to her lips, silencing her as he went on.

"So far you been so busy getting to be a good nurse and being a good daughter to me you ain't had time to find out that you're a woman, and a damn good woman, too. And that's the part that is hard for me to talk to you about.

"You're a damn good-looking female person now, Sally, but there's gonna come a day when you're really going to bloom out--just like a mountain flower. And when you do, feller's heads are gonna snap right off their shoulders when you go by. On top 'o-that, men are going to see you, and for lots of different reasons. What I'm trying to tell you is that you should keep your head. I always like to think that I was the right man for your mother, and I hope I treated her the way she surely deserved, and what I'm trying to find the way to tell you is that if you have patience and believe he's out there somewhere, the right man will come along for you. Your mother always said a woman has a way of knowing. I think you're enough like your mother that you will too.

"Remember, girl, I maybe never told you this like I should have, or when you could have used it, but I was always proud of you, and I always will be. I'll believe in and love you forever, no matter what." Victor Archer, his eyes brimming with tears of love for his daughter, pulled her tear-stained face to his and gently kissed her on the forehead and each cheek. She returned his kisses, and then he was gone. And before Sally knew it the train was pulling out.

Sally smiled in quiet recollection of her father and recognized what she saw in the mirrors was what her father had spoken about. She knew that she no longer had to let life pass her by. She was honestly ready for it. She also understood what her father had said. She was ready for its challenges as well.

Sally stood and allowed the robe to slowly creep from her shoulders and down over her body, fully revealing her as it fell to the floor. She stretched and slowly turned before the mirrors, showing herself in aroused grace, and half complaining, half-imploring, muttered to herself, "Oh, Mr. Right Guy, where in the world are you? I am so damn ready!"

"Yes, my dear, you most certainly look like you are," said a grinning Gwen, who had just slipped into the room and had been an unseen witness to Sally's announcement. "You seem to have been enjoying this unusual little room of mine, and quite remarkably, all by yourself!"

"Well, it certainly is different," Sally returned, a deep flush on her face.

Gwen went on, "Now, if you really want to find the true depths and expressions of this 'Crystal Palace' of mine, you must share it with an intimate friend. Even taking a bath can become a succession of unlimited and exotic opportunities and pleasures."

As Sally occupied herself with straightening the cosmetics, Gwen began gathering the bath towels. Reaching out her hand as though to pick up a towel, she tentatively placed and allowed it to warmly linger on Sally's bare shoulder and drift somewhat aimlessly but inquiringly down and across her breast before she directed her attention to pick up a final bath towel... Gwen, noting Sally's ambivalent reaction, looking searchingly at Sally's reflection in the mirror, continued, "We must hurry and dress for the evening. Later on I can show you so much more about this room and the excitement and fun there can be experienced in it."

"If you're perchance wondering about Avery and I being different, you are quite right. We are very different. When

Avery takes a holiday here, he uses the regular facilities at the other end of the flat. I'm quite sure that he doesn't realize that this flat has two bathrooms, much less dream how lavish and playfully sinful one of them is--or for that matter--what sinful joys may take place in this end."

Gwen realized that not only had her tentative advances prompted no reaction, her suggestive conversation had also been completely lost on the unresponsive Sally as well. Gwen decided that she still wanted Sally's friendship regardless of her personal preferences, and suppressing and dismissing her own physical interest, returned to the kitchen to leave Sally to her dressing.

Gwen sliced off some lamb that she had in the refrigerator, and, along with some green vegetables and a couple of boiled potatoes, gave Sally her first introduction to English 'home cooking.' Privately, Sally was not impressed. She had been warned that English fare would be rather bland, and the warning had been right. Still, she knew that she certainly had no right to complain. She was lucky to get a meal at all. War rationing had put all of Britain on a diet and very few people were able to share their meager allowances. Avery had sent along a number of packages of tinned food, and Sally had also brought what she could find at the military commissary to add to Gwen's larder. After they had finished eating and doing the dishes, Gwen suggested that they start out the evening by dropping in at the 'Highland Hart Pub'. They could always move on if they found the pub not to their liking, but if the right crowd was in there it would take care of the rest of the evening without their venturing one bit further.

CHAPTER SEVENTEEN

THE STREET WAS CEMETERY QUIET. Sally kept a firm grip on Gwen's raincoat belt as they moved along through the night's inky darkness with the confidence gained from the many times Gwen had found her way through the blackout to her favorite haunt. As they crept down the flight of stone steps to the lower level pub, Gwen told Sally that she would be perfectly safe in the pub but that if she did find it a bit uproarious to try to keep close to her.

Sally was sure that she would be quite surprised if the 'Highland Hart' was much different from the taverns, saloons, and roadhouses back in Colorado. It could be no more exciting than what she had seen of English pubs in the movies, where a room full of young men lounged around and sang country airs while they threw darts for exercise and drank Porter or Stout.

Still trying to accustom her eyes to the brightness as the door and then the blackout curtain swung open, she found herself swept up in a crushing bear hug and in the same motion jerked off of her feet and swung into the air. Then a great red beard crunched into her face. Abruptly, she was tossed high in the air like a blown feather and then caught and gently returned to the floor.

The red beard thrust back into her view, gaped open into a vast and toothy grin, and issued forth a mighty exclamation. "And McTavish ha' give ye a bonnie welcome to ta' pub o' his countrrr'men! Ma kin, bonnie Gwen, ha' toll' me ya be a Yank, ba' it na make a difrrrance! I ha' give to ya ta' kiss o' ta' heather! Ye are a bonnie Lass, an' ya will be in ma charge!"

Sally staggered back against the wall in wide-eyed disbelief. She had walked into the pub, and in a matter of seconds found, she was not sure that one part of her was in the right place. Even her shoes and undies seemed to be on back-to-front.

"Wh-what was THAT????" she stammered.

Gwen was helpless with laughter. "Sally, meet my wee giant cousin, Cedric McTavish. THAT was his gentle welcome. He approves of you. He has taken you to his heart--forever. He was really quite gentle. You should see him when he dislikes someone. He would still have thrown you up to the ceiling, and then he would have walked away while you were up there and let you find your way to the floor by your own self."

The rest of the evening turned out to be just as much of a riot as the reception. Cedric's regiment, back from nearly a year of intense service in North Africa and now standing down from weeks of intensive training in the western moors, was at their pleasures and that meant piping, drinking, dancing, and whatever else Scots conceived of as pleasure. Sally never realized that grown men could dance with such frenzy and drink with such abandon.

Nothing seemed beyond their imagination in trying to out-do one another. One moment she was an awed spectator; the next, she found herself snatched up and wildly swept from one kilted, hairy-kneed, sweating merrymaker to another. Then, as suddenly, the gambolers abandoned her and the other women and madly scrambled to reassemble at the bar. There, amid a mass of teetering and tottering arms and legs, great glasses were held high and voices of questionable quality but great enthusiasm strained mightily to send their shrills the three-hundred and more miles to the Scottish highlands from whence they had sprung and now sang of in drunken piety.

No one heard the air raid alarms over the clamor of the Scotts. Had the bomb been a sound-seeking device, there would surely have been one less Scottish Regiment on this earth. As it was, the German nuisance air raid had been so quick that the Wardens had not been able to silence the Scots in time to lead them to the shelters.

The First indications that an air raid was in progress came when the Pub's exit doors were blown down the stairway into the basement-pub and with the sounds of the two empty floors above being swept away by the concussion. The first reaction of many was to finish their glass and their song as they were swept from their place at the bar and across the room to the more out-of-the-way and protected area of the tables where Sally, Gwen, the other women, and the less exuberant Scots remained. That no one was hurt was a miracle. The Piper Sergeant was heard to tell two British Axiliaries that more damage had been done during a missed step in the dancing of the Regimental Highland Fling.

It little concerned the assemblage that the street side of the pub was now inside it and the ceiling and floor above seemed only to be looking for the proper place to fall before joining the rest of the building--and the party.

Searching about, the merrymakers unearthed the barman and found him, while shaken and somewhat deaf, still able to stand. By that evaluation, they certified him capable of serving. They quickly cleared a place in the room so they could stand about the bar as well as begin the dance again. Discovering that the Head Piper had not lost his pitch and leading tick, they agreed that they had not finished song nor drink. And thus it was that Cedric and his comrades showed Sally the grit of the defenders of bastion Britain, for within a few minutes the celebration was again in full romp.

The Air Raid Wardens and Police made no headway in their pleading and efforts to budge the gathering until they threatened to use a fire hose on bare knees and hairy legs. But by that time most of the pay had been spent and all of the refreshments had been consumed, so the enthusiastic warriors wearily and unsteadily scrambled through the debris to the street above. After a few happy moments of playful staggering about, hugging, patting, pinching, and goodbying, the merrymakers were transformed into a precision rank and file at the word of the Piper Sergeant. They smartly stepped off down the street in the early light to the mournful sounds of the pipes, their arms swinging in exact unison.

As they rounded the corner, the Head Piper let off and set himself to draw a great breath for the next passage. In that moment of silence, a great sound seemed to emerge from deep within the bowels of the earth and, like a volcano straining for its freedom, grew more violent in its struggled for release.

Following this earthy report, the great and bellowing voice of the Piper Sergeant resounded, "Mistar Cedric McTavish!"

"Aye, Piper Sergeant McIntyre?"

"Ken ya na' contrrrol ye'self? Ye know ya na' ta' pass the gass. Er 'e war wa' ya did, wel' ya are in formation . . . ! Shame, Mun!"

As the sounds of the departing Scots faded into the early morning light, the others moved off in their own directions, leaving the deserted street to Gwen and Sally.

"Did you have a good time?" Gwen asked.

"A good time? I've never been through anything like this in my life! I wouldn't have missed one second of this for all the world!" Sally cried.

"Yes, pardon the pun, but wasn't all of it a blast? We need to go home and wash some of this dust off and get some rest and a little sleep. Would you like to try for another pub tonight?" She saw the answering gleam in Sally's eyes and the infectious smile that crossed her lips. "Yes, from the look of you, my dear Sally, I guess I had better start planning where we're going right now.

CHAPTER EIGHTEEN

The droning engines of the aircraft flying high over North Africa were having a lulling effect on Harry as he contemplated the months of intensive preparation that were behind him--right from the very hectic beginning at "S" Station--a once private estate--in the Yorkshire Dales.

On his First day at "S" Station, Harry and eleven other candidates for O.S.S. assessment training and critical activity evaluation had been assembled before the Director.

"Our responsibility," the Director said", is to discover your special skills, unique abilities, and individual talents so that we may put them to their best use. "To conceal the nature of this work, we have given out the explanation that this is an Military Rehabilitation Center. The residents of the nearby communities have been accepting this fiction and are firmly convinced that you are all serious mental cases.

"Just as our facility has a cover story, so many of you will need one. During your training period most of you will prepare to claim to have been born at some place other than your actual birthplace, educated in places other than where you attended school, worked at occupations other than those you did, and lived in locations other than where you are from. Members of our staff, from time to time, will try to trap you into breaking your cover by asking casual questions about you when you may least expect. Don't get caught! That one time could also be your last!"

Harry knew that he had been under surveillance from the moment he arrived. He could feel the eyes of the instructors on him from the time he climbed out of the back of the six-by-six truck. He felt scrutinized as he responded to the staff officers and as he handled his new name and identity. He knew that his friend Major Keesling was now just a memory and name in his past. He began to wonder if Keesling was Keesling or if that had also been a cover. One morning he met Colonel Middleton and was obliged to salute him. He felt that he had handled the matter well in not showing any recognition and that he apparently had slipped by without the Colonel recognizing him. Harry was wrong. The Colonel did recognize Harry and he gave him a passing grade as a result of the encounter.

Harry found himself gauged for his initiative and resourcefulness by having to overcome field problems with inadequate equipment and only his wits. He was given construction problems in which his assigned helpers were actually staff members instructed to obstruct and annoy him. It was no consolation that no one had ever completed the problems in the allotted time. One of the most important and hardest ordeals was the difficult Stress Interview test. Harry was grabbed from his bunk in the middle of the night, roughly hurried to a dark room, and summarily seated in an uncomfortable stool with a spot-light directed into his face. He was subjected to a rapid-fire, merciless

Reflections

cross-examination by a simulated Gestapo board. Every trick in the book was used to expose flaws in his cover story, to trip him up in a contradiction, or to rattle him by yelling, "Now we have you! You have just admitted you have lied! You will sign the confession of this, or you will be tortured and shot!"

Harry was never allowed to relax. He was ordered to sit upright, to cross or uncross his legs, to refrain from wiping sweat that was running down his face--anything to irritate and confuse him. While his inquisitors found no inconsistency in his story, Harry felt pushed far beyond what he had thought to be his emotional limits. When the interrogation was over, the examiners conferred and solemnly announced, "It is our decision that you have failed to meet the minimum requirements of the test, and therefore we must fail you".

Harry sat totally stunned and drained, unable even to show any signs of irritation. As it was, his near-stupor saved his place in the training program. Unlike three of his more overwrought fellow trainees, he was passed on.

As he felt the plane's strain as it changed altitudes, Harry reached down and unthinkingly pulled at the laces of his jump boots. Relaxing as he felt the aircraft level off, he squirmed around, trying to make himself more comfortable in its cramped quarters and faintly smiled as he remembered what he had been "passed on" to; the 'Next Stage.'

Maude's Glen without a doubt had to be the greatest cover name of the war. Behind this sleepy little Lancaster village, hidden in the folds of the wooded hills in the northwest corner of England, was anything but what the name suggested. Yes, Harry thought, more like Mahem Glen.

From the first moment--as he had tried to step down from the truck and found himself jerked down and painfully slammed to the ground by a "helping hand"--he discovered he was in the midst of a non-stop school in close combat, gutter, and back-alley fighting.

A knee to the groin, a sideswipe with the heel of a hand to the Adam's apple, and a doubled fist between the shoulder blades were in the offing for the unprepared.

Harry memorized a cipher system. He learned how to improvise a shortwave radio out of no more than old razor blades and damaged radio parts; and he learned how to build makeshift firearms. He was initiated into such other arts as cracking safes, handling explosives, blowing bridges, derailing trains, and photographing secret documents.

He was moved through a scare house that outdid any chamber of horrors; particularly since he carried a machine pistol loaded with live ammunition and was graded on his reactions and "kills".

His final examination was frighteningly realistic. Through the cooperation of Scotland Yard, The British Secret Security Service, M-5, and the O.S.S., each trainee was assigned to infiltrate an English factory to steal secret papers. If Harry was caught, the intelligence units would clear him. However, it was most imperative that Harry had learned his trade well since there was a very real and far higher-than-average chance that he would be shot by company security guards if he should blunder.

While he passed this test, one shocked company official ordered a complete shakeup of his aircraft factory's security when the British Secret Security people revealed that a trainee had forged a security pass and had spent several productive nights photographing vital secret drawings and specifications without being questioned in any way about his activities--or his very non-British accent.

Harry thought that after the completion of the training and examination he might be given a few days to relax in London, but instead found himself at a jump school refresher course near Winchester.

In three days, he made a balloon drop, a daylight plane drop, a low-level drop, and then his graduation jump, which was a night jump into a small lake. That the lake was to be less than eight feet deep at any point gave little comfort to the six-foot-two-inch Harry; that the lake was to be infested with frogmen in case there was any trouble with the chutes and landings did not reassure him either.

His recollection of the jump was that as soon as he felt the presence of water near him, he smashed at the chute release and free fell into the water. He was elated to find that the water was only two to three feet deep, and a wave of euphoria swept over him. He congratulated himself on his success--a little too soon. As the chute silently settled down over him, it tripped him into the shallow water and nearly drowned him before he could cut himself free. The attending frogmen never materialized. In typical inter-service action, they had been ordered to assemble at the lake's other end.

The lurching of the aircraft, as it struggled to climb over the thunderheads, brought Harry back from his reminiscence.

The long months of preparation finally appeared to be over, and along with three others, he waited in the belly of the modified British Wellington bomber, surrounded by his gear, and huddled under a blanket.

Harry realized that he had been staring at the compartment's red "Off Target" light ever since the plane had lifted from the carrier's deck and headed into the wind off the west coast of Africa.

He shivered with the comprehension that his eardrums were pulsing in the rhythm of the throb of the engines as they strained to climb ever higher. The Flight Sergeant came back and gave each of the team an oxygen mask and showed them how to hook into the oxygen lines on either side of the compartment, as they would be climbing to above 18,000 feet to get over the storm. They were still over two hours from their destination.

Harry looked around at the other members of the team.

The slight, dark complexioned, little man, who answered to the name of Jen Paul, must have been French. He spoke the language with complete ease and seemed to understand more about the war than any of the rest of them. Paul kept to himself.

The hulk of a man who was sleeping next to him was another story. He was Dutch; he was at least six-feet-six-inches tall, probably weighed over two-hundred-eighty pounds and was pure blonde muscle and ferocity. He called himself Janish Van Keelen. He admitted to having been a butcher for some time, and blood was something he was very used to. He made it very clear that his business now was to kill and that Germans were his fare.

As they had boarded the plane, Janish announced that he expected to begin killing Germans very soon and would be sleeping so he would be well rested for that pleasure.

Harry remembered that Janish had nearly been dropped during the Stress Interview part of the training. When told that he had failed the program, by the Gestapo-dressed instructor, Janish had responded by picking him up and throwing him through the window.

It was then hastily decided that this was not an indication of failure under stress; rather, it was a positive sign of highly organized enthusiasm, and as such, reason and justification for advancement. Because he placed such importance on his origins and could not remember any part of his cover identity, Janish was allowed to remain "Janish".

Harry's final cover was also quite simple. As he came from relative obscurity and had no ties in occupied countries to conceal, it was decided that his actual identity was as good a cover as he could come up with, so he remained Harry Morgan.

He had trained with Jen Paul and Janish for nearly six months and found comfort in the precision, understanding, and teamwork that they had developed as they moved through the program. He had expected that whatever assignment he was given would also involve them and that they would be a complete unit unto themselves. He had assumed that at the time of their mission one of them would be charged with the responsibility of leadership. Deep within himself, he hoped that he would not be chosen, while at the same time he anxiously looked for additional qualities to emerge in his companions, which would build his confidence in their chances for survival, and perhaps success.

While their courier plane was being loaded at Bristol for its flight to the carrier in the Atlantic, Harry had been surprised that a fourth member of the team was added at the last minute. He became even more astonished when he found that the fourth member--their team leader-was Major Al Keesling, once again wearing First Lieutenant's bars.

Harry made every effort to avoid recognizing Al. It was Al who drew Harry aside and told him that it was all right to recognize him, saying,

"Harry, it's okay to know me. After all, you still only know me by my cover."

A relieved Harry responded, "You mean it's all right for us to talk about our time in London, and well, you know . . . Harrow?"

"Sure, why not? There's nothing to hide. No military secrets there. Come to think of it, no secrets at all."

Once their flight to the carrier had begun, Al became serious and spoke about their assignment in North Africa. They would be briefed by a French underground intelligence officer when they got to the carrier. The final details would be worked out as part of the objectives of the mission, which they could expect to take place at any time within the next seventy-two hours.

CHAPTER NINETEEN

"Gentlemen! Your attention, please? We have a mission of some interest and considerable importance to discuss. We have less than twenty-four hours to prepare our plan of action and to move out on it. Please gather about and make yourselves comfortable. The smoking lamp, as they say on this carrier, is lit, but there will be no talking or questions until the mission has been presented. I shall be known to you as Colonel Barnaby. I am British and that is all that you have to know about me! Now, for the plan!"

As the Colonel pulled the covering from the map on the compartment wall, Harry surveyed the room and its occupants. In addition to Keesling, VanKeelen, and Paul, there were four of the British members of the attack bomber crew that would to fly them from the carrier to their mission, four American members of the crew of a second air transport that would pick them up and fly them out to safety, and a tall, slender man dressed in coveralls. It was this new member of the group that the Colonel called to the front of the room.

"Gentlemen, I wish to introduce you to a member of the French Resistance in North Africa. You will know him as

Captain Jean Monier. As a bit of background information, Captain Monier tells us he has been in French Morocco, Tunisia, Lybia, and Algeria for most of his life. During the last ten years he has been employed as a telephone and communications specialist by the French Provincial Government and has worked extensively in Tunisia and Libya. He is considered an authority on the network of communications in all of western North Africa, eastward to the Tunisian-Libyan border.

"Since the Nazis have imposed the Vichy government on France, he advises us that he has used his position to intercept the communications and codes in use between Vichy-France and her colonies. He has been able to tap into the German and Italian communications emanating from Tunisia and connecting with Rommel's forward positions during his advance on Tobruk. When he finally notified us he was ready for the sub to pick him up, he made sure that he had the blessings of the liberation movements in Tunisia and Libya, as well as the latest information on German and Italian troop positions and movements.

"He has just been brought out from Tunisia by submarine and destroyer, and I understand that while the underwater passage at first rather unnerved him, by the time he had cleared Gibraltar and rendezvoused with the destroyer, he had become somewhat of a submariner. Nevertheless, he has the latest information that we will need for this undertaking--which brings me to the subject of why you have been brought here.

"Since late in 1941 the Americans have had a number of operatives, ostensibly vice-consuls and their aides, attached to the United States Legations in Casablanca, Algiers, Oran, Tunisia, Lybia, and Benghazi.

"These people, for the most part, are known to the French and Provincial Police, as well as to the Gestapo, and are maintained under loose surveillance--until now.

"On November 8th, two days from now, Operation Torch, the invasion of North Africa, will start. You can be sure that the moment this invasion becomes apparent to the local authorities, these American operatives will be rounded up and promptly dealt with as spies, which means they will very likely be tortured and/or shot.

"Your mission is to fly in, parachute down, and gather up our people in Benghazi and meet at the old Foreign Legion air strip marked 'K' on the map, call in your support plane, and fly them out to Egypt. Not too complicated, Eh?"

As the implications of these details began to sink in, Harry checked the reactions of his teammates. He felt his pulse quicken and perspiration break out on his upper lip.

Al was taking some cryptic notes, which he later studied and burned. Paul sat erect and seemed to give his complete attention to the Colonel.

Janish had become very animated and was sheathing and unsheathing his boot knife. He began to upset the concentration of the others, and Al had to remind him that the assault was not in the wardroom, but more than a thousand miles away. The Dutchman settled down, apologized, and said that he would make up for his commotion once they arrived in Libya.

The Colonel went on. "Captain Monier tells us he has been monitoring German, French, and Italian radio and telephone transmissions for the past six months from clandestine radio station 'Betsy' overlooking the harbor of Tunis, and has arranged to jam the entire French, German and Italian telephone communication system. The Resistance people have pledged that the jamming will be complete. Confusion will reign, gentlemen.

"We are creating a diversion which we believe will make the Germans believe that we are preparing an invasion of Sicily. We are sending false signals of the torpedoing of two of our supply vessels and a light escort cruiser in the waters between Sicily and Gibraltar. So that the Italians and Germans will not wait for a confirmation from one of their submarines, we will also announce the sinking of the offending submarine. You have less than two full days from now to have your charges out of Bengasi. Now, Captain Monier will give you additional information."

Monier moved to the front and outlined the route that team would take.

In response to Janish's question, Colonel Barnaby again resumed charge of the briefing and advised that the agents in Casablanca, Tripoli, Algiers, and Oran were going out by submarine with other teams. Their objective, Benghazi, was the farthest behind enemy lines; therefore, they would have to go out through Egypt.

"After this briefing we shall have you inspect the conformation of the two modified aircraft.

"The one that will be delivering you will be a slightly modified Wellington British Bomber with 'joe holes' or releases through the floor while the pickup plane will be an American modified C-47 Transport craft, with large side doors and harnesses for members of your team to help load personnel.

"The Wellington will deliver its load and return to the carrier while the C-47 will leave the carrier, land on a short airstrip which you will establish, pick up its cargo of personnel, and fly on to Cairo, or at least somewhere in Egypt behind British lines.

The rest of the afternoon was spent securing equipment, inspecting the two aircraft, and going over responsibilities and plans. After a hearty meal of English eggs and American beefsteak, everyone turned in. Sleep was difficult because by now the carrier was moving at maximum speed for Africa so that when darkness arrived, she could be in the most favorable position to send off the modified attack bomber and its "cargo".

"'Ave at it, blokes. Get your kit together, now! The Flight Sergeant interrupted Harry's recollections.

"It's about ten minutes from your drop point. The Dutchman and Frenchy is awake, and we 'ave the equipment all hooked up for the drop. Here are your signal devices. The pilot says good luck." The Sergeant took a quick look over the group and tested all of the static lines. He released the catches of the cover over the "Joe Hole" through which the men and their equipment would drop.

The red signal light had blinked out, and the amber colored "Ready Light" had come on. Harry and the others made one last check of their weapons and straps and made sure that their helmets were properly on and that the all- important chin straps were pulled tight. The amber light blinked out, and the green "Target Area" light flashed on.

"Target area," the Sergeant yelled into Harry's ear. "We'll be circling around once; then, when we level off and I slap you on the arse, out you go! Eh?"

Harry nodded. He felt the plane bank and curve. The engines were throttled back and the cabin became deafeningly still. The Sergeant flipped the cover off the 'Joe Hole' and motioned Harry forward. The wind howled through the opening, and it was all Harry could do to force his legs out of the hole. Harry ran over the jump instructions: hold straight, head on chest, legs together, and pull on the shrouds.

"We're on the approach," the Sergeant warned. Harry nodded again and noticed that the rest of the team were hooked up and intently watching him. The plane leveled, and began its long glide, and suddenly . . .

"Get your arse on the move! Good Luck, Yank!"

Harry shoved forward and down with his arms. The propwash spun him like a ball. As he tumbled he felt the sharp tug on his harness from the static line and then he heard the rifle-like crack of the parachute opening. He grabbed at the lift shrouds and pulled down as hard as he could to lessen the swaying motion and to break his spin.

Moments later, Harry peered upward into the murky night as he heard the plane roar into life again, its engines straining to regain altitude. He wondered where the equipment was and whether the rest of his team had gotten out safely. Suddenly he was struck by his complete isolation. He was more alone than he had ever been in his entire life!

"Night is night and it's always dark. Keep your damn feet together, your ass tight--and land lucky!" Harry's stateside jumpmaster's words were running through his head as he searched in the darkness for a place to land. He hoped he would be lucky, and he was. The information that Monier had brought on the landing sites was accurate.

During his orientation on the carrier, Monier had said, "We will jump into an area which is about two kilometers from the highway. The terrain will be sandy with only scrub brush and few large rocks or gullies. There should be no trouble with our landings, and, with the homing devices which we have, we will be able to assemble without any difficulty. From there, we can quickly move on to the contact point with the Resistance people." Much to the relief of all, it had worked out just that way.

After they had assembled and gotten their bearings, they set out for the abandoned airstrip that they would use on their flight out. They had purposely not dropped over it because they did not want to take a chance on local patrols stumbling onto their plans. They found the airstrip within thirty minutes, buried the flares and transmitter that they would later use to bring the support aircraft in, and then moved off toward the highway and their meeting with the local resistance group representative.

Al had taken charge. Monier served as a scout because he knew the route to the rendezvous point. Al had lingered behind to check the location of the transmitter and to make sure that Janish had properly covered it. He hurried along to catch up with Harry as he and the others trotted alongside the highway. They headed for the lights of the distant city.

"Harry, how's it going?"

"Oh, all right, I guess. Are we on schedule?"

"Yeah, close enough. You know what you gotta' do when we get there. You gotta make it fast. Abher don't take no screwing around. I can tell you that from experience."

"You know he is here? I thought this was your first time here!"

"Yeah, He's been here for a while, remember, Frenchy-Arab, Arab-Frenchy, but it has been very hush, hush. Monier don't even know about him."

"Oh? What's he doing here already?"

"Never mind, you'll find out soon enough."

They had been trotting along for about twenty minutes when Monier signaled a halt.

"What's up?" Al asked.

"I see the small light off to the side of the road," Monier said. "It flashes the required three times. We shall return the signal?"

"Go ahead! Everybody get low in the ditch," Al said. "You saw the direction, give them the four flashes, Jean."

A moment later two flashes were seen, followed by three, then by two again.

"That's it! Come on, Monier, let's go bring him in. Harry, you, Paul and the Dutchman wait here and cover us as best you can."

Almost as quickly as they were gone, they returned with a man cloaked in the robes of a Riff warrior. "Everybody set?" Al said. "The Captain is taking over now. Whatever he says, we do."

Al handed over a message pouch. After a brief exchange and muffled conversation with Al, the Riff warrior turned to Harry. He pulled back his hood and said, "It's good to see you again. I heard that you made it, and I'm glad to have you along."

"My God, it is you! You're Walter . . . ."

"Uh-huh", the warrior interrupted. "I'm Captain Abher. We can talk about old times later. We know each other and that's all there is to it for now!"

A speechless Harry stood and watched as Abher, Keesling, and Monier went on ahead to meet with the endangered operatives from the embassies.

Paul and the Dutchman had begun preparations for their part of the operation, and Harry put his wondering aside and swung into his part of the action.

Each of the three had carried a part of the signal device, and each of the three had a job in its positioning.

Before leaving, Captain Abher pointed out a survey benchmark from which Harry and Paul measured a course due north for exactly one hundred meters. At that point the Dutchman began digging a hole on a slight rise. Because the device had to be buried and wired for self-destruct in the event it should be discovered and tampered with, Harry and Paul had to use great care in its assembly so as not to detonate it.

After all of this had been done and the unit and its batteries were buried in the hole and a covering of sand was smoothed over it, only the antenna of the signal device showed above the surface. Harry activated the clock which would delay the start of the signal for thirty-six hours, which was shortly before the pinpoint bombing of the fortifications around Tunisia and Benghazi were scheduled to start. The transmitter was designed to operate for eighteen days, after which it would self-destruct. It was expected that Morocco, Algeria, Tunisia, and Libya would have been taken by the Allied armies by then.

Paul and Harry returned to the roadside to wait for Abher, Keesling, and Monier. The Dutchman had remained behind to cover the protective land mines that had been planted around the signaling device. He had told them to go ahead so he would not have to worry about them as he armed the mines.

The returning Dutchman noiselessly leaned over to Harry and whispered, "Harry, I feel in my bones there will be Germans tonight. We will get some."

"Jan, there aren't that many Germans in this part of Lybia. This is Vichy France controlled. The Germans are in the Libyan desert."

"I know, but I think I get one tonight. I smell some blood. Maybe I get a couple for you, too, Harry. I know we find some Germans before we get out from here. Don't you worry, the Dutchman smash them with his bare hands for you!"

"Okay, whatever you say, Jan. Don't forget Paul. He might have some ideas about the Germans. How about it, Paul?"

"I don't think we meet the Boche tonight, but I go with the Dutchman if we do. I help him plenty!"

The Dutchman had been looking down the road, and, turning quickly, said, "An automobile! It comes very fast from the city. It must be our people coming back. We must lay here in the ditch and be sure."

The car, moving without lights and fast, nearly sped on by them. At the last moment, it screeched to a stop.

"Quick, get in!" Keesling barked. "They must have been waiting for us! There's a German patrol vehicle behind us. We've got about ten minutes to ditch this car and call the plane in." The car, a German minibus, had, in addition to Abher, Keesling, and Monier, five other passengers. Harry, the Dutchman, and Paul squeezed in, making it eleven in all.

They sped to the unmarked airstrip. Monier said he knew of a concealed location nearby so he would hide the car. The others turned on the transmitter and prepared the small landing flares.

Their one chance of escape lay in the possibility that the Germans would not stumble onto the deserted airstrip. Twice they heard a German patrol car race by on the nearby road. The wait was excruciating, even though they heard the plane's engines in less than fifteen minutes.

The flares were lit and the eleven men hurried to the end of the landing area. Within moments, the plane was overhead and then drifting in for its landing. As it taxied up and turned to head down the strip for the takeoff, the group scurried out and began clambering aboard.

The operatives were all loaded. As the Dutchman, and Harry and Paul who put on the restraining harnesses at the open side door as they scrambled into the plane, the night suddenly exploded into searing and brilliant flame.

"God Damn it! Mortar Ground Flares! They found us! Come on, let's get out of here!"

Harry could hear Abher and Keesling yelling from outside of the taxiing plane as he crouched at the door.

"Harry, help," Al yelled. "Stop your damn day dreaming up there! For Christ's sake, pull us in!"

Al, Abher, and Monier ran alongside the plane and desperately reached for a hand to help pull them in. The plane lurched wildly, and a mortar shell exploded right at the opening of the side doors. Harry took the impact of a near miss and was nearly thrown from the open door. except for the restraint of the harness, and then slambed across the fuselage of the plane and nearly through an open cargo door on the other side. Paul was also blown backward, but up into the cargo area... The explosion was deafening as the mortar shells continued to burst in the plane's path. Still the three ran alongside, reaching for hands of help that Harry could no longer offer to them.

The Dutchman shoved Harry out of the way, and, practically pulling Keesling's arms out by the roots, threw Al into the plane.

"Harry, grab on my arm. I get the Captain in, too. Harry, you help me...."

The explosion of the next mortar shell cut the Dutchman off in midsentence, blowing him out of the plane and tearing out nearly half of the side of the plane as it strained into the air without Captain Abher, Monier, or the Dutchman.

As the plane clawed its way into the sky and away from the hail of bullets that followed and vainly searched for it, the flight crew and others made frantic and finally successful efforts to put out the fires that the explosions had started. The aircraft had lost both doors on the explosion side. The covering around the small door on the other side of the fuselage had been largely blown away, leaving gaping holes as large as a man. The communications to the rear of the aircraft were gone but the hydraulic flight controls seemed to have been spared.

One of the engines must have caught some of the shrapnel, as it seemed to be misfiring and laboring. Small rivulets of oil streamed across its wing mounting. Although there was a jagged tear in the skin of the port side wing, the wing tanks were not losing fuel. While the flight crew was assessing the damages to the aircraft, the passengers began taking stock of their conditions. Since the operatives that were picked up had been the first on the plane, they had been farthest away from the blast and, outside of some mild concussion, they were not injured.

Paul had caught nasty shards of metal in his right leg and arm and was bleeding profusely. Hastily and deftly applied tourniquets and dressings applied by the flight crew stopped the bleeding. He was given a shot of morphine and lapsed into unconsciousness, and appeared to be resting as comfortably as possible.

Keesling, though breathing regularly, was totally unconscious and seemed to have no injuries other than a swelling on his forehead. There was a small trickle of blood from his nose and the corner of his mouth.

Harry had been thrown across the compartment and halfway through the skin of the plane on the other side by the force of the explosion.

Monier was nowhere to be found. Later on, no one could recall that he had gotten into the plane. They never saw what happened to Captain Abher, but it was assumed that the force of the explosion had killed him along with the Dutchman, since Paul later reported that he had seen the Dutchman reaching for the Captain the instant before the mortar shell hit.

The struggling plane leveled off, and very shortly the co-pilot crawled back from the cockpit and after a hasty survey of the damages drew the crew chief aside and told him, "Holly Jesus, what a mess you guys got back here! The skipper said to get these guys taken care of quick. He doubts this crate will hold together for any more than a couple of hours, and we might not even get them far enough into Egypt to get behind British lines. What are the condition back here?"

"We're not sure yet, sir. We're still finding them. Some are in pretty tough shape," a flight crewman said.

"Here's another one under all this stuff," the Flight Sergeant said. He pulled Harry free of the twisted metal.

"Is he dead?"

"I can't tell yet. No, I don't think so, but he sure as the devil might be. He's one bloody hell of a mess. I can't get his hands off his face. He's just one lump of bone and blood!"

"Here, let me give you a hand. Let's get him over here where I can get some light on him. He's the one who got it at the door, ain't he?"

"Yes Sir, he's the one. I guess he couldn't keep up with the pressure and the shelling, and all."

"Suffering Jesus, his whole bloody face is gone. No, look where his hands is up. He's still got his eyes. That's about all, though. If he hadn't got hit there that way at the opening, Sir, these other guys what's missing, and the one we think we seen killed could of made it. They can thank him for what happened to them--what with his bad luck."

"Yeah, he just set there and stared out at them what was hollering to get in."

"I hope the bloody son of a bitch lives."

"You're right, Sargent! He should remember what happened here for the rest of his life."

SPECIAL MEDICAL OBSERVATION
MEMORANDUM
February 11, 1943.
Cairo, Egypt.
British Expeditionary Forces Evacuation Hospital.
Memo: To British Seventh Rehabilitation Facility,
Great Wakering, Essex, England.
Major Avery E. Martin, M.D., Neurology Section.

Subject:

The following specified serviceman is scheduled to be forwarded through your Facilities for evacuation and subsequent transfer to American Forces Central Hospital at Harrow.

Orders:

Transfer your operation to American station to continue treatment, as well as to instruct American forces in treatment of similar battle-related cases. Process at your earliest discretion...
First Lieutenant Harry William Morgan, O-23452, U. S. Army.

Detached Service Assigned OSS34-/42)......
Patient is cleared to you for transfer and additional corrective plastic surgery of facial and hand lacerations.
Warning:
Patient is morose, suicidal, and totally blind.
Past evaluations give reason to believe that the continued blindness is emotional based
and not due to physical damages. Patient to be kept in restraint and under observation at all times...You are to review case and conduct further treatment and handling.
Patient and complete files to follow.
End of Orders and Memorandum.
Refer file, observations, review, and decision to:
Bartholomew Wells-Smith, M.D., Colonel. Commanding.

CHAPTER TWENTY

Dr. avery edward martin, md, Neurosurgeon, rolled his chair back from his desk. "Miss Nickles", he called, "Do I have any tobacco in your office?"

"No, Major, you got it all yesterday. Surely you can find enough in all of your pipes to carry you through another five or six hours. Your ration will come in by 1400 hours."

Avery scowled and began to rummage around his office. He had already gone through his desk and felt quite sure that if Nickles had really tried to look she would have found some undiscovered cache in her desk or in the files. It had been his life-long habit to squirrel away sweets and tobacco. He began another search in his uniform closet and discovered three American Hershey bars and two tins of Potter's Sweets. He promptly returned them to their hiding places. He was about to admit defeat when his eyes came to rest on his riding boots. He shook them out and was finally rewarded for his persistence. Two carefully wrapped tinfoil packets of Turkish tobacco landed at his feet. Wondering if he might be improving at deceiving himself, or, if he might be becoming even more absent-minded than he had thought, he gathered up his find.

He couldn't recall ever having put even one packet of tobacco in his boots. Nevertheless, he could now splurge and turn his office blue with the comforting aroma of one of his two great loves--a pipe of fine tobacco--while pursuing the other--reading an interesting case history.

"Miss Nickles, fortune has smiled on me", he called out. "I have found two packets of tobacco, and I shall have a most enjoyable morning. Is there anything of interest in our basket?"

"No, not a great deal, Major. Some bulletins for you to read, some surgical records for your approval, some requisitions for supplies for our section, and a file that was forwarded from the receiving section about that blind American officer who came in on the ambulance train last evening."

Avery tapped his pipe of tobacco. "Uh, yes. Well . . . very good." After a few moments of silence devoted to packing a pipe, striking a match, lighting the pipe, and drawing-in the first heady puff of the tobacco smoke, he said, "What American officer is that, Miss Nickles?"

"Remember the special correspondence you received on a First Lieutenant Harry W. Morgan who was to be forwarded from the evacuation hospital in Cairo?"

"Oh, yes, but that was well over two months ago. I had supposed he was no longer to be sent here. Bring me the file and cut off all calls for the next hour or so. I will need to concentrate my efforts on bringing myself up to date on him. He was that secret service or M-5 type person, wasn't he?"

Avery spread the pages from the file across his desk and began sorting through the service and medical records of Lieutenant

Morgan. He surreptitiously glanced up to watch Lieutenant Nickles return to her office, only to find that she was watching him and smiling in a disconcerting manner. Realizing that she had been noticed, she diverted her gaze, curiously blushed, and quickly left, closing the connecting door behind her. Avery returned to the papers and did his best to ignore the flush that he had suddenly felt.

He read on:

First Lieutenant Harry W. Morgan, O-23452,
United States Army;
Nationality: American.
Unit: O.S.S. Assignment: Joint British-American Pre-Torch Mission. Theater of Operations: North Africa (Tunisia-Lybia). Service Authority: British Expeditionary Forces.
SPECIAL MEDICAL OBSERVATION MEMORANDUM
February 11, 1943.
Cairo, Egypt. British Expeditionary Forces Evacuation Hospital.
Memo: To British Seventh Rehabilitation Facility, Great Wakering, Essex, England.
Major Avery E. Martin, M.D., Chief, Neurology Section.
Subject:
The following specified serviceman is scheduled to be forwarded through your facilities for evacuation and subsequent transfer to American Forces Central Hospital at Harrow. First Lieutenant Harry William Morgan, O-23452, U. S. Army.

(Detached Service Assigned OSS34-/42)......
Patient is cleared to you for transfer and additional corrective plastic surgery of facial and hand lacerations.
Warning: Patient is morose, suicidal, and claims to be totally blind. Past evaluations give reason to believe that the continued blindness is emotionally based and not due to physical damages.
You are to review case and conduct further treatment and assume full responsibility for subsequent handling.
Complete US Army Form 20
and all service and past medical files enclosed – Patient to follow within 24 hours, or on earliest Evac. Available. Patient to be kept in restraint and/or under observation At all times.
End of Orders and Memorandum.
Refer file, observations, review, and decision to:
Bartholomew Wells-Smith, M.D., Colonel. Commanding.

―――――

Avery noted Morgan's training since he had arrived in England. His general physical condition was listed as having been outstanding at the time of his mission and injuries, over six months ago. Emergency treatment had been given at the Cairo Evacuation Hospital and more extensive surgery performed later at the British Army Medical Hospital in Alexandria. The reports indicated that the plastic surgery had been successfully done and the stitching had been confined to the area above the hairline wherever possible. It predicted that in another six months there would be little to show that Morgan had ever experienced any facial damage.

    Avery frowned and shook his head as he read. Morgan was completely ambulatory, but it was still necessary that he be maintained in restraint. Morgan had resisted all efforts of the doctors to examine his eyes. The cursory examinations that had been made, however, indicated no systemic reason why Morgan could not see. The records indicated that whenever the bandages or dressings were removed from Morgan's eyes and face, he demanded that they be replaced. He even went so far as to tear up sheets and pillowcases and clumsily bandage his eyes and head. Any effort to reason with him was met with anger and refusal. He had withdrawn for days, accepted only the most meager morsels of food, and refused treatment that was not enforced. He had made three clumsy attempts at suicide and had repeatedly indicated that he had nothing to live for. It appeared that there was deep guilt and conflict within him and that he had purposely regressed in his attempt to shield himself from the world he feared to confront.

    The record recommended that Major Martin make a personal evaluation based on his extensive training in the fields of neurology and neurosurgery, psychiatry, and his understanding of the treatment of combat and battlefield fatigue. It directed him to assume the responsibility for the continued observation and treatment of Morgan and ordered that Avery provide for the transfer of Morgan, himself, and a working staff of his choosing to the newly opened British-American hospital unit near Harrow.

Avery penciled in a note that this was the station that the American nurse, Lieutenant Archer, had been assigned to. After a few moments of consideration, he made another note to himself to arrange to have her added to his staff again, when he arrived, along with Morgan, at Harrow. He felt that Archer would be most valuable in the treatment of Morgan.

The history of the events leading to the injuries of Morgan was totally inadequate. It mentioned that there had been an explosion in an aircraft and others, as well as Morgan, had been injured. Some men were listed as missing in action and it was believed that there had been fatalities. A brief note in another hand indicated that Morgan felt directly responsible for the injuries and loss of life. There was neither reference to the sequence of events that had occurred nor any mention of why Morgan continued to object strongly to any effort to unravel the happenings on the night of his injuries.

Avery noted that Morgan has received extensive facial surgical repairs, and he was pleased to see that the plastic surgeon, an acquaintance of his, had extensive experience in cosmetic surgery, and had noted in his prognosis that Morgan's facial scars and injuries should be completely unapparent within a year or so. He had also noted, along with the attending physician that Morgan had not responded in any other respect.

One medical officer had noted that Morgan would not discuss what had happened and refused to allow others to talk to him about it. He also observed that while Morgan showed these attitudes outwardly, inwardly he seemed to be in the grip of the events and through his psychological blindness was castigating himself for what he viewed as his cowardliness during the mission. Avery carefully gathered together the notes that he had been making and put them back in the folder. Carefully closing the file, he sat quietly and tried to think it all out. Where to begin?

He turned his chair to the window and gazed out across the sand and blowing grass to the Channel. Looking at this English moat that had protected the British Isles for nearly a thousand years from the incursions of the continent had always given him a measure of strength. But for some reason, it wasn't enough today.

He wished he could become involved with interests other than his medicine and his stock of pipes and tobacco. He had begun to agree with his sister, Gwen. She had told him, "Avery, you simply can't go through life a medical book with ears, a mustache, and a pipe. You need to find that people are more than case histories. Love them for everything they are when they're well. They exist then, too."

He had laughed awkwardly the time she said, "Avery, go fall in love. Make a fool of yourself! Learn to love, to feel passion, to feel your blood race through you with a wild, crazy pounding. Learn to throw yourself at someone and not care what happens--only that you are with them and they are with you. Find out what it's like to reach out and touch a soul, to feel what it is like to be alive with the need for another special person in a very special way. I want you to feel and know with your heart as well as your analytical mind."

Avery had always thought she was a madcap, but he also realized that she knew something about living life in a way quite different from his, which was fulfilled only through his work.

"My dearest brother, she once said, "You would be the finest physician on the earth if only you could unbend. Compassion is an intellectual exercise for you! You hurt because you can't help or save all of them, not because you really understand what's being lost. You sympathize, yet you don't empathize, because you don't really feel, or know how to feel!"

When he objected, she rushed on, "Oh, pooh, Avery! What you are feeling is inadequacy, recognition on your part that you are not the perfect healer with all of the answers. Their pains and deaths diminish your stature, but they do not get anywhere near your soul. When you are able to understand, to identify with the rest of us, you will be able to really feel. You'll be able to share and to help, and you won't diminish or die as much as when you can't."

Over the past three years he had seen more than three lifetimes of misery. This senseless war had given him a measure of the empathy Gwen had said he lacked. He had become too sensitive to his patient's needs, a sensitivity that was a drain on his strength. He had died a little with every death, had inwardly wept a little with every pain. Each soul became his responsibility, and through that responsibility he shared a part of their anguish. Fortunately, when the opportunities presented themselves, he had begun to learn to share in the joys of their recoveries. He was learning that his inability to save them all was a human rather than a personal inadequacy, but it didn't stop the anger that welled up within him when he had done all that he could do and still they died or faced the rest of their lives with bodies or minds scarred and forever devastated by the ravenous appetite of war. His realization still didn't remove the burden of his struggle and responsibility from his shoulders.

Avery realized that he was not having a very good morning after all. He felt tired and old beyond his forty years. His pipe had gone out and so had some of his vitality. The practice of medicine seemed to have lost some of its luster and he, some of his desire. For the first time in his life he questioned his qualifications and his right to interfere with the bodies and the lives of others. Realizing that his whole attitude had gone sour, he decided to take a quieting walk on the beach. He scribbled a hasty note of his whereabouts for Nickles and left.

As Avery walked down the south beach, he noticed that a storm was forming out over the Channel. Flashes of lightning streaked across the darkening sky, and flights of sea birds darted in over land in search of cover. He looked up to one of the high banks and waved to the two Home-Guard coast watchers. A small brown dog fell into step with him and, except for occasional forays after gulls, happily shared his excursion. A coastal defense boat bobbed along on the horizon and an observation plane lazily slipped in and out of the clouds. Only the sounds of the sea, the birds, and the occasional yap of the little dog came to Avery. He began to feel a little better.

Gwen had always been wild, and Avery worried about her, but it now seemed that she was the one who made sense. He could almost hear her saying, "Find a Girl! Any Girl! If you can't think how to speak to her or how to touch her, then just look at her. Watch what she does. See her, feel for her as a person. Learn to want her; try to think about lusting for her. Damn it, Avery, crave for something before you wither up and die!"

He had tried to distract her by replying, "But, Gwen, that may be well and good for someone your age, but I'm nearly twenty years your senior. I'm past forty! I'm afraid that young ladies of any age just aren't for me--nor I for them. No, I have my medicine and my fine pipes and tobaccos. I will be content. As a matter of fact, it might do you well if you would take a more serious view of your own life."

"Rubbish!" Gwen had said. "Just because you're so advanced in years, as you put it, there is no reason to shelve yourself with your dusty old books! There is more to you and to life than what you've permitted yourself. There is joy in life; there is joy in sharing yourself with someone else. It can be beautiful for you because people will come to love you for your tenderness and understanding as well as your mind and medical talents. And, on top of that, your medical talent will grow from your expression of your new compassion."

"But, Gwen," Avery protested, "I find my practice to be quite rewarding. There is an excitement that . . ."

"It wouldn't hurt you to experience another excitement, Gwen interrupted. "The electricity that people can feel for one another when they sincerely touch and contribute to one another. It might come as a shock to you, but it would be good for you. You have so much to share and if you don't share it, you're being just plain selfish, even to yourself."

Avery recognized that Gwen was going to have her say, and he also found that he wanted to hear her out, so he sat back in silence as she continued to lecture him.

"You can add a whole new dimension, and other people will feel and share it, too. You might get hurt, and you might have to really believe and trust in somebody beside yourself for a change, but you can't go on living this silly closed life of yours! You've got to realize that you need someone. You don't have to be hedonistic, but the way are you are now is downright monastic! Avery, you can find a whole new reason for being if you'll only open up and let someone in. There has to be some one person in the world that will care that much about you. For your own sake, Avery, please let people find you; let that person find you. Please?"

Avery reached the end of the beach and turned back toward the Medical Station. He found wetness about his eyes that he knew was not the mist of the surf. He knew that the hardness in his throat and tightness in his chest were not from the cold.

The Morgan file, the calm efficiency of Miss Nickles, his recollections of the thoughtful admonitions and prescriptions of his sister, Gwen, his weariness with the uselessness of the pointless war--all came together. He felt stripped of his defenses and crushed with the awareness that he was alone--and miserable.

Avery finally knew that he needed more than medicine and pipes and tobacco. He needed help; he needed understanding; he needed, for now, a friend he could share with--confide in. He needed a "girl", a lady friend to watch and yes, maybe, even to touch.

He smiled to himself, feeling maudlin yet relieved, and wondered if he might start by trying to see Nickles a little more as a person than as an efficient Lieutenant-secretary-nurse. At the very least it might prove a grand experiment. If nothing else, an ideal intellectual exercise.

"Major Martin is in conference. May I take a message and have him return your call?" Lieutenant Nickles picked up her pencil.

"Have Major Martin call the receiving section when he is able. Lieutenant Morgan is demanding to talk to someone in authority. The transmittal directive that came with Morgan says that Major Martin is to make the initial contact and evaluation," she repeated. "I will see that Major Martin receives the message."

Miss Nickles hung up. She felt that the message was urgent enough to interrupt the Major, so she let herself into his office with the intention of placing the note on his desk and slipping out. The office was deserted, but there was a note on the corner of the desk. She put down the note that she had written and picked up the one that Avery had left. She went to the window and looked down the south beach, where she could just make Avery out as he made his way back toward the medical station.

She smiled her approval of this most reserved but kindly man, who was playing throw and fetch with a scruffy looking little brown dog.

Miss Nickles' father had been a member of the King's Livery. He had been Chief Gamekeeper and Master of the Hounds at Windsor and had instilled in his daughter a profound respect for breeding and education. It was easy for Elizabeth to carry over this appreciation for Major Martin. In her view, his detached manner and outward confidence qualified him in every respect. She found herself wistfully wishing that her station was such that she could offer him more than the silent ministrations of a servant. It would be nice to share in a personal conversation with him.

There had been a time when she had hopes of moving up in station. She had been born in the 375th anniversary year of the birth of Good Queen Bess and had been christened Mary Elizabeth in her honor. As was the custom in 1908, because the consort of the reigning Monarch was named Mary, she was known by her second name and through her childhood was called Beth Nickles. She was a bright child and was singled out for special education as a clerk for the Service of the King's household.

She had worked as a handmaiden from her twelfth through her fifteenth birthdays in order to learn the procedures of the royal household. From her fifteenth birthday through her twentieth she attended at the expense of the Crown, a young ladies' school to prepare her for the position as private secretary to either a royal household or to a royal princess. Part of the training for this position required that she be a registered nurse, which she became by her twenty-fifth birthday.

At this point, the course of history took charge of her life, and with the death of George V and the ascension of the bachelor King, Edward VIII, there was no place for all of her specialized training in the royal retinue. Fortunately, her case was noted by the Lord Chamberlain and provision was made for her to be commissioned as a Lieutenant in the Royal Corps of Nurses. She enthusiastically accepted the commission and, due to her extensive training, had been immediately assigned to the administrative position of secretary, aid, and surgical nurse to Major Martin at the Great Wakering Hospital Station in Essex.

Even though Essex was recorded as the driest part of the British Isles, this statistic did not extend to the beaches. Devastating showers could rush in from the Channel in a matter of moments, and while they did not endure for any great length of time, anything in their path was utterly drenched in seconds. It took no experienced weather eye to see that within moments this would be the case at Great Wakering, and that Major Martin was ill prepared for that certainty.

Seeing the impending disaster, Elizabeth quickly found the Major's umbrella and great raincoat in his uniform closet. Hastily returning to her office, she slipped into her own great coat and grasping her umbrella as well hurried out the door to reach him before the deluge.

As she ran, she wondered why she was doing this. If he ran, he could reach the station before the rains got to him. On the other hand, she justified her actions because of the Morgan message. Only a tiny bit of her awareness admitted that she was running to him because she liked the thought of doing so, and she hoped that the weather had given her an acceptable reason.

Avery had been plodding along, in his concentration oblivious to the oncoming rainsqualls, when his dog-companion sounded an alarm. Looking up, Avery saw that the rain was advancing in gray sheets. He saw Miss Nickles awkwardly hurrying toward him at great speed. Moments later, she staggered to a faltering halt and wordlessly thrust his raincoat and umbrella at him. In breathless fatigue she opened her umbrella and sank to her knees on the sand.

Avery quickly slipped into his raincoat and huddled down beside her and the little dog, under the protection of their two umbrellas mere moments before the sheets of rain arrived.

"I say, good show, Nickles!" Avery shouted through the wind and the rain. "I should have become quite wet if you had not come to my rescue." He hesitated and then continued, "You really shouldn't have gone to all this bother, Nickles, but I do thank you. I seem to have found a new friend in this little dog."

Appearing to examine the dog, she said, "I had a message to deliver, but when I found that you were not in your office, I looked out of the window and saw that you would become quite drenched if I did not hasten to your assistance".

It occurred to Avery that he was touching this woman and that her touch was pleasant, even stimulating. She had reached over to settle the squirming little dog and in doing so had brushed his arm.

Lieutenant Nickles was pleased that the Major had settled down beside her and was attempting to protect her from the driving rain. She enjoyed the intrusion of the little dog as it seemed to permit them to be close without calling attention to the closeness. She had touched his arm as she tried to settle the dog, and she knew that she had lingered before she withdrew her touch. She found that she was having to consciously control her trembling as she felt their close contact through their bulky uniforms.

Thirty-seven year old Mary Elizabeth Nickles, heretofore a spinster, glanced up at Major Avery Edward Martin and felt a new hope thrill through her. She crowded as close to him as she thought she dared and settled down to wait out the storm, secretly hoping that the rain would never stop.

Elizabeth softly closed the door between Dr. Martin's and her office. With a tender and curious sensitivity she leaned against the door, her cheek lightly pressed to it. Her fingertips traced the rough joining of the doorjamb. She dreamily recounted the events of the past few hours and, in reflecting on them, found it incredulous that so much could have happened to her in so short a time. As she grappled to put some stock and order in herself, she found that she was unable to recall anything about them that had not thrilled her to the core, or helped set her somber life on what she dreamily looked to the promise to be a new and exciting course. She had been overcome by her own release and flow of desire and had scarcely been able to see how he had been affected. She was sure that Major Martin had not been acting out a planned course, but had been guided by his instincts that led him to an awareness of her.

When the dog, frightened by the heightening storm, broke away from them, she received new and exciting sensations from the closeness and contact of their bodies as they frantically reached for him. With the animal no longer there to serve as a point of interest, she had feared that they would become embarrassed at their unexpected closeness. But she found, as the rain squall quickly grew to a savage, full force channel storm, blowing away first one and then the other of the umbrellas, they were left unprotected and clinging to one another with little time for such thoughts. Following the dog's lead, they scurried for the protection of the high cliffs that guarded the beach.

The sound of the dog's shrill yapping led them through the low brush that shielded the base of one of the cliffs, where they discovered him huddling in the opening of a small, well-concealed cave. They found that while the cave was small, it would protect them from the storm.

The cold and dampness pressed in on them, and Avery held Elizabeth ever closer in his efforts to warm and protect her. A short time later, when the dog moved deeper into the cave they found themselves alone.

Soon the dampness and cold were replaced for Elizabeth by her pleasure at the closeness of this man. She realized he was trying to warm and shield her from the elements by holding her tightly to him. It was maddening for her. He had awakened and aroused her. She was enveloped with sensations that she would never have permitted herself had she realized that they could exist. She found that she desired this awkward and unassuming man in a way that she had never thought of. Despite her moral bewilderment, this desire reached to the core of her body.

She wanted to be near the Major, to be a part of him, to serve him, to crawl closer and within him, and yet to surround him. She wanted to find and to know with him all of the things that she had never found any reason to experience before.

She wanted to be free of the limitations of being a conventional human. She suddenly craved Avery with an almost animal wantonness. This rutting heat that he had loosened in her had turned her from a wasted, timid, thirty-seven-year-old, into a fiery, passion driven vixen. She knew she must have him, even if she never found another moment in which she could face him--or herself. Somehow, she had to bedevil him into this world of wild lust that he had created for her. She would never be able to endure the feeling of having lived a useless and unrewarded existence unless she gave herself to this man.

She felt she could gladly die, but before she did, she must live. If that meant pain, agony, or nonconformity, she knew she would gladly bare mind and body to him. But she must live! And Avery Martin must be a component of that living.

He had stripped away all of her reserve and produced an awareness that was like nothing else she had ever known or expected--a hundred times over. It was a grand celestial, sexual insanity! And, as though her unspoken prayers held the key to her envisioned world, and all that she now longed for to happen should come within his power to command, she discovered that her supplication for a share of life and a chance to experience and glow in her need to live had been set in motion.

Both he and she were guided by a flow heretofore foreign to either of them. From the first awkward moments of contact and the subconscious and awkward love attempts that followed, they found a blending and sharing. There was a harmony and poetry of motion and it seemed that neither of them knew the source. Elizabeth felt that their exquisite adventure, their uniting and joining, this wonder of wonders, had been pervaded by a power beyond earthly means.

Reflections

She felt somewhat uncomfortable offering thanks to God, but considering herself not quite a child of the devil, she pensively smiled as she lightly patted the closed door and whispered a heartfelt thanks to whoever might like to take credit for the recalled interval. She would never forget one second of that afternoon for the rest of her life.

Moving to her desk, she brushed the wet sand from her uniform and shook her bunned hair loose to comb the grains out. She gathered all of the golden hued bits together and, putting them into a medication bottle, carefully sequestered the now-treasured vial in a corner of her desk drawer. Then she gathered up the balance of Lieutenant Harry W. Morgan's file for her Major Martin.

As she opened the door to the Major's office she found herself beaming with pride and optimism. Lieutenant Morgan's recovery was assured. Major Avery E. Martin could do anything! She suddenly wondered what the 'E' in the Major's name stood for. Finding herself a bit flustered that she would be wondering about such trivial things, she dismissed the consideration from her mind for a later time, although her thoughts were still very much with Major Martin. Yes, whatever he touched simply responded, came alive, and became beautiful and so very right!

"I say, Miss Nickles, is the chap who is making such a row down in Receiving the one whose file you left on my desk for me to read . . . ah . . . before?"

"Yes, Major." Lieutenant Nickles beamed. "The very same one. First Lieutenant Harry W. Morgan of the American Forces. Receiving reported that he is really quite unmanageable, and they are most anxious that you come to their rescue and take him off of their hands. As a matter of fact, the nurse on the floor told me that they would rather send him back to Egypt, not wanting to slip anything so badly disposed off on you. She said that the most merciful thing she could think of would be to put him in a soundproof, padded room! Blind or not."

"He does sound like a bit of a problem, Avery said. "I should expect that this quiet seaside is far from prepared for his sort." Avery reached for the file again and paused for a moment. "Yes, Miss Nickles, it appears that we will be traveling and joining the Yanks at Harrow."

He found the directive that gave him the authority to conduct the treatment of Morgan, to transfer the operations to Harrow, and to decide who would assist him. "We will have to drop down to receiving to settle him down, and I will have to make some preliminary evaluations to support my decision to transfer him and ourselves to the British/American medical station at Harrow, but that is just a matter of going through the motions. I believe that I should like to have you check the whereabouts of Lieutenant Archer, that American nurse that we had with us for a time. I seem to recall that she posted there from here."

"Yes, I am quite sure that it was Harrow, sir."

"She went to visit with my sister, Gwen, on the way, didn't she?"

"Yes, you mentioned that your sister had confirmed her visit in one of her letters. A fine, very fine nurse. All of the ladies on our staff were quite taken with her. She was so unlike what we expected of the American women. As a matter of fact, I cannot recall that she chewed gum at all!"

"Yes, Miss Nickles", he said absently, "I completely agree with you, but I will leave it to you to help her to refrain from doing it in public."

"I beg your pardon, Major?"

"Nothing at all, Lieutenant. Nothing at all. Just thinking about our case . . . ."

"If you say so, Major. Shall we leave now?"

Avery turned his attention to Nickles. His face unusually grave, he looked searchingly at her for a long moment before answering. "In a bit, Lieutenant. Ah . . . there is something that I need to say."

"Yes sir?"

"Ah, yes. Well, it is about the rain, you know."

"Yes, sir, it surely did rain today."

"Yes. It did. As a matter of fact, there was a good deal of wind out there, wasn't there?"

"Yes, Major. There wasn't any sunlight today to speak of, either."

"Nasty day, all right. I should never have gone out and caused you to have to come out and rescue me from the rain. Should have had more sense, you know."

"I was quite pleased to be able to come to your assistance. I should do it again if you were out and did not forbid me."

"Oh, I shouldn't do that, but at the same time I feel rather badly about your getting wet, and . . . well . . . ."

"Yes, Major?"

"What I am trying to say is that I feel rather shameful about the way I went about, eh . . . ah . . . . Drat, Lieutenant! My conduct was unbecoming an officer, particularly in regard to my relationship to a fellow officer. I expect that I shall have to prepare a report and reprimand myself."

"Major, I took no affront, I . . . ."

"If you wish to prefer charges, I shall not stand in your way. I can only think that were it not for my need for your technical and administrative services in the handling of this Morgan case, I should suggest that in defense of your honor you immediately request that one of us be transferred or that I be relieved of my post."

"Major!"

"No, Lieutenant, while I have the muster for it, hear me out so that you can make your course of action known as soon as possible. As I said, I will not stand in your way."

"Major, I believe that it was I who has acted badly. I was in the presence of a superior officer, and I conducted myself in a wanton manner. It is I who should expect the reprimand. I was unmilitary in my attentions to you. While I found those moments most enticing, I should respect that there is no room for such exquisite pleasures in the proper relationships between officers. In that I fully agree with you, but I must respectfully request that you accept my resignation from your staff. I have shamed your position, and I shall withdraw."

Elizabeth was unable to conceal the tear that crept down her cheek and the sob that came to her voice while she spoke of her need to resign and the shame that she felt she now had brought to the Major. She felt the tears force their way from under her clenched eyelids and down over her hot cheeks and saltily into the corners of her mouth. Her sobs bubbled up as little tortured gasps of despair.

She struggled to control herself, and, as she did, her concentration was so intense that her first awareness of the Major's reaction was when she felt his hand carefully cupping her chin. He softly said, "My dear Lieutenant. No, Miss Nickles. Drat! Elizabeth! Let us not have any more thoughts of tears. Unless you are showing such sorrow because you are truly angered with me and I have wronged you, let us continue as the medical team we are while on the station. And let us not lose sight of that grand team of another kind that we have found we may become when we are away from here and our time is our own.

"We have much good work to do, and let us not let this stop us from being fine friends. My dear sister, Gwen, has told me that I needed to find a good friend to share myself with. I should like very much to have you be that good friend. I should like very much to have you think well of me. If you can find it in yourself to do so, I should like to have you think of me as something other than the doctor or Major whenever the need for military formality is not necessary. Can we make a go for it?"

By now Elizabeth had lost nearly all of her composure and felt her heart nearly explode with happiness. She smartly stepped back and delivered a most snappy salute to her superior officer. "Yes, Sir. Oh, yes, yes, yes sir!"

A smiling and suddenly worldly-wise Avery returned the salute, and rumpling his mustache, suggested, "Then come along with you, my penny-bright-Nickles, and we will set about curing this foolish American."

"Yes, sir. He has no idea what he is in for, does he? You and Lieutenant Archer will be much more than he can have bargained for."

"Yes, my dear. We *all* shall share in conquering and curing this cantankerous colonial."

"Good show, sir. Mind that you take your raincoat. It could blow up another one of those unexpected storms, you know."

"Yes, Elizabeth. And you too. And let us not forget the umbrellas, either."

CHAPTER TWENTY-ONE

"I AM MAJOR MARTIN, STATION neurosurgeon and psychiatrist, and this is my assistant, Lieutenant Nickles. I believe that you have an American chap here that has been asking for me." Avery showed the head nurse the Morgan file and went on: "I should like to have Lieutenant Morgan brought out of the ward. We will make our preliminary examination and evaluation here."

"We'll have him here as soon as I can get an orderly!" the obviously relieved head nurse said. She pulled a wheelchair out of its line and stuck her head into the men's latrine. "Come on, Tommy, off the W. C. with you, now. We are going to rid ourselves of Mr. Congeniality! Hurry it up, now!"

Seconds later a red-faced boy of no more than twenty, hastily buttoning his pants, dashed out of the latrine and down the hall in hot pursuit of the racing, wheelchair-driving head nurse. "Hold on, Mum. I am as ready as you to see him off. Just let me get me buttons fastened before I fall over me drawers."

Avery leaned over and observed to Nickles, "I am beginning to get some sort of an idea of how accurate your telephone report about this young man is. It seems that we may have a bit of a sticky problem with him. I expect that our evaluation had better be quick, and we had best move to the American station before he totally rubs raw and reduces whatever goodwill that has been created between the mother-land and the colonies over the past two-hundred years."

"Yes sir, I have my medical records pad. We can make your report as you go along, and it will be all ready to copy, file, post, and move on with. Dear me, Major, here they come with him now! He most certainly is bandaged around the head."

"Careful, Tommy. Wheel the young man into the examination room and turn him around so that he can be looking out at the doctor. Now, get down to the linen locker and bring along some fresh supplies for the room in case the Major needs to have them for his examination."

"Lieutenant Morgan?"

"Yeah! Who's asking?"

"Major Avery Martin. Your assigned medical officer. I have Lieutenant Elizabeth Nickles, my assistant, with me. I have gone over your file, and, while I find it interesting . . ."

Harry grunted.

Ignoring Harry's indifference, Avery went on, "I suggest that there may be some information that has been ignored or which may not have been entered correctly. Tell me, Lieutenant, what you believe your condition to be, and how you foresee your subsequent treatment. If possible, we will take your suggestions into consideration."

Harry's head jerked up, and even though shrouded in bandages, appeared to be trying to locate Avery's whereabouts. "Well! It's about time they found you. I was beginning to

Reflections

think I was going to be stuck in here for the rest of my life. So, you want to know what I think about my condition? I can't believe it! 'Till now all anyone ever did was tell me about my condition, like they knew all about how it was to be blind and how it was to go through all the crap I have gone through. I'll tell you! I can't see! And I don't give a damn if I ever do again! I should have a tin cup. That's all that I will ever be any good for from now on. People have been pushing and poking around on me and scraping here and there. And all the time it comes out the same. I'm blind! Just forget about me. Run me off into a corner. One day I won't be there anymore and no one will miss me. You won't have to bother about me, either."

Harry dropped his head back on his chest. Quieting down, he went on, "I can solve my own problems. I was the one who got me this way. I don't have anybody to blame but me. Don't get involved . . . ."

"Now, Lieutenant . . . ", Avery began.

Harry grew rigid and seemed to glare right through his bandages as he yelled at Avery. "All Right! Damn it, Major! You're pushing me too far, too. You asked me and I'm going to tell it to you just the way it is, and then you can leave me alone. I don't need any help! I couldn't get all the rest of them, anywhere, to pay attention to me. They keep patting me and clucking over me and telling me 'everything is going to be just fine and that I should have all kinds of faith in them and their fancy doctor who I'd be seeing. I suppose that's you. Huh! Damn it! I'm the one who's blind!

"How in hell do you know what I feel like in here? You ever been blind? No! There's no one else in here with me, and there is no room for anyone else in here with me. I want you all to leave me alone. I'll take care of myself, and if I can't do that, then just stay the hell out of my way because I got me this way and I will do my own thinking and handling of this mess I am in.

"I got this way because I believed in something too damn much, and I lost. What makes you think that you can make up for that? I lost, damn it! You didn't!

"If you want so damn much to do something for me and give me all this help, then leave me alone and stay the hell away from me. I don't need anybody!

"Everything I ever had that anybody had something to do with ended up with them either getting hurt or expecting too damn much from me. I'm tired of it all. Why in hell should you help me? What in hell can you do? You think you're some kind of God damn God or something?

"God! God? There wouldn't be this damn war, and I wouldn't have lost my friends and I wouldn't have been part of killing them if there was a God! And maybe I wouldn't have to be blind for the rest of my life. If there was any God or if there was any justice, I wouldn't be here. I'd have it all over with by now, but that ain't the way it works out."

Elizabeth attempted, "Please Lieutenant . . . ."

"Aw lady, please just shuddup!" Harry snarled. "Who are you? Just what the hell do you think you can do? Don't waste your time; don't waste my time either. Just leave me alone. I can take care of myself. Get the hell out of here! I don't need either one of you--or anybody like you!"

Clumsily propelling the wheelchair so that it bumped its way into the corner, Harry closed the conversation with a

Reflections

parting "Get out. If I want to die, at least have the good graces and sense to quit watching me. Now get the hell out of here! Leave me alone!"

A graven-faced Avery and his unbelieving nurse noiselessly backed out of the room and silently closed the door as Harry remained motionless, blindly staring into the darkness of the room.

"Miss Nickles, inform the ward nurse to prepare Lieutenant Morgan for immediate transfer to Harrow. Telephone Command and have the transfer orders cut for the first thing in the morning. Move on the Lieutenant Archer assignment as fast as you can as I shall need to know what you come up with. We will need to transfer all of our other caseloads and files to Major Sloan's section to close our office as soon as possible."

"Yes, sir. I'll take care of everything. He is a bitter one, isn't he?"

"Hmm, yes, dreadful."

"Can we help him? Do you think we can get through to him?

"I believe so. There's some very good fight there. It just seems to be channeled off in the wrong direction."

"How my heart goes out to him. He seems to carry the total agony of all of the war with him. It's not right, sir."

"No, Nickles, it is not right, but nevertheless it is there. Yes, I believe that we can help him, but we must find some way to earn his trust. I am even more in agreement with the reports in his medical record. I am convinced that he has not actually lost his sight, but that he has lost his purpose, and along with that his need and will to see. He remembers in his darkness the pain that he saw when he could last see, and at least he can hide in his darkness and not have to take a chance of seeing something that he cannot handle. It will not be easy, but I believe we will do it."

"We have a lot of work to do, sir. I'll have the office ready to close in the morning."

"You are really stout, Nickles, err . . . , Elizabeth. Yes, I dare say that we will be up all night getting the work done, but the sooner we get to Harrow, the sooner we can begin on Morgan."

CHAPTER TWENTY-TWO

"Major martin! guess who's our first visitor? Never mind, I'll just bring her in right now so you won't have to."

Lieutenant Nickles hung up the phone and all but dragged Sally toward the Major's office.

"It is so good to see you again, Lieutenant Archer." She happily exclaimed, "We had dearly missed you at the Essex station. The Major and I were so glad when he was able to add you to his staff for this assignment. We--but I must not chatter on so. The Major will want to tell you himself about what we all have in store for us here. Here, let me open the door for you. There!"

Nickles pushed Sally into the Major's office, nearly bowling him over.

"Now, now, Nickles. Your enthusiasm for Lieutenant Archer may create our next casualty. Dear me, but you are exuberant!" The clearly pleased and smiling Major turned his attention to Sally, and warmly accepted her salute. Shaking her hand, he exclaimed, "Let us see if we can find our way clear of our hyperkinetic Nickles. Come over here where I can get a good look at you, and we can all sit down and bring ourselves up to date. You do look as though being back with your own people has done well for you."

Nickles chimed in, "Yes, see, her uniform is spotlessly clean, and it is starched and pressed beyond belief! Dear me, how clean your station must have been!"

Sally squeezed Elizabeth's hand and then patted the sleeve of the Major's coat as she said, "Yes, it was good to get back, but I certainly did miss all of you. I never thought that I would look back at Essex and Great Wakering with any fond recollections, but whenever I thought of the wonderful people that were there, I really found myself quite homesick for you. I'm so glad we are all together again, at least for a while."

"Yes. Well, it may be for more than a while", Avery replied. "Your and our people have moved with uncharacteristic speed when they heard that we were coming here with your Lieutenant Morgan, and they decided that we should help them set up a section which will deal with some of the things which we have been experiencing with our lads that are coming back from North Africa."

Avery walked to his desk, picked up a handful of files, returned, and dropped the files on the service table in front of them. He went on, "In the last war they called these cases 'shell shock.' Now there is a new phrase, 'battle' or 'combat fatigue,' but it all comes down to the same thing. These men are suffering from emotional stress brought on by the pressures of war, pressures that none of them were ever prepared for, pressures that we are going to have to identify and help them to cope with. We have precious little experience, and by and large your people have even less. Yet, there is more than enough theory floating about to fill the English Channel, but beyond that, very little concrete fact to work with.

Turning to Sally, he said, "I have had you reassigned to my staff for a number of reasons. We were pleased with the work that you did during our earlier association, and you have had formal training in the area in which we will be working."

Sally nodded in agreement as Avery continued, "I believe you will find a great challenge in the case we brought with us. I wish to assign you as his Nurse in Charge, and have you handle the main contact as he is an American officer. Make no mistake. He is a most difficult person. In fact, he is as uncooperative, rude, boorish, selfish, and disgusting in his attitude toward himself and everything around him."

Elizabeth injected, "I would like to help him pull his own trigger! He will be most challenging for you, but from what I know of you, you won't let him win out over you."

"Quite true," Avery agreed. "Of course, Nickles and I will be working with you, but for the time being and the most part, you will be the sole contact with our Lieutenant Morgan. It will be up to you to put the will to live back into his heart and the will to see back into his eyes. We are sure that he is physically healthy, and there is nothing at all wrong with his sight. He simply has regressed and is hiding. He believes that he let other people down and that he as much as killed a number of his friends. But whether he did or not, he is well in body. It is our job to see that he realizes that he can also be well in sight, mind, and heart."

CHAPTER TWENTY-THREE

HARRY NEVER KNEW JUST WHEN she came into the room for the first time, but suddenly he felt a new presence. The first time had to be when she came to introduce herself, but did nothing. He knew she was there, but yet she made no effort to speak. There was something different about her, but even then, she could have been part of the 'treatment.'

A lot of people had intruded upon him during the past weeks and months. None of them had made any impression; none had been able to reach into his world. He had repelled all of them and that was the way he wanted it. He had nothing to give and nothing to share, and he wanted nothing from anyone. If he didn't want to shave, or eat, or talk, why the hell should they care? It was his darkness, his world. He didn't need them, and the sooner they realized that the better off they would be--and so would he.

There was that absurd-sounding Major Martin, who was supposed to be a doctor who specialized in his kind of case, and his clackety-heeled nurse, Lieutenant Nickles. When he heard her clattering down the halls, all he had to do was listen a little harder and he could hear that Limey doctor sucking on his infernal pipe. Harry wondered if he ever lit it. He could smell the odor of the pipe, but he had never been able to detect the scent of burning tobacco.

Of course, there had always been the orderlies and other nurses and their weak attempts to 'cheer' his day. He had tolerated the 'dressing nurse' who changed his facial bandages, but only because it was in his view absolutely necessary. Otherwise, this attention was senseless. Why didn't they leave him alone?

He had seen death explode right into his face and felt it all around him. Hell's fire! He had been the 'right hand' that death had sought out. He had not helped kill the enemy. He had watched if not participated in 'death's' execution at least two of his own close friends. Harry, beyond all others, knew his inability to act had caused Janish to die. In his mind, his fear, his cowardliness had assured the death of Walter Abher, Janish and the disappearance of Jean Monier. Beyond that, Al Keesling and Paul had been gravely wounded.

Harry had not been able to forget the exchange between the airmen: "He caused the death of at least two with his freezing up."

"Yeah, the bastard. He's something else."

"You're right about the bastard! I hope he seen and remembers it all."

And he had seen it all, and then, as he realized his part in the misery around him and caught the look of disgust that the airmen held for him, he let his own wounds screen the world from him. The darkness set in. He took refuge in the darkness of a world that saw no wars, heard no screams for help, felt no pain or fear, and shrank from no pointing fingers of guilt.

No. They could never reach him here. He felt secure in his realization that the harder they tried to pry into his chambers, the easier it became for him to wall them out. He needed nothing from them. There was nothing that they could do, nothing that they could give that he needed or cared about.

It was his birthday. At least, that was what someone had told him. He had been stoically sitting, trying to decide whether that was something he should take note of. He could consider it as another victory for himself since he did not have to share it with them. If he wanted to think and have a birthday, he could do it very well here in his own world. As a matter of fact, he realized that he had been enjoying himself and that he might well have been smiling because a voice that he had never before heard drifted into his hearing, saying, "Captain, I'm pleased to see that you have found something to enjoy and smile about."

"What?" a startled Harry asked.

"Are you thinking about when you were a boy and had a nice birthday party?" Her voice was soft.

"I don't know what you're talking about."

"Oh. I thought that when I looked at your chart earlier this morning, I read that this is your birthday."

"Well, what of it? That don't give you any cause to butt in on me! You're new around here! Aren't you? Why did you sneak up on me like that?"

"I didn't, Captain. I just thought it might be nice to talk to you for a little while."

"I'll bet! What do you want, anyway?"

"Sorry, Captain. I don't think you have anything I want. I'll be on my way. Thanks for letting me share your birthday for a few moments. Goodbye."

"What was that supposed to mean?"

"Nothing at all, Captain. I won't bother you any more today. Maybe another time." And the soft voice drifted away as an even deeper darkness and silence closed in on Harry.

Harry realized that she was the one who had come into his room and had watched him without trying to talk to him. "God, they sure go out of their way to try to get these 'shrinks' on me. I wonder if there was one with her?"

Harry fumbled for his cane and swung it around, trying to dislodge his imagined compartment mates. Eventually tiring of this effort, he hooked the cane back over the chair and slouched down to catch his breath.

The tension and exertion had tired him more than he had realized, and as he rested he also became settled by the warm rays of the sun that streamed through the window into the glassed porch. As he dozed off to sleep, he muttered, "Who the hell did she think she was calling me Captain? That woman might think she's some kind of a nurse, but she can't even read the information on my chart. It sure as hell didn't say anything about me being a Captain there. I'll bet my butt on that. God, they'll do anything!"

"Well, Archer, what have you decided about our Captain Morgan? Has he bitten your head off yet?"

"No, although I can't say that he hasn't tried. He's been so busy throwing up a wall around himself and striking out at me that I believe he hasn't noticed that I have been calling him Captain for the last three visits. Of course, the visits haven't lasted more than a minute or two at a time."

"That short, eh? Do you feel that you have made any headway at all with him?"

"Yes, Major, the first time I stopped I am quite sure that he sensed someone was in the room, although he made no effort that I could see to communicate. The next time--his birthday--I spoke to him for a few moments and he accused me of spying on him, so I came away with the impression that he realized I had been in the room before. At any rate, he challenged me, which I felt was good."

"Yes, I agree. Go on."

"When I spoke to him yesterday, he asked me what had happened to Lieutenant Nickles. He said he hadn't heard her 'clacking heels' coming down the halls lately. I told him that she was busy doing something else, but that I would be glad to have her come down to see him. Then he said that I should forget he mentioned it. This morning he wanted to know if Major Martin had gone back to wherever he came from, and I told him you were still here and would be glad to see him whenever he wanted to see you."

"What did he say about that?" Major Martin asked.

"He just sort of grunted. He really didn't say anything, but at least he didn't blow up like he has in the past whenever someone mentioned something that related to his condition--or to doctors."

"Not very complimentary, but considering the circumstances, we will have to view it as an improvement. I am rather taken with the fact that he still seems to ignore your calling him Captain. Are you sure that no one else has called him Captain and that his only contact with this reference to him is through you?"

"Yes, I am quite sure that I am the only person addressing him by his new rank."

"Lieutenant Nickles suggested that he may be hearing you call him Captain but that because of his dislike for himself, he will not accept that he has been promoted, particularly on the heels of what he considers to be his abject cowardliness."

"I agree, Major. He certainly has ignored each reference to his Captaincy. It may be too painful for him to accept."

"Yes, Archer, and it may be too challenging for him to continue hiding from. Somehow or another, he must begin to come to grips with himself. He must realize that he has to make the first move toward his real recovery. He has accepted himself as having failed not only his companions, but more importantly, himself. He is still quite willing to use us, more particularly you, as a sympathetic contact with the outside world, while he hides behind his mask of blindness. He is not blind. He is only blind to himself and refuses to come to grips with the fact that his are the same fortunes of war that all of us face."

Half-protesting, Sally returned, "He has been badly beaten, wounded, and seems to believe that anything that he has ever put his faith in--from as far back as his childhood--has proven to be undependable. He shows that in one way or another; his idols, his family, and his aspirations have not held true for him.

Either people have not been what he expected them to be or they expected more of him that he was able to be. He has never had a happy life; I am pretty sure of that."

"Yes, Archer, it's a shame, but the fact still remains that he has to come to grips with himself. In a way, it's too bad that he is so very brilliant. He has the ability, the intellect, and somewhere in there--though still totally undiscovered--the social grace to be a very effective if not a magnetically dynamic person. But he must try. We--rather, you--cannot live for him. You cannot carry him. He should have sense enough--and we must help him find it--to leap to follow your lead. I chose you to help him because I knew you to be tough, fair-minded, and determined. I saw that you would have an understanding of his American ways and that you would be able to stand up to his tactics of aggression on the one hand and sympathy-seeking on the other."

"I don't find him a bad person, Major. I find him very much in need of help. He desperately needs a friend. I don't think he ever received any appreciable affection during his childhood, and in the years that have passed since then he has been either rebuffed or ignored and has become totally distrustful of even the most sincere attempts to be close, helpful and friendly. It is as though he has never learned trust. He certainly knows nothing at all about love! He so dearly needs to find just one person that he can believe in. He has so much to come back from, and the pain and hurt just oozes from him."

"You know, Archer, you have to be careful. You have feelings, too."

"Yes, but I can handle whatever he needs for a while longer. If he will just relax and try to trust. He hasn't even asked me what my name is yet. I know that we can eventually give him the self-assurance that he needs to carry on for himself. He has become important to me, Major. I have the strength, and I will share it with him as long as he needs it."

CHAPTER TWENTY-FOUR

SETTLING HERSELF INTO THE CHAIR Sally opened the blinds and switched on the microphone. She dated the activity report sheet and observed that over four weeks had passed since she had come to Harry Morgan's world of darkness. She had watched him--mostly without his knowledge. She had talked to him from time to time. He was so alone and yet he resisted all attempts to befriend him. Since his promotion to Captain had caught up with him, Sally had casually addressed him as Captain Morgan from time to time during their conversations. As far as she could determine, he had continued to ignore the reference.

Despite his acidic abruptness and rudeness, she had developed sympathy for him. She had found his company had progressed from intolerable to acceptable and sometimes satisfying. In the meanwhile, Harry had discovered that his days dragged until she stopped by.

Unaware that he was being observed, Harry sat in his 'aloneness' in the sunroom. The day seemed cold and remote because he could not feel the sun and because 'she' had not come by. He was certain that something was wrong because she had not come around today, and he was sure that she had not been around on the day before, either.

She probably was tired of his rudeness, he thought, and had found other duties to keep her from having to come near him. Yes, that was it. He had only himself to blame, but that was the way it usually went. He wondered if she would ever return. His anxiety grew. Had she been transferred?

In the past, Sally had witnessed little or no concern on his part for what happened around him, but of late and particularly this time he seemed to be increasingly nervous. She turned up the volume of the microphone so she could hear his grumblings.

"Damn that nurse, anyway! What in hell right did she have to come around here and bother me? He squirmed around in his wheelchair. "I didn't need her nosing around here. Now that she's wormed her way into my life, where the hell is she? Just like the rest of them. Nowhere around when you need them! Well, to hell with her, too! I wish she'd never come around here in the first place."

Even though she felt compassion for him, Sally couldn't help grinning in mild amusement at his comment about her "worming" her way in. At the same time, no matter how essential her observations were, she felt embarrassment because of her eavesdropping.

Harry continued, his anger obvious, "Her intrusion is an indignity! I can't get away from her, and I can't make her leave me alone. I just have to sit here like a damn vegetable waiting for somebody to come and put me in the sun like a damn house plant. She did it to me!

He pounded his fist on his knee, "I could have lived forever without her, and now here I am; I can't get through a damn day without her! And I don't even know her name!"

Harry sagged, now painfully aware that someone could reach him. And yet the person had never so much as touched him. All of the others--the nurses, the doctors, even the orderlies--had been making a full-time job out of patting and poking him. But not her! No! She had never even touched him!

"What in the hell is happening to me?" Harry asked aloud. "Before, I could keep the whole world out there and find solace in doing it. Now I can't even keep one nurse out of my mind!" Somehow, he realized, she gave him great comfort. Try as he might, Harry had been unable to keep from looking forward to her arrival and to the cool, yet coaxing interest that she seemed to show in him.

Sally switched off the microphone and drew the curtains. But instead of going to confer with Dr. Martin as she had intended, she decided to stop for a few moments of conversation with Captain Morgan. She believed he showed pangs of remorse. He appeared ready to try to relate to the world. She felt his awareness of and anger at her was a good sign. She was aware that he had been keeping track of time by the warmth of the sun, and more recently, by her visits. She had therefore broken the pattern of her visits to observe and learn his reactions. She silently let herself into the room.

Harry had arrived at the conclusion that he must be going soft. The last thing he wanted was to have any kind of a "visit" with anyone. But there wasn't much doubt about it. She did sort of visit with him. Except, she wasn't visiting him today! Had she been around at all yesterday? Or the day before that? He squirmed in the wheelchair knowing that he was no longer as secure in his dark world as he had been before this nurse person had invaded its sanctity. "My God, he muttered, "I don't even know her name."

Sally started to move toward him. She thought he was going to try to get out of the chair. Instead, he settled into a new position, and in a low voice, said, "If I could only see just enough to make out light from dark. I could at least see the sunrise." He was silent for a moment. "But what the hell good would that do? I'd have to take my bandages off to see that much. They could see me for what I am and all I could see would be if it was light out. They could sneer and look at me. They could say, 'There's that damn bloody bastard. He froze up and all his friends got killed because of him.'"

He grabbed as if to tear the protective shield of cloth from his eyes, but instead pressed his hands over his eyes as he sobbed, "If only she hadn't come along and destroyed the only security I ever found. Why did she do this to me? Why did then leave me here with her around? Nurse! Where the hell are you?" Help Me!

"Right here, Captain."

God! He wondered. How long had she been standing there? How much had she heard? He had to master his feelings to protect himself from her further intrusion, but he was unable to deny that he had found great relief at her presence. In a faint effort to show composure he said, "You, er . . . been busy?"

"Yes and no. Why do you ask?"

"No reason. It was nothing."

"Oh, did I forget an appointment or something? Had I promised to be here sooner?"

"I told you, it was nothing."

"Whatever you say, Captain. Can I get you a blanket? It's rather chilly out here, particularly now that the sun is not out."

"No, I'm comfortable. I . . . I've got to ask you something."

"Yes?"

"Why did you call me Captain just then? You did it before, too."

"Because you are a Captain. You've been promoted!"

"Not very likely. Why would they do that?"

"Because you earned it."

"If I earned anything at all it was a court martial! I let all of my friends get killed! I deserved to die, and I couldn't even do that! I'm not a Captain! I . . . ."

"Easy, Captain. You didn't kill anyone."

Harry tried to get up, but she gently pushed him back into the chair, and then touched her fingertips lightly to his lips to silence his protests. "Believe me, Captain," she said, "Those casualties were never your fault. You did the best you could, and you have to accept that."

Her words were lost on Harry. Her first touch thrilled through him like nothing ever had before. He grasped her hands in his and pressed her fingers to his lips. "Please help me", he pleaded. "I want to come out of this darkness, but I don't know how."

A half-hour later as Sally Archer rounded the corner of the corridor on her way to Dr. Martin's office, she came face to face with Elizabeth, who, with a rather long and disturbed face, announced, "Oh, Miss Archer. Dr. Martin would like to see you in his office."

"That's just where I'm headed. Any idea what he wants? Any information or files that I should bring?"

"No, nothing like that. I really don't know what he wants to talk to you about, but I can warn you from his grumping around his office this afternoon, his news is not of an optimistic nature."

"Well, maybe I have something to report that will make him feel better. It looks like . . . well; you'll hear it when I report to Dr. Martin."

"Ah, Lieutenant Archer, how good of you to come so promptly. Please take a chair. Can I interest you in a spot of tea?"

Avery drew a chair into position for Sally. He glanced toward the other end of the desk to be sure that Elizabeth and her note pad would also have a comfortable place.

"Thank you, Major. Lieutenant Nickles tells me that you have some rather distressing news. Is Gwen all right?"

"Oh my, yes. Nothing seems to disturb her. I venture to say that the whole German Luftwaffe could drop into her garden and she would merely call the gardener to dispose of it. No. It's not about Gwen."

"I'm glad to hear that. I enjoyed her so very much when I spent that weekend with her in London."

"No, I'm afraid it's about our young American. That Lieutenant Morgan fellow."

"You mean Captain Morgan", Nickles reminded.

"Oh, yes. I stand corrected," Avery absently agreed. "It looks as though we are going to lose him."

"Lose him?" Sally and Elizabeth responded.

"Yes. It appears that his army feels that regardless of the degree of training and specialization that he has, unless we can give them some significant indication that we are making headway with either his sight or his emotional recovery, they intend to arrange to return him to a hospital for the emotionally impaired in the United States."

"Ohhh!" Elizabeth said, dropping her pad and pencil into her lap. "Is there nothing that we can do?"

"Not unless we can report that there is some progress or change in his attitude. How about you, Archer? Anything to report?" Avery asked.

Hardly able to contain the excitement of her discoveries of that afternoon, Sally responded, "Yes, I have something that we can report that will help our position."

"You do?" Elizabeth said, snapping back to her usual prim attention.

"Yes. I think he is expressing a new kind of anger for him. I am quite sure he is frustrated. I believe that it is due to the fact that his blindness now has become an irritating nuisance and a considerable obstacle to him. He is beginning to look beyond himself. I think that is something that you can build a favorable report about, Doctor."

"Now, that's more like it, Archer. Have you made some headway in getting him to respond to your interest and visits?"

"Yes, Major. But I'm not sure if I fully understand all of what has occurred."

"Why is that?"

"Well, it seems that the relationship is developing into something somewhat beyond clinical or even professional."

"Really? I don't believe that I follow what you are saying. Do you know what she is saying, Nickles?"

"Yes, sir."

"You do? Well, it must have something to do with women and their way of thinking. Yes. No! He is a man and must certainly be thinking like a man. Oh!" Avery's face reddened, and he tugged at the corner of his mustache. "You mean that you think he feels something personal toward you?"

"Yes. I'm concerned that that may be the case."

"Well, after we have seen to his recovery, we can work on turning his interests into more mundane directions, can't we, Archer?"

"I don't think it will be all that easy, sir."

"Eh? I confess you have lost me again."

Elizabeth, not able to believe the denseness of her Major, but remembering her own long suffering adulation for him, exasperatedly said, "She means that she feels something personal toward Captain Morgan as well. Isn't that right, Lieutenant?"

Sally turned her attention from Avery to Elizabeth. "Yes, you're as perceptive as ever, Elizabeth. I find that I have a feeling of more than just compassion for him. And there is something else that keeps gnawing at me."

"What's that?" Elizabeth said as Avery, quite perplexed by the developments, sat back in his chair.

"I have the strange feeling that I have known him from somewhere before," Sally said.

"Oh, Sally!" Elizabeth said. "Maybe it was in another life. I hear that there are many charted cases of reincarnation where people are brought together centuries after having been together before. Just the other day, in the Daily . . . ."

Sally thoughtfully said. "I don't think this is the case, this time, Elizabeth."

"Oh?" Avery said. "I should like very much to be able to begin to understand this case again. I confess that I had not expected these turns of events. You say that there is an, ah . . . , ah . . . , infatuation? Between the two of you? And now you believe that you have been introduced to him before? Most unexpected to say the least. Remember? I warned you earlier about yourself in this matter!"

Drawing comfort from Avery's expressions of concern rather than alarm, Sally went on, "While I was observing the Captain today, I overheard him talking to himself. He was angry with himself and with me because he could no longer enjoy the refuge of his self-enforced darkness."

"Really?" Avery responded.

"Yes."

"Was there anything else, Archer?"

"He was complaining to himself that he didn't even know my name, and even then he in his darkness asked me to help him."

"Yes! Yes! And . . . ?"

"Well, when I touched him to try to console him, he took my fingers in his and kissed them . . . ."

"He did?" Elizabeth exclaimed so loudly that a startled Avery dropped his pipe. He ducked down to retrieve it.

"What did he do? What did he say next?" Elizabeth begged.

A misty-eyed Sally looked at Elizabeth for a moment and then softly said, "He said he wanted me to help him. He said he was afraid, but that he wanted to see again. He said he needed me."

At these words, Elizabeth fell back into her chair. Then a loud 'thump' was heard to come from under the desk.

"Ouch," said Avery. Wearing a sheepish but pleased smile, he emerged from behind the desk, pipe in hand, and gingerly rubbed his head. "Good show, Archer. You've won through! He jolly well will see again! We'll win out after all!"

CHAPTER TWENTY-FIVE

Avery took one last pull on his pipe, poked it into his breast pocket, and then peered into the sunroom. He had hoped to find Harry asleep or at least otherwise occupied so that he could make some undetected observations of his own. Before he got through the door, Harry called out, "what can I do for you, Doctor? It is Doctor Martin, isn't it?"

Avery answered, "I say, how can you chaps always discover that I am about before I even know where I am, myself? I am ready to believe that you can see more through your bandages than the rest of us can with our eyes wide open. How do you do such things?"

Harry--not about to tell the Major that between the slurping sound of his pipe and the strong tobacco aroma, that he was about as stealthy as an asthmatic elephant –let it pass. "I guess it's an extraordinary sense we develop under these conditions. You just have to work a lot harder being silent."

"Righto. I say there, Captain, it appears that we are alone and I should like to have a few words in private with you."

"Oh you would? About what? What's up?"

"Well, part of it has to do with what we have scheduled for you today. Today is an important day for all of us. It is over 2 months since we came over here, you know. The tests that you have taken prove to us that you have sight in your eyes, and the reports that we have prepared support our decision that later this afternoon we are going to remove your bandages."

"I don't know, Doctor. 'You think maybe it's too soon? Are my eyes strong enough to handle bright lights yet?"

"No, not bright lights, but you will be all right as long as you continue to stay indoors for the next little while. You will have to wear smoked glasses for a period of time, and that will give your eyes a chance to further strengthen."

"Well, I guess I'm just nervous about it all. Is Lieutenant Nickles going to be here when the bandages come off? And by the way, who is that American Nurse you have coming in to see me? I don't even know her name,"

"Really? She is first Lieutenant Sally Archer, an American Registered Nurse who we had on our staff at Great Wakering because of her specialized training in anesthesia and psychology, and who I asked to have added to our team because I felt she would be highly useful and understanding of your colonial ways."

"I've really have never seen either of them yet, either."

"I fancy that I should take that personally, Captain. You have never seen me, either. Haw! Haw! Only a joke, you know. Why, yes, they will both be here, but you must realize that you will not be able to see clearly for the first few days."

"What can I expect to see then?"

"In the subdued light of the room which you are being transferred to, you will be able to distinguish light from dark. You will be able to see outlines. You should be able to see the outline of people and the general color of their clothing, but it will be a little longer before your optic equipment will be strong enough for you to distinguish facial features."

"Does that mean that I may not be able to see again?"

"Not at all! It merely means that we are going to be able to see who you are for a few days before you can see who we are."

"Then I'll be able to see as well as ever before too long?"

"Yes, as well as ever."

"I guess I'm pretty lucky at that. I had begun to think I would never want to see again, and now I can hardly wait. Some change, huh, Major?"

"I fully agree with that, Captain."

"Say! You know, you're right. I never have seen any of you. I wonder if you will be anything like I imagine. It'll be interesting when I finally get to see all of you."

"Well, Captain, the anticipation, and mystery is not all yours. Remember since you have come into my care, you have never permitted anyone other than the surgical dressing nurse, Miss Johnson to see your features, and then only partially at a time. Neither Nickles, Archer, or I have ever seen you without bandages."

"Yes, that's true isn't it? But I just wanted to be left alone. That's changed for me now. Thank God. I surely must have been hell to handle."

"I categorically agree with you. I must tell you the staff, particularly the surgical nurses that have had to dress your wounds and damage eyes, have had no easy time of it."

"No, I suppose not."

"I can also tell you that you have been the most difficult person that we have ever had at the Essex station or here at

Harrow, and your people here at Harrow were becoming increasingly anxious to return you to Essex, if not to North Africa, if not to send you to a physically impaired hospital in the United States."

"That bad?"

"Yes, Captain. Very much that bad."

"She'll be pretty, won't she, Major?"

"Eh? Who'll be pretty?"

"Archer!"

"Oh! Well, you know, I never thought much about it. Yes, I suppose you could say so."

"You don't sound very encouraging about it at all, Major."

"Well, I don't suppose that I do. She is a most outstanding nurse, you know. I expect one of the very best I have ever seen. Most efficient and dependable, but…"

"Not much to look at…"

"Confound it, man! I have never considered nurses for their looks. How would it be if I were to go about the hospital observing if this or that nurse were, as you say, 'pretty?' I would get little or no work done. To be perfectly frank, by some standards, a great number of the staff would have to be 'put on the hook.'"

Recognizing that he had pressed Avery into an awkward position, Harry attempted to soften the mood as he said, "What I meant was, I have become rather interested in Lieutenant Archer because she has been so patient with me these past weeks. I was wondering what you could tell me about her. I wondered if there was anything you thought I should know about her. I guess it was only natural that I would wonder if she was attractive, and what she looked like. I was just looking for your opinion."

"Oh! Well, she is an outstanding professional nurse of the very highest quality. Of all the nurses I have served with only Lieutenant Nickles is on an equal footing. In a matter of appearances, I would say she is quite nice for an American person. She is efficient, dedicated, most dependable to work with, and according to Lieutenant Nickles, has a delightful personality. She is highly respected and thought of by your medical people. I can tell you little more. Beyond that, you'll simply have to make your own judgments in the matter."

Thankful that he had completed what he considered to be a most difficult assessment, Avery turned to leave, only to be stopped short as Harry called after him, "What was the other part you wanted to talk to me about, Doctor?"

"Oh! Yes! In my haste I forgot all about it. It concerns Archer, as well, although she knows nothing of it yet. I would like to keep it from her for the moment, and you can help me do that."

"I can? What's she done now?"

"Nothing. Well, that's not true. She has done quite a lot and is certainly deserving, although I expect that it would never happen to one so young in the British service."

"What would? You've totally lost me. She's not leaving, is she?"

"No."

"Then what's the big mystery?"

"Archer is not a Lieutenant."

"I thought she was an Army nurse. What is she, a civilian?"

"No, it's really nothing like that at all. She's a Captain now just like you are, but she knows nothing of it."

"A Captain! Great! And she doesn't know about it? How come?"

"I haven't told her. As her temporary commanding officer, I have the responsibility of conferring her new rank on her, and I want you to tell her later on, much as we had her tell you of your promotion, and… Shhh, here she comes with Lieutenant Nickles. Mum's the word for now. I'll let you know when and where later."

Harry lounged back into his wheelchair. It was hard not to grin. He marveled at how much his world had changed for the better. It was all because of Archer. And now she was a Captain.

"Will I ever have fun with her now, Harry thought. "I'll have to remind her about who has the seniority around here, though. Yes, I gotta see this!" And then, as he felt the orderly begin to wheelchair him towards examination office, he became more excited. "Boy! There is so much I gotta see… Starting with her."

"Are we all here?"

"Yes, Major," Lieutenant Nichols reported.

"Are you comfortable, Captain Morgan?"

"Yes. Doctor? Is Archer here, too?"

"Yes Captain, I'm right here beside you."

"Oh! Are you going to be doing something, too? I mean, will you be close by?"

"Yes, I'll be right beside you all the time."

"Major?"

"Yes?"

"Can Lieutenant Archer be the first thing I see when the bandages come off?"

"Yes, I guess so, but you must remember what I told you."

"I know. I won't see much. But what I do see I want to be her. Okay?"

"Very well. Miss Archer, why don't you let the Captain hold on to your hand while Nichols, Lieutenant Johnson, and I begin to snip away at these bandages? Lieutenant Johnson will be leaving as soon as the bandages and dressings are removed"

"Well, are we all set, ladies? Oh yes… And gentleman."

"The blinds are drawn, Elizabeth said, "the lights are adjusted, I have all of the instruments ready and so are we".

"Ready for a go at it, Captain?"

"Let's go. I'm sort of scared but let's go."

"Hand me a bandage scissors and adjust the light so I can see a little better, Nickles. Good".

For the next few moments there was little sound other than the precise sounds made by the instruments, which were occasionally interrupted by the murmurs of Avery and Elizabeth, along with Lieutenant. Johnson, as they remove the bandages that have been Harry's refuge for these many months. As he felt the bandages removed, Harry became more and more anxious. He clung tightly to Sally's hand. Through it all she quietly console him and diverted as much of his attention from his near terror as possible.

When Avery got down to the final eye pads he paused and said "Captain from now on it will be first names. We have gone through much and we have too much more to go through together to stand on formalities so I will address you as Harry. I suggest that you call me Avery. If the ladies are so disposed, let us call them Sally and Elizabeth. I also suggest that in the privacy of this group we be known to them as Avery and Harry as well. I suggest this because very much is at stake here for all of us I want the most comfortable circumstances possible to prevail. Is this an acceptable arrangement?"

"I think it is an admirable and thoughtful suggestion, Dr." Sally responded

Harry trying to bolster his own nerves by making a private joke said, "I think that's a great idea. You can never tell who's liable to answer when you say Captain around here, anyway."

Avery paused waiting for Elizabeth to comment, who dabbing at her tears, finally managed, "yes, I'm ready, doctor".

"Good. Harry when Elizabeth and I have removed these last two pads I want you to remain with your eyes closed until I give you further instructions it is important that you understand everything I tell you so if there is anything that is not clear, question before acting. Do you understand me so far?"

"Yes, Avery."

"Good. Sally will have to let go of your hand in a few moments, and I fancy from the look of the grip that you have on it, it will be a welcome relief for her."

"Will she have to leave?"

"Dear me, no. If you want to be able to see her when we finally clear your eyes to open she will have to be directly in front of you because I do not want you to shift your eyes to either side, nor do I want you to turn your head."

"I am to look straight ahead?"

"Exactly. Then keep your eyes open for only the period of time that I tell you and when I tell you to close them you must do so."

"Okay, I'm ready."

"I will check certain of your reflexes and reactions with your eyes still closed and when I am satisfied that you properly prepared I will then have Sally move directly in front of you for a few moments. We will increase the light in the room so that normal vision will be able to identify objects at five or six feet, but only to see what effect it will have the closed eyelids. If everyone is ready let us move on with this."

Harry exclaimed "I must sound childish as hell…"

"No, Avery responded. Frightened, maybe…

Lieutenant Johnson removed the last of the pads, threw them into the wastebasket, after which she left the room.

Avery said, "If you will free yourself from Harry's grip Sally I would like you to stand precisely here in front of him. Elizabeth, when I tell you I want you to increase the light level in the room but only at the rate and to the intensity that I indicate. Then be certain to watch in case I signal to decrease it for any reason whatsoever."

"We are about there, are we, Avery?"

"Yes, Harry. It won't be long now I'm starting my examination now and you are reacting exactly as I expected you would your involuntary responses your eyelids reaction the twitching – it's all just what it's supposed to be. I'm going to lift each of your eyelids and take a momentary look into the back of each of your eyes and then we will give you a moment of rest while I play with the lights."

"Am I supposed to have seen or felt anything yet?"

"No, not particularly. You could be seeing a sort of grayness now as I'm peering under your eyelids but if you don't it's nothing for you to become alarmed about this just means that it would take you a few more minutes to respond when we get to the next step."

"I saw something gray, I think!"

"That's just fine. I told you that you were responding just the way we expected. Now relax for a few moments."

"Elizabeth? Do you have the new dressings here?"

"Yes, Avery, they are here."

"Are you comfortable, Harry?"

"Yes."

"Anything else?"

"Yes I'm still nervous as hell."

Glancing to see that Sally was properly placed, Avery signal for Elizabeth to turn up the lights. As the shadows which had heretofore concealed Harry's face as effectively as the bandages, melted away each of the team intently searched the features of this man of mystery.

"Why, Harry there isn't one scar showing anywhere on your face! Elizabeth exclaimed. "Dear me, but you are really a very handsome man. Yes... Yes... All the scars that you have are very well hidden above the hairline. Your nose and cheekbones have been so cleverly reset that, if it were not for the medical records that Dr. Martin has I would not be able to detect that any work had been done in either place."

"I look okay? I'm not full of scars?"

"No, Harry, Avery responded. "Our surgical nurse Miss. Johnson and I knew all along that you had no scars. I felt it best to not make an issue of it with you because you had a lot of other things to work out before you came to grips with having no 'badges of courage' as our Horse Marines and other saber carrying cavalryman used to say."

Avery drew his pipe from his pocket and, using it stem as a pointer scratched himself alongside his ear. "No, Harry you have nothing at all to worry about on that score. You're coming through this very nicely. As Elizabeth said you look quite well."

"No scars? Huh! Sally, how do I look to you? Do I look okay...? Sally?"

"You... Look... Fine. You... You're just fine."

"Are you sure? You sound strange. Like you're not telling me everything. You're sure I'm okay?"

"Yes, Harry, you're really okay. You're just everything Elizabeth and Avery say you are. You're coming this with flying colors, and you going to be back on your feet before you know it."

"Those are the words I've been waiting for! Avery? When can I open my eyes? I've got to see the three most important people in my life or I'll go out of my head."

"We have been ready for about a quarter hour. And remember, let's go slowly about this and don't expect too much, just light and dark and blurry outlines. If everyone is in place, now's as good a time as any to commence."

Harry was not sure that he had remembered how to raise his eyelids. He thought he had felt the right muscles go into action but nothing seemed to happen. Then he realized that he never had been able to really feel his eyes open or close; he just sort of thought them that way. If they were open he saw thing; if they weren't, he didn't.

As grayness started to register it in his mind, he realized that he was again looking at the outside world. At first it was just the same as the darkness – uniformly gray – and then it started to become variegated. He discovered that part of what he saw was not gray. He tried hard to recognize what it might be, and then he found that he could not. He had lost touch for the world during his self-imposed withdrawal from reality.

Even though his newly uncovered eyes were barely capable of receiving blurred images Harry could see at last. What he saw was not the room and the people in it nor was it Sally. What he saw was the distortion that he had conjured for himself. He finally saw that it was not a world that oppressed and hated him out there, but a world that was still unconcerned and unaffected by him.

There had always been love and opportunity, and those who could care. Now, as his sight began to clear he realized that the things he had sought to retreat from had been within him and that the sooner he reached out and shared with the people around him, the sooner he would be free of his fears.

God! How much he owed that woman how much he loved that woman! He would totally recover, and he vowed that, regardless of how she looked or acted, if Sally would have him he would dedicate the rest of his life to her.

A half hour later Avery supervise the placing of light dressings over Harry's eyes and left orders for Harry to be put to bed, given a light sedative, and kept under close observation. While he had no abnormal concern for Harry sight recovery there had been considerable emotional trauma that day. Avery did not intend to take any chances on any unforeseen reactions occurring.

As Avery talked to Harry and the night nurse, Elizabeth and a solemn face Sally slowly returned to Avery's office. At first Elizabeth's enthusiasm completely overshadowed Sally's pensive and uncommunicative mood, but before long the latter's distant responses brought Elizabeth up short.

"Sally! Whatever is the matter with you? I would think that you would be overjoyed at the success that you can take a great measure of the credit for. Harry's going to be well, and you are very much the cause of it. Whatever can be the matter with you?"

"It's nothing. I guess I'm just tired."

"Fiddlesticks! You have never been tired before, and I have seen you fill in at the emergency room at Essex when you had just finished three back-to-back surgery schedules. No. Something else is bothering you!"

"No, really. It's nothing for you to worry about. I'll be all right…"

"See! There is something wrong! Is something to do with Harry Morgan, isn't it? What has he done to cause this reaction in you?"

"It's nothing. I'll work it out."

"Sally, – please."

"No, I'll work it out by myself. It's nothing that you can do anything about, anyway."

"Well, maybe you are right. But if you need me at all, I will be up until all hours in my quarters tonight. I have a letter to write to an aunt, a hand wash to do, and I have not pressed a skirt or blouse for tomorrow. I'll be up all night, so please come by if I can help."

"Okay, I'll see."

Elizabeth lightly touched Sally's arm as she said, "Remember, in spite of my chattering I listen well and hold secrets as dear and close as a Parsons box".

"You are a kind friend, Elizabeth. I may take you up on your offer later on. But I'd rather work it out for myself. Tell the Major... Avery... That I'm really tired and I'm going to my quarters. I'll see all of you in the morning, okay?"

"As you say, but remember, Harry isn't the only person in this world that might need some help, and you aren't the only person in this hallway that can give it!"

Sally forced a grin at this parting remark. Once out of sight she could no longer hold in her emotions. She broke into muffled sobs and she hurried to her quarters where she threw herself on her cot, weeping as though her heat had broken.

Elizabeth glanced at the clock on the shelf. It was nearly twenty-three hundred hours and she was certain that she would have heard from Sally by now. She wondered if she should take the initiative and search her out. Yet, Sally had told her that she might come to her room. For her to encroach on Sally under the circumstances seemed improper. She repressed a blouse that still seemed to have a wrinkle or two; but the time still dragged on.

Elizabeth decided that she would give Sally another thirty minutes and then she would go see what was disturbing her friend. She knew anguish when she saw it, and she was not going to let Sally suffer without her support. That was final. As a matter of fact, Elizabeth decided there was no need to prolong her agony. She hung up the blouse and just as she reached for the door she heard a faint tapping. Preparing to welcome Sally, she was surprised to discover Avery standing in the hall.

"Major Martin! I declare, you gave me a fright. What are you doing here? Is there something wrong with Captain Morgan?"

"Elizabeth, you gave me quite a start as well, to open the door that way. Upon my word, I did not expect you to be inside with you hand on the knob waiting for such an occasion. Let me catch my breath. I say, I can't even recall why I came here. No! It isn't Morgan, it is Sally Archer."

"Sally?"

"Yes."

"What has become of her? Is she ill?"

"I don't know. I only know that about an hour after the two of you left Morgan's ward, I chanced to walk through the corridor past her quarters and I distinctly heard what I took to be someone crying as though their heart had come apart."

"Yes?"

"Well, I hesitated to knock on her door to discover what might be the problem, but then decided that it was not rightfully of my concern."

"Not rightfully of your concern? How can you say that? Lieutenant Archer has been assigned to you and has been as devoted to you as anyone I know."

"I know. I was wrong, so I mustered up my nerve and went back to her room. But when I got there I couldn't get up the courage to knock. So, I came for you."

"You did the proper thing. I will go down to her room and see what can be done I suggest you return to your office and I will come down there as soon as I can."

Elizabeth knocked at the door.

"Yes?"

"It's me. Elizabeth. Can I come in?"

"It's very late, isn't it?"

"Yes, but that doesn't make any difference among friends."

"All right. Just a minute."

As Elizabeth walked in she said, "I brought us some warm milk from the night kitchen. Shall I set yours here on your side table?"

"That's very kind of you. Here take this chair with the cushion. It's not as hard as the folding one and it doesn't sag as much of my poor old Army cot. Sally took the milk and sipped it. "Mmmm, this milk is just what the doctor ordered, Elizabeth you are a dear friend."

"I try to be. And that's why I am here."

"I know, I know."

"I won't bandy about the bush with you Sally. Your eyes are as red as Churchill's nose. You have been crying, and do not deny it because Major Martin heard you… Right through that door when he walked by a short time ago."

"I told you it was nothing that you could do anything about. I have to work it out for myself."

"Of course you do, but sharing it with a friend often helps you to see a way out that doesn't ever show itself until you talk it over with someone. Now, what is it that can devastate you so completely?"

"All right. But you must promise to tell no one else."

"I can't do that, Sally. I have to tell Major Martin. He knows that you have been deeply troubled, if not hurt, and he is just as concerned about you as I am. As a matter of fact he is waiting in his office for me. When I leave here I am honor bound to give him at least an idea of what has been troubling you. But you should want him to know, anyway he is your commanding officer and he thinks a great deal of you."

"Elizabeth. I can't…"

"And another thing. It strikes me that you are acting in the same way that Captain Morgan has! How can you possibly come here to your room, crawl into your shell, and cry your eyes out over something when you have seen how destructive the same conduct has been for him? No. It simply won't work. As a matter of fact, I want you and me both to go down to the Major's office and talk it all out together. If it involves anyone of us it is a professional manner, and he needs to be involved."

"Elizabeth, I can't. It's a personal thing that I have to work out and…"

"Sally, remember this involves a patient, doesn't it?"

"Yes."

"And whose patient is it? Yours? Mine? I'll wager not!"

"No, he's Doctor Martin's."

"Well you have no choice. At least you have to give Dr. Martin the generalities, particularly when he knows that there is something amiss with you, and that it has occurred at a time closely associated with the revealing of Captain Morgan's face. Do you know Captain Morgan, Sally?"

"Yes."

"And that has brought on all of this grief for you?"

"Yes, it has something to do with it. And yes, I suppose you're right I am obliged to report."

"I'm glad you can see it that way. Beside Dr. Martin is very understanding and once he knows about something he will do everything possible to work it out for everyone's benefit."

"I don't see much of a chance here."

"Let us not prejudge. Come, finish your milk and we will go down together, and if nothing else, assuage Dr. Martin's concern for you."

"All right."

Elizabeth opened the door and Sally and she entered the office.

"Major? It's us, Sally and Elizabeth."

"Well, by Jove, I am glad to see both of you again. We seem to be making quite a day and now a night of it."

"Sally has something to tell you, Major."

"Yes, Major. Elizabeth has convinced me that since what has been disturbing me is something that could affect Captain Morgan I should report it to you."

"Good! I confess that I was not intending to eavesdrop this evening, but I did overhear you sobbing as I chanced to pass your quarters, and it greatly disturbed me. I confess that I had not realized that you had been troubled."

"Well the problem is new, and yet in a way it's old." She hesitated.

"Go on, Sally where did it begin?"

"Well remember when I told you that I felt I had known Captain Morgan before?"

"Yes, I remember."

"Yes, Elizabeth agreed. "It was a day before yesterday shortly after lunch."

"Well, Sally said, "I discovered this afternoon that I did know him from before and where I had known him before."

"This afternoon?" Avery asked.

"I discovered who Harry Morgan is. Sally returned. "I never knew his name before and I never really clearly heard his voice before, but when I saw his face in that dim light I realize that I had seen it once in much the same sort of light."

"Where?"

"When? Elizabeth chimed in. "Who is he?"

"Yes for heaven sakes," Avery said.

"Before I go into that, that's not the reason that I have been troubled and confused, and sitting red eyed in my room all evening."

"Then, Elizabeth said, "What is the problem if it isn't who the Major has assigned you to care for?"

"Oh, Elizabeth. This is the part that is so hard. It's that it is my problem and yet I can see where the problem greatly concerns Captain Morgan as a patient."

"Sally, Dr. Martin is the one person can help you. He was a practicing psychologist before he entered service. Weren't you Major?"

"Why, yes. Yes it seems so long ago, but I did have quite a practice as I recall. Come now Archer; let's have a go at drying your tears. Now what's the problem?"

"My problem is that I am hopelessly in love with Harry Morgan! He has become the most important person in my life and if he realizes who I am he will either reject me or retreat into his darkness. Either way I'll lose him before I ever have him."

"Well, who is he?"

"You remember my telling you both about what happened to me on the boat coming over here. How I got beat up?"

"Yes. Was he on that boat?"

"More than that, he's the man that nearly killed me. He's the one that beat me up."

"Good Lord!"

"Oh Sally, you can't mean it. Are you quite sure?"

"Yes, Elizabeth, I am absolutely sure it is Captain Morgan. It's him all right! There is no question about it. It's him."

"Do you wish to press charges against him? You know you still can if you can make a positive identification."

"No, Major. That's the last thing I want. I honestly love him. I'm more afraid of what will happen to him when he discovers who I am and I'm sure that he will as soon as he gets a clear look at me. That's my problem."

"Hmmm. I'm beginning to see what you mean. I am glad you decided to bring this to me. Go on."

"I have forgiven him. I forgave him the instance I recognized him. I'd forgive him again and again because I sincerely believe that when he attacked me he thought I intended to harm him."

"Then your concern is for his reactions?"

"Yes, Elizabeth. I don't want him to turn away from the world, and I don't want to lose any chance at him. I want to love and care for him and I don't know what to do."

Sally slumped into silence while Elizabeth blindly stared out the window. Avery looked from one to the other, loudly struck a kitchen match with his thumbnail, drew noisily as he lit his pipe, and settled the issue as he announced:

"My dear ladies. This is really quite a fundamental problem, and we have a quite simple answer. As you, Sally, know perfectly well where you stand in regard to Captain Morgan, and as you and Elizabeth are totally concerned with the outcome of this case then we will best remember that this is, after all a medical case, so we shall treat it as such. Harry Morgan is my patient. I expect to discharge a normal, responsive patient, capable of receiving affection and of returning that affection particularly when that affection, yes love if you will, is so important to someone that I have such a high regard for.

"I quite clearly recall claiming victory over his blindness, and I intend to include in that victory much more than just that. We will come out of this just fine.

"In short just leave it to the Doctor. I may not understand much about you ladies, but I do have some knowledge about what makes Captain Morgan 'tick'. After all I did prescribe you as an important part of his treatment, and you can see how far we have come and how nicely we have done. Don't worry your heads about it for one moment more! It will all work out just the way we expect it to. Won't it, Elizabeth?"

Avery noted the look of relief on Sally's face. He turned to Elizabeth for her answer and was created by her smiles and her tears. He smiled back at her and feeling quite pleased with himself, found himself curious about the possibility that he and Elizabeth could someday be bound with a sensitive regard for each other like Harry's and Sally's.

Avery leaned forward and scowled at the file on his desk. "Morgan Harry W., Captain, etc., United States Army etc. etc. etc. that was the whole trouble of it. Just too much 'and so forth'.

Just as fast as one part of this case seen to be clearing up another part popped up out of nowhere. This is clearly an example of what he would have to call to the attention of his sister, Gwen. She and her 'feel a little, Avery!' He had begun to feel and where was he getting himself? He had a patient that he had become personally interested in; he had a nurse who was too much in his mind as a potential companion; and to top it off, he had involved a competent American nurse in a program of treatment which had irrupted into a genuine hearts and flowers melodrama. Clearly he needed to make some swift decisions. But what?

First and foremost, he had to consider his patient. Regardless of the effect his decisions had on the others he had a responsibility to see that the treatment of Captain Morgan stayed on the right track.

Earlier when he made his rounds, the ward nurse told him that Harry has slept comfortably. Avery had briefly noticed Sally during breakfast, and while Elizabeth had reported to him on his others cases there have been no conversation with either of the women about Morgan. It was as though the whole world was on hold, waiting and looking to him to start it rotating again. He needed something, something to get things rolling again. But, what?

CHAPTER TWENTY-SIX

"Avery?"

"Yes, Elizabeth."

"The orderly from Captain Morgan's ward brought this note for you."

"From Morgan?"

"Yes. The orderly said he dictated to him for you."

"What is it?"

"Not much that I can make any sense out of. The orderly said he thought he was addle-headed, but Captain Morgan repeated the message and said you would understand it."

"Well, read it."

"'I think this would be a fine day to promote something, don't you?' I don't understand…"

"Never mind, Elizabeth. I do, and it is the answer that I have been searching for. Yes. We will have to promote something."

"Avery? Are you quite sure about all of this? I fail to understand the meaning of any of this."

"You will soon enough, Elizabeth. Be a good lady and run down Lieutenant Archer and bring her to Morgan's examination room. Now, off with you while I rummage through this drawer. Where is that tin I put it in?"

"Avery, what tin?"

"The Potter's Sweets tin! But never mind, you know nothing of this, too. Go on ahead. I'll find it, and then I'll see you in fifteen minutes, and a short time later you will know what all of this is about. Now where is that tin? Here it is… and… Yes, everything is still safely in it."

Avery waited for Sally and Elizabeth in the corridor. "I say, it is a pleasant morning, Sally."

"Yes, doctor. Elizabeth said you wanted to see me."

"What else did you tell her, Elizabeth?"

"Nothing. You have left me confused on all counts."

"Good. Well, we are going to see if our patient's eyesight has improved. I want to plan out what we are going to do before we go into his room."

"Yes, Sir."

"Good. Sally, I want you to stay in the background until I motion for you to come into his area of sight. You may talk to him, and we will include you any activities in conversation; however, I do not want him to see you until I say when. By then I will decide as to the exercise progress."

"Exercise?"

"Yes, Elizabeth. He will only require smoked glasses, and then only for a short period of time, if my diagnosis is correct. I am going to have him try to read the eye chart, and if that is not too tiring, I will have him read a bulletin or some other sort of print."

"Is he going to be ready for small type reading, Major? Won't it be too much of a strain on him?"

"No, Sally. It won't be that much to read when I give him the paper to read. Elizabeth, you adjust the stand light so it will illuminates the paper, and you, Sally, remained just beyond the ring of light where you can observe his features closely. Do you feel up to it?"

"Yes, Sir."

"I fancy that you have your ginger up, though I wager that you should not even need it. Well, we will see. We all know what we're going to do so let us be about it."

"Good morning, Harry." Avery said.

"Good morning. It sounds like all three of you are here, right?"

"Right, sir." Elizabeth agreed.

"Elizabeth. Sally is here with you, too?

"I'm here, Harry."

"You sent a note with the orderly?" Avery questioned.

"Yes, what did you think of it?"

"An absolutely smashing bit of genius."

"Are we going to start it now?"

"No, not quite yet. I want to check you over and then have you do some simple eye exercises, take a look at an eye chart and then see if you can handle normal room light and then I may have you try to read a bit."

"Sounds great."

"Elizabeth, let's get these bandages off for the last time. Avery remarked. "Let's take a bit of a break. Rest your eyes, Harry."

"Yes, I'm beginning to feel the strain a little."

"Actually, it's not the kind of eye strain that a physical injury to your eyes would cause and that we would have to be sensitive to."

"No?"

"No. Right now you're feeling the same sort of fatigue in your eyes that you would experience in your legs if I were to have you run 100 yards. Your biggest concern is reversal of muscle atrophy. The best thing we can do for your eyes is give them some protection from excessive light and plenty of things to see and to read. Now that you have had a short time to rest, I would like to get into this other manner you reminded me of."

"Are we all here?"

"Yes, Major," Lieutenant Nickles reported.

"Are you comfortable, Captain Morgan?"

"Yes. Doctor? Is Archer here, too?"

"Yes, Captain, I'm right here beside you."

"Oh! Are you going to be doing something, too? I mean, would you be close by?"

"Yes, I'll be right here beside you all the time."

"Major?"

"Yes?"

"Can Lieutenant Archer be the first thing I see when the bandages come off?"

"Yes, I guess so, but you must remember what I told you."

"I know. I won't see much. But what I do see, I want to be her. Okay?"

"Very well. Archer, why don't you let the Captain hold on to your hand while Lieutenant Nickles and Nurse Johnson and I finish clearing these bandages?"

"Is anyone else in here with us?"

"No, Captain, after the bandages are cut away Nurse Johnson will be leaving and there will be just the three of us and you. Well, are we all set ladies? Oh yes… And gentleman?"

"The blinds are drawn, Elizabeth said. "The lights are adjusted, I have all instruments ready, and so am I."

"Ready for a go at it, Captain?"

"Hand me a bandage scissors and adjust the light so I can see a little better, Nickles. That's a good girl."

"Good! Good! You did very well with the eye chart."

"Elizabeth? Sally? Let's all gather around so we can hear about this idea that has been exciting Harry all morning. I fancy from his smile, he has a surprise for us, eh?"

Harry took the paper that Avery handed him. After finding he was able to read the oversized print, Harry began:

> **By order of the President of the United States, First Lieutenant Sally Ann Archer, ON–344600, is forthwith promoted to the rank of Captain in the Corps of Nurses of the Army of the United States and is henceforth entitled to wear the insignia and receive the benefit of that office. The effective date of this promotion is April 1, 1943, signed, Fern R Hawthorne, Colonel, Corps of Nurses, Army of the United States.**

Avery quickly produced his Potter's sweets tin and removed a tissue wrapped pair of bright silver Captain's bars from it.

Handing them to Harry, he said, "I suggest that you as the ranking Captain in this room confer these bars of Office on your new comrade of rank, while Elizabeth and I congratulate her."

As Harry attempted to open the clasp of the bars in preparation for pinning them on Sally's uniform he realized that he was shaking. He still had not looked at Sally. He wanted to keep that moment of his first sight of her isolated and preserved in his memory for all times.

He had discovered that his sight was distinct, but was quick to tire. Seated in his wheelchair, as he mastered his nerves and the balky rollers of the clasp guards, he turned his eyes towards Sally and saw the hem of her white skirt. She was taller than he expected. Remarkably symmetrical, too. As he moved his eyes progressively higher he found that his notion of her physical size and appearance were somewhat in error.

In general, he found her more in keeping with a woman, comparable to his own size expectations. She was certainly taller than he had anticipated. And from what he could see, yes, classically proportioned.

"I expect the new Captain Archer had better bend down so that you can pin her new rank on her unless you wish to get out of that wheelchair and stand." Elizabeth injected.

"I'll stand," Harry responded as he boosted himself out of the wheelchair. He found himself looking just over Sally's white nurse's cap. Her lovely Auburn hair swept back on one side, nearly covered one of two questioning crystal clear, blue eyes.

Concentrating on his task, Harry nervously pinned the bars on Sally's lapels, took her right hand shook it, stepped back, and saluted the new Captain. As Sally returned the salute, both she and Harry looked fully into each other's face for the first time.

Oblivious to the presence of either Avery or Elizabeth, Harry stammered, "You… You… You are you!"

Not quite sure how to respond Sally said, "Yes, I guess you could say that. I'm me"

"No. I mean you're the girl from the boat."

"Yes."

"I mean, I hurt you. Out on the deck, there…"

"Yes, I was on the deck."

"I think I nearly killed you, them. I hit you so hard I could have killed you!"

"I got over it. I lived. I'm here."

"You helped me, here? After what I did?" Harry looked about the room but Avery and Elizabeth were gone.

"That was a long time ago," Sally returned, calling Harry's attention back to her.

"I begged you to help me see again, and after I nearly killed you! I was involved in killing all those others, and I nearly killed you, too."

Harry dropped himself back into the wheelchair and sat staring at the floor.

"You didn't mean to hurt me, Harry. I know you acted out of fear that I might be someone attacking you. You were just protecting yourself."

"Don't you see? That's just how I killed my friends in North Africa. I was afraid of being attacked. I was afraid. I was looking out for myself. It's the same damn pattern."

"Please, Harry, it's not that way at all."

"No? Then what way is it? Now that you know me you'll shun me. You'll hate me like everyone else does."

"No, Harry, nobody hates you. I was angry with you for a couple of weeks. But I didn't hate you – ever."

"But that was before you knew who I was."

"I didn't hate you a few days ago."

"What's a few days ago got to do with it?"

"It was when I began to feel pretty sure I knew who you were."

"You did? Christ! What must you have thought of me? After what I did to you. I told you I needed you and everything!"

"I believed you. I wanted to."

"Why should you want to do that? Why should you want to ever see me again?"

"Because I care about you, Harry. I do."

Harry looked up in disbelief. "You what?"

She gently took his face in her hands, leaned forward and softly kissed him on his eyebrows and gently on his lips and said "Because I care about you, you silly man!"

Harry was speechless. He nodded his head and pressed Sally's hands to his cheeks. After he found himself and his breath, he looked up at her and with tears in his eyes, smiled and said. "I love you, Sally. I hope you can realize someday just how much I love you and how much I need you."

"And I love you, Harry. I have from almost the first moment we finally talked on the sun porch. I loved you. And I had so hoped you would love me."

Harry rose from his chair, gently drew Sally into his arms, and tenderly kissed her.

Reflections

Avery quietly drew the blinds of the one-way glass of the observation window and happily reached over and squeezed Elizabeth's hand. They moved on down the hall to his office where he and an adoring Elizabeth spent the rest of their afternoon assembling a glowing report on the progress and condition of Captain Harry W Morgan, with considerable mention of the contributions of Captain Sally Ann Archer, RN.

CHAPTER TWENTY-SEVEN

The recognition between Sally and Harry appeared to serve as a medical, if not a social catalyst for the heretofore-morose Harry. Each day his condition improved remarkably, and by the end of the week he suggested that he would like to visit The Old Spotted Dog Inn and Mrs. Worsham again. Sally, Avery, and Elizabeth would be able to accompany him, and the whole idea was readily agreed to by Avery…as soon as transportation could be arranged.

CHAPTER TWENTY-EIGHT

LIEUTENANT ELIZABETH NICKLES WAS UNQUESTIONABLY quite proficient at a great many things, Avery Martin told himself as he stood waiting in the drive in front of his office. She certainly was the most capable nurse and secretary he had ever worked with, as well as the most enthusiastic. Indeed, he concluded, she had now added resourcefulness to her attributes.

As he continued his vigil, he recalled that he had been wondering for some time how he could get Captain Morgan out of the hospital ward for a change of scenery, and at the same time keep him within easy reach of medical observation and treatment. He had expected to have him take daily walks through the nearby meadows, but the late February weather was unseasonably wet and cold, and hardly conducive to rehabilitation of a patient, so recently, subject to such serious depressions.

The hospital unit was out in the countryside, and while Harrow was the closest village, it was a full 15 miles away. The tram that struggled there once each day was generally packed, and was rumored to have never made the trip without at least one time delaying breakdown. Again, hardly conducive to a patient's rehabilitation, regardless of the ailment.

Avery smiled as he recalled that he had not realized that he had been mulling the problem over aloud, until he heard Nickles, who had popped her head around the corner from his outer office to say, "Why don't you use your own transport?"

Avery swung his chair around. "Eh? Whatever are you talking about, Nickles?"

"I only suggested that if you want Captain Morgan to get to Harrow, then why don't you drive him there yourself in your own transport. You have one, you know."

"I do?"

"It was assigned to you when we arrived here, but we have been so busy that I expect you forgot about it."

"I expect that I never gave it any thought. I don't drive very often, you know. It's probably one of those American things with the steering wheel and all those pedals on the wrong side, anyway. I don't feel that Morgan is ready to drive, and I drive so little I should be quite dangerous behind its wheel. I haven't a military driver's license, anyway."

"I have!"

"You have a military driver's license?"

"Yes, it's required, you know. As a matter of fact, I have been trained to drive both our regular style of vehicle as well as – as you put it – the wrong sided American machines. My card shows that I also had training in chauffeuring Lories and even city trams."

"How very remarkable."

"It was part of my qualification requirements to be assigned as your military aid, as well as your surgical nurse and secretary.

I was required to be able to drive for you. This shall be my first chance at it, you know."

Thoughtfully nodding his head, Avery, mused, "that would certainly make things a lot easier. I wonder what we have to do? Do you suppose it would take long to have a vehicle brought around?"

"I have already checked that out," Nickles reported, "and all that needs to be done is for me to go to their motor pool and sign out whatever you want, and I can drive it right over here. Probably no more than thirty minutes."

"Then let's do it. Today is Thursday. Make the necessary arrangements and we will spend Saturday in Harrow. Have Captain Morgan signed out of the hospital to my care. He has wanted to visit and introduce us to an acquaintance he has there, and this will be a fine time to go."

Avery paused for a moment of thought, during which Nickles had the strange sensation that he was appraising her from head to toe before he went on, saying, "Lieutenant, be sure to have a couple of pillows and a supply of blankets and robes packed in the luggage compartment."

"Yes, Sir. Would that be all?"

"Let me see… No, before we leave be sure that you have two or three thermos of tea and a substantial hamper of food provisions. I am still quite suspicious of these American automobiles."

"In what way is that, sir? I have found the most comfortable."

"No, Nickles, that's not what I mean. We could suffer a breakdown and we simply can't take a chance on his chilling and having a setback. After all, he has not been out of a hospital in well over six months. Be sure to get a vehicle big enough for four because I want Captain Archer to go along, sort of as a nurse for Morgan, but also as a companion for you."

"Yes sir," Elizabeth responded. "I'll take care of everything."

Avery turned his attention to the pamphlet on his desk, otherwise he would have seen the smile on Nickles' face as she left, commenting to herself that Harry and Sally would have very little time left during which Sally might serve as her companion. Most certainly other arrangements would have to be made for her companionship, and if she had anything to say about them, Major Martin would find himself sharing greatly in Lieutenant Nickle's companionship and plans.

Avery's reverie was broken by the sound of the automobile's tires crunching the gravel as Nichols smartly brought it to a stop in front of him. Seeing that Harry and Sally were already in the backseat, he opened the front passenger side door and started to sit down.

"Better get in the back seat, Sir." Nickles suggested. "I expect that it would not do well for the ranking officer to be riding around the station in the front seat with the driver."

"Really, do you think it's all that important?" Avery questioned, disappointment registering in his voice as he got into the back and pulled the door closed behind him.

"Well, at least until we get past the guards of the gates, I do."

"You may very well be right, however as soon as we get beyond the brow of that hill and clump of forest, someone will have to moved up there. There is simply is not enough room back here for all three of us."

Returning her attention to the driveway before her, dropping the car into gear, and moving off of the smoothness of a Rolls-Royce chauffeur, Nickles cocked her head to one side and returned over her shoulder, "Whatever you say, Sir."

CHAPTER TWENTY-NINE

Harry vigorously pounded the front desk bell, and happily shouted up and down the length of the Parlor-Lounge and Tea Room, "Hello? Isn't anybody about at this Inn today? We are four very important people, and we refuse to be kept waiting while the keeper of this establishment dallies around and dozes off over her Toddy and Tea! I demand to see the owner, and I demand a full explanation of this tardiness – at once!"

The moment of total silence that followed his declaration was interrupted by a voice that came up from the lower kitchen stairway, and was heard ascending the stairs in ever closer and greater volume, punctuated by the angry stomping of feet on each tread.

Irritatedly, the voice said, "and who do you think you might be, coming into a body's establishment with your high and mighty manners and demands? I don't give a fig if you are Lord George, himself, I'll have you show some respect for the establishment and its proprietor, or by Old Nick himself, I'll have the Constable after the lot of you!"

Harry hurried his friends around the corner where they could observe but not be seen, and then turned away from the kitchen-way door so that when the angered proprietor emerged all she would see what was their uniformed backs.

Turning to the irritating intruder, "Now, you young Spratt, who do you…"

Harry said, "Hi, Mum".

"Oooh, my dear God, it's my Harry! God, love it, it's him! It's my dear boy, Harry! He's come to see me again. It's one of my two 'Yank boys'! Blessed Pete, I can't believe my heart, soul, and eyes. You, dear, dear boy. Let me sit you down and bring you some tea and cakes."

Grasping her and holding her from scurrying off to her kitchen as much as for hugging her, Harry laughed, "Hey! Mum! Hold on a minute! Later. I'm not going to run off the next minute. I have some friends I brought to meet you that are really important to me. You are going to love them, too. Now <u>try</u> sitting down and acting nice, for a change. You can run around and wait on everybody to your hearts content later on."

Assuring himself that Mrs. Worsham was finally secured in one of her parlor chairs, Harry beckoned his three friends from around the corner and amid much beaming, bowing, handshaking, and smiling, managed to complete the introductions.

A short time later, when the tea table was set, the water boiled, the pots and the cakes served, the innkeeper settled down to provide the finest hospitality and service she could for this young man she had grown so very fond of.

He had again answered her prayers. This time by coming back to see her so that she, a childless woman in her middle age, might discover for the first time the joy of having a favorite son come home. And as Harry looked about him, he too felt that warmth and sense of homecoming. Certainly, this is all the family a man could ever want.

CHAPTER THIRTY

After the early tea had been cleared, and Mrs. Worsham had brought Harry and his friends up on the latest news and local gossip, she moved to her knitting bag, suggesting that the four might like to take a stroll along the stream that wound through the park that Harry had enjoyed during his earlier stay.

Elizabeth, thinking that Sally and Harry were never going to get a chance to be alone, nor she with Avery, unless she took charge, was about to make a suggestion of her own when to her surprise, Avery declined the walk, saying, "Oh, thank you ever so much Mrs. Worsham, but while we are so close at hand, I want to motor on to Windsor where there is a lovely old deserted Abbey Lieutenant Nickles and I have talked about. I should like to show it to her, as well as walk through the nearby Warren that she has told me her father managed for King George when she was a child. At this point, that activity might prove rather strenuous for Captain Morgan, although your local stroll should be quite therapeutic. Besides, we should be able to be back by afternoon tea time, provided my suspicions of our American vehicle's reliability do not prove to be true."

As Sally and Harry stood on the veranda of the old Inn watching Avery – this time beginning the trip in the front seat – being driven off towards Windsor by Elizabeth, they knew they shared the amusement of the totally out of character unpredictability of the otherwise placid Avery.

They, along with Mrs. Worsham had seen the look of amazement that registered on Elizabeth's face when Avery announced his intentions for the afternoon. Clearly, Elizabeth couldn't have been more in agreement if he was following a script she had written for the day's activities.

Mrs. Worsham, who had been watching the olive drab staff car disappear over the crest of the hill walked to the end of the veranda and cautiously scanned the sky. Pointing off in a general northerly direction, she exclaimed, "you best not stray too far and long from the Old Spotted Dog."

"Why?" Harry questioned. "It's the best day I've seen all spring."

"That well may be, my boy, but my eyes – and my rheumatism – speak loudly to me that there is a good deal of rain not too far off, and maybe a good bit of wind along with it. I hope your friends are not caught out in it while walking over the warren."

"Speaking of friends, how did you like them?"

"The two that just went out of your sight over the hill are the finest of our finest. I am happy for you that you found them, and happy for them because I suspicion they are finding one another because of you."

"You really like them, do you?"

"I said, I do. Do you not believe your English mother? The gentleman is a bit formal and on his reserve, but give that lady a bit of time with him, and she'll have him awakened up to her, right enough."

Harry nodded, and turning to follow Sally, who had moved on ahead to the pathway, which led from the porch to the stream and on through the park.

Mrs. Worsham continued, "Are you not concerned of my opinion of all of your friends?"

"Well, Harry said, "I didn't want to put you on the spot, but… Of course, yes… I am."

"And well you should be! Treating me so ill, I shouldn't even tell you, and if it were not for the sweetness of yon lass, I should run you off to the Meadows without telling you that she is the dearest creature you've yet shown me, or I've yet seen in all my years."

Harry returned his attention to Sally – now stopping to admire the emerging spring flowers that were struggling alongside the path – exclaiming, "Wow! You're really sold on her, aren't you?"

Dorothy Worsham, stepped closer to better confront Harry, and stretching herself up to her full height of barely five feet and an inch, reached up and firmly grasp Harry by his two ears as she, in mock seriousness solemnly stared into his eyes.

"My dear boy, I'll take her part with you every day of the blessed week – and twice on Sunday. You don't deserve the caring and love I see in her eyes for you. You must be a doubly wicked young man for you to have charmed her heart away from her – as you have cast your spell on mine. That you should have the good wishes of all of these fine people is more blessing than one man should be entitled to in ten lifetimes."

Turning him loose, she stepped back and including Sally in her view and charge went on, "And on top of that you have mine for the lot of you. Now, be on your way before the rain and the wind conspire against your walking even as much as to yonder gate. Scat, now!"

CHAPTER THIRTY-ONE

AVERY CHUCKLED IN AGREEMENT WITH himself, as he twisted about in the front seat of the staff motorcar for one last look in the direction of the Inn before Elizabeth drove out of view of it. Things were working out quite well.

He could see Harry and Sally headed for the path that would take them across the meadow to the heights of Stanmore Commons. The gradual climb to its 800-foot high crest would be good exercise for Harry.

There would be no need for Avery to be concerned about Harry for the balance of the day, and Avery could direct all of his attention to the tour of Windsor Castle's St. George's Chapel. (Elizabeth would most certainly be exhilarated by this finest example of Perpendicular architecture in England).

He knew they would not be able to tarry though, because he must save time for her to drive on through Windsor's Great Park to the forest preserve that included the Warren that her father had tended while he was His Majesty's Gamekeeper.

So, putting Harrow behind him as he prepared and lit his pipe, he said, "Elizabeth, do we need to ask for directions?"

"No, Avery. I know the area quite well. I lived near Windsor for a number of years, and yesterday I made notes on the roadways we will need to use to get there. We should arrive within an hour with no difficulty."

"Capital! I say, the weather does appear threatening ahead of us. Do you think we shall have time to stop at St. George's Chapel? It might be well to motor right on to the Warren, you know."

"Oh, no! I should very much like to see the Chapel with you, Avery. The glens and woods in the forest will still be quite lovely in the afternoon. I would like to chance it. Besides, there is the old woodcutter who has a cottage that my father used to take me to when I was a girl. If worse should come upon us, we can look in on him for some shelter.

"Very well, to the Chapel then, and from there to your mysterious forest.

CHAPTER THIRTY-TWO

"Well, Elizabeth, that didn't take at all long, did it? What did you think of the old Chapel?"

"Oh, Avery, it was so very lovely. I spent much of my life around here, and scampered all over the acres and acres of castle grounds, but I had never been in the Chapel before. It's very old, isn't it?"

"Yes, much of it dates from the 12th century. As a lad, I went to school at Eaton, across the river there. I recall that I was always impressed with the splendor and stateliness of the Castle's ramparts, and particularly the Chapel. It seemed to me that they filled all of the countryside and bespoke of royalty without uttering as much as a sound. Yes, I have always felt very proud that I am British whenever I think of Windsor."

As Avery was speaking, Elizabeth slowed the motorcar, and turned from the paved highway onto a side-road. Within a few miles she again turned from the side-road down a lane between rows of hedges that stretched on, like two rows of attending soldiers.

Occupied with driving and the selection of the portions of the lane that she would drive on, Elizabeth remained silent, as did Avery who had become completely fascinated with the primordial beauty of the countryside.

Before long, they came into a large clearing that the lane skirted, leading to an opening in the forest that grew thickly along the clearing's far side.

"This is one of the edges of father's Warren when he was His Majesty's Gamekeeper here, Avery. This clearing is where I played, alongside of that brook you see below the near meadow. Father would walk all around its edges, looking for the signs of poachers. Then, after he had satisfied himself of what the signs had to show, he would toss me up on his shoulder and we would head off into the woods, along that lane over there."

"I am surprised that you can drive a motor-car up here? Being so far from where people live and sport about, I would think that this would be all overgrown."

"That would normally be true, Avery, but with all of the war shortages, His Majesty has allowed wood cutting and forest's clearing to be done on his land holdings for the poor and the old people. The road is kept open by the Lorries that come back here to clean the woods out of fallen limbs and trees. From the looks of things, they must have been here sometime of late because the road is still quite open. We should be able to drive all the way back to the last clearing, just below the woodcutter's cottage."

They drove on for the next few minutes, entering into the heavy woods, and following the lane that had now reduced itself to a just manageable path that twisted and turned on through the woods. Finally, this came to an end as it reached another, but much smaller, clearing that barely provided room enough for

Elizabeth to turn the vehicle around and face it back the direction from which they had come.

"I hope you have your walking shoes on, Avery. This is as far as I can drive you, but it's not much farther to the Warren's barn. As a matter of fact, if you look closely through the woods, you can make out the corner of the old barn. It has a small veranda on it, and we can sit there and have our tea and biscuits. Be a good fellow and bring the thermos and blankets while I take the picnic lunch from out of the motor-car's baggage compartment."

"I say, Elizabeth, you have thought of everything, haven't you."

"Yes, Avery," Elizabeth answered, turning away from him to conceal a tiny grin that was slyly working at the corners of her mouth. "I certainly hope I have." And going on to herself, she murmured, "I may never have another opportunity like this, dear Avery, and I do so want to realize more from this 'friendship' of ours than a keepsake medicine vial of sand and 'a love that almost was' in a damp cave along the channel coast."

"Her reflections were interrupted by Avery's, "Elizabeth, I believe we had best bring our umbrellas, too. I thought I felt a drop of rain a moment ago, and I shouldn't like you to get wet." Closing the door of the motorcar and the lid of its baggage compartment, Elizabeth led the way up the narrowing path. "It's only a short distance beyond this thicket of laurel to the barn, she said." Yes, I felt a drop of rain too, but we are just about there.

"See the old barn? Isn't it picturesque? It was so warm and cozy. I could hardly wait to see it again. It's been so many years, you know. Let's arrange our picnic on the veranda."

Moments later, having pushed their way through the thickening weeds and undergrowth, they clambered up onto the stone-floored veranda that quaintly circled three sides of the old barn. Mows of clean, if not age-old hay overhung the timbers like silent spectators looking on as Elizabeth hurriedly inspected the two empty stalls on the first floor, and in the process alarming a sleepy whip-poor-will that had been nesting in one of the mangers.

In the meanwhile, Avery put the thermos and other things on the heavy, rough oak table, and hung their umbrellas over a harness peg in the barn wall. By the time he found, arranged, and had taken a seat on one of the heavy benches that he had discovered slid under the table, a reverie-indulged, Elizabeth had returned and had thrown a cloth over the table, unpacked the hamper of sandwiches, apples, and biscuits, and was pouring two hot cups of tea from one of the thermos bottles.

The temperature, unseasonably warm for February combined with the increased humidity that portended the impending storm, had caused both Avery and Elizabeth to find the restrictions of their militarily tailored uniforms to be uncomfortable. As she bustled about preparing the table for their picnic, Elizabeth had unbuttoned her jacket, and after his exertion in moving the table and benches about, Avery had done the same, as well as loosened his tie.

Satisfied that everything was arranged to her liking, and taking a relaxing sip of the steaming tea, Elizabeth leaned back on the bench that Avery had set against the barn's wall for her, and sighed, "Couldn't you just sit here forever and forget there ever was a war out there, Avery? It's so quiet and beautiful."

"Yes, there have been many times in my life that I would have given a king's ransom for a retreat like this. I really cannot remember when I have felt so at peace with the world, myself, and ah,--my immediate surroundings."

Elizabeth reached across the corner of the table that separated them, and patted Avery's hand. "I'm pleased to hear you say that, Avery, because I feel very much the same way. I have already had one of the most memorable days of my life, and it is hardly the middle of the day."

The touch of Elizabeth's hand brought a ripple of pleasure as well as a mixture of anxiety and uneasiness to Avery. He realized that his current discomfort stemmed from his sudden recollection of the other time he experienced that sensation; when Elizabeth and he were together on the beach, and later on in the cave.

His uneasiness was not dispelled by the further realization that he was even more alone with her now, because on the beach there had been that scruffy little dog to share their isolation. He found himself torn between wishing that the dog would re-appear around the corner of the barn, a tantalizing realization that there was very little likelihood that anything or anyone would intervene in their lives for the next few hours, and the awareness that he was totally unprepared for what he, at the same time feared, yet hoped, might happen.

Elizabeth returned to her position on the bench. She closed her eyes, allowing herself to breathe deeply of the clean, forest scented air, and within moments had dozed off into a half awake, half asleep dream fantasy in which Avery had swept her from the bench and up into the mows of cushioning hay.

As her emotions crept closer to her surface, she began to softly smile and breathe deeper. None of this was lost on a watchful Avery, who, deciding that their luncheon had been completed, and noting the worsening weather, silently rose from his bench and noiselessly as possible moved to where Elizabeth slept, and bending down, gently whispering in her ear, said, "Elizabeth? Are you awake?"

As Avery's intrusion into her dreams found perfect timing from Elizabeth's point of view, she responded with considerable warmth from the satisfying depth of her dream, "Yes, Avery, I'm right here. What do you want?"

"I have a suggestion, if you don't mind."

"Anything." Her eyes still closed and trying to fit the words and purposes Avery was saying to her with the dream that she was striving to keep alive. "Anything at all, Avery."

"Very well, Elizabeth. Before it gets too much later, don't you think it would be wise to continue on to pay your visit to the old woodcutter's place?"

Her eyes now wide open, at the same time buttoning and arranging her military jacket, Elizabeth returned. "Yes, Major."

As Elizabeth pushed back the last of the branches that shielded the cottage from sight, her anxious flight into her childhood came to a stuttering halt.

"Oh, Avery—it's—it's not there. The cottage is gone. I so wanted to show it to you. I wanted you to see where I was a happy, carefree, little girl. And now it isn't there anymore."

"Now, now, Elizabeth, could it be that you have forgotten just where the cottage was? I believe there is a small building over there in the midst of that thicket of trees. It looks rather overgrown, but I believe that it will qualify as a cottage."

Taking the lead, Avery moved ahead, through the overgrowth of brush, and onto the tiny porch that still hung precariously to the front of the stone and timber, one room cottage. Finding a vine and grime covered window, Avery peered inside.

"It appears to have been unoccupied for some time, Elizabeth." Avery reported. "Shall we try the door lock and see if we can get in?"

"There never was a lock on the door, Avery. Just latches with a leather thong pull. We would be more apt to have trouble with the old hinges. Let's push together."

The old door, creaking somewhat in mild protest, swung back, opening the room to the meager daylight that had forced its way down through the heavy foliage of the forest, showing Avery and Elizabeth that the sparse furnishings were very much the same, and in the same places, that she had remembered from her childhood.

Pulling Avery along, she stepped through the doorway into the room and took stock of her surroundings.

"See, there's the great old feather bed back in the corner, the wash stand over there, and the table we used to eat at with its tallow lamp is still next to that back window. The two chairs and the little footstool that I used to sit on are <u>still</u> drawn up by the hearth. Look, even the wood-box is overflowing with dry wood, the matches are here in their can, and the tinderbox is full--I guess waiting for someone to lay a fire.

"Look, Elizabeth. Above the mantel. Two splendid old clay pipes. I'll wager that many a fine pipe of tobacco was shared before this fire."

"Avery, how wonderful of you to have found them. Look here at the initials cut into the bowl of this one."

"A. C. Does it have some meaning to you?"

"Yes. Alfred Cosgrove. He was dear Uncle Alfred, the woodcutter. He wasn't a real uncle, only a little girl's honorary uncle."

"This one says--it's hard to make out through the wear of fingers and the stain of good tobacco-- C. N. Another friend?"

"Yes, Avery. A very dear, dear friend. C. N. stands for the only person that up until now I had felt free to love in my life. C. N. stands for Christian Nickles, my dear father.

"Avery, you have made me so very happy today. First the lovely trip through Windsor, and now coming here and finding this clay pipe; this memento of my father's life. I never before had even one scrap of his; not a picture, not even a farthing that he had carried in his pocket, to know was his. It was as though I had been completely cut away from him when he passed on. And now, you dear man, you have discovered a portion of my heritage for me to cherish and safeguard for the rest of my life."

Then, with marked deliberation, Elizabeth took the pipe from Avery's hands and, after carefully putting in on the table, reached up and drew his face down to her level and kissed him heavily on the cheek. Shocked and flustered at her own boldness, she quickly moved away and busied herself looking into the dusty nooks and crannies of the cottage.

"Do you know what became of your 'Uncle Alfred'?"

"What do you mean, 'what became of'?"

"Only that it appears that no one has been here for quite a long time, and I wondered if you knew if he moved away, or if he, as it were, passed away?"

"I really don't know. It has been so many years--probably over 20--since I was here, and father has been gone since 1934. I guess I just thought that Uncle Alfred would always be here, just like the lovely trees. What made you ask?"

"Come look through this window overlooking that hummock, it appears that there may be a marker of sorts at its crest. Shall we go out and see what it is all about?"

"Well, Elizabeth, that would appear to clear up the question of Uncle Alfred".

"Yes--I didn't realize that he could die. And so long ago. Nearly five years."

"He certainly had a long life. If he was born, as it says here he was, in 1850, he was nearly 90 years old. My word, but that speaks well for the simple, sequestered life combined with a good pipe from time to time (Elizabeth looked askance in Avery's direction). How remarkably stout!"

"Yes, Avery," she replied, "If that's the way you want to look at it. But, I can tell you that he suffered dearly from lack of companionship between my father's visits to him.

"You noticed that the pipe with my father's initials on it was filled with tobacco as though it were waiting to be lit. Well, it was. When we would come up here Uncle Alfred would beg us to stay, if even for only a moment longer. Each time we left the last thing we would see of him as we dropped from sight over that rise in the pathway, was his parting wave as he cleaned out the ashes in father's pipe and filled it with fresh tobacco for our next visit.

"Poor Uncle Alfred patiently waited in vain, some four fruitless years, for father to share that next smoke with him. And nothing came of it because father had already passed on. I missed my father greatly, but imagine how it must have been for Uncle Alfred to have waited for one last bowl of cheer, and then to have been cheated of even that bit of happiness by the double slamming of death's door.

Not quite sure how to express his sympathy and understanding for Elizabeth, Avery, still looking at Uncle Albert's headstone, awkwardly took her hand in his, and began as if to speak, but was silenced as Elizabeth continued on; "No, I have come to a decision, and this makes it even clearer to me. I give you fair warning, Avery Martin; I will have what I can of my life before my life is done with me. I'll no longer stand back, alone in a woods of my own; I'll not miss my chances and become another Uncle Alfred.

"I love you Avery Martin, and while it pains me greatly to be so bold, it would pain me to my grave and beyond not to have spoken my heart to myself and to you. Now, if you wish, I'll drive you back to our army and the war, and not another word need ever be said. But I shall still love you, Avery Martin. Forever on."

Elizabeth searched Avery's face in the gathering afternoon darkness, and finding no signs that she could read in it, accepted defeat and sadly moved to return to the cottage and the path to the motorcar.

She tried to slip her hand from Avery's tightening grasp, and turned to him to find that he was pulling her into the circle of his arms, and was holding her close to him. At the same time puzzled by his silent actions and thrilled by the nearness of him, she began to feel the tensions that had taken charge in his body. She could feel him trembling.

As he continued to hold her ever closer and she in turn drew as close to him as she could, wrapping her arms around him, and turning her head so her cheek pressed against his chest, she felt his face and then his lips pressed into her hair.

For a long moment they stood, measuring one another through the infinite number of ways two bodies, finally in harmony and consort with one another can, and having experienced and given and accepted one another in this new intimacy and awareness, she gradually turned her face toward him. As she felt his kiss follow her until its exciting warmth found its gentle way through her hair and to her temples, she in turn lightly caressed him with her lips along the line of his collar, and on up the side of his throat.

As he kissed her eyes--first one and then the other--she in turn nipped at his chin, and he, responding to this sensuous urging, kissed her high upon both cheeks, the bridge of her nose, and finally, having paid homage to all of her features, and silent supplications, lustily pressed his lips, fully and sensitively upon her trembling and eager mouth, to breathlessly share a kiss with her that spoke in a language beyond the power of words of the measure of the ultimate regard, need, trust and passion that each held for the other.

As her pressing warmth and closeness reached Avery, his response and reaction soon became evident to Elizabeth, and she, while never having known anything of the nature of what was occurring about and to her at the moment, instinctively recognized and responded to what was happening, and consciously began to draw great warmth and increased ardor from his stimulation.

Their lips, as with every other part of their bodies that strained for contact with the other, eagerly savored the excitement that they had released and were giving to one another after two near-lifetimes of lonesomeness, and diminishing hope. How completely captivated with one another, this uniquely celibate pair were--in each other's inaugural embrace of awareness--would be difficult to measure except for the fact that they were totally oblivious to the rain.

The rain, only an occasional drop when they walked out to the hummock behind the cottage, had, in the intervening moments, begun falling heavily and was now being driven in sheets by a wind that was rising to gale-like velocity.

As it was, they were quite drenched when Avery, trying to wipe the water from the hair and face of the now bedraggled appearing Elizabeth, said, "My dear, I think we best do something about all of this water. You are becoming frightfully wet, and I suggest that it would be wise of to return to the cottage."

Nodding, Elizabeth disengaged herself from their embrace, but still holding fast to his hand hurried down the path and around to the porch on the front of the cottage.

Looking at Avery, she exclaimed, "I think we had better try to wait this storm out here, but while I'm all wet, I'm going to run back down to the barn and get our umbrellas, blankets, food, and thermos bottles. Can you get a fire started while I'm gone, Avery?"

Avery shook his head in despair. "Elizabeth, I have never started a fire in my life. Well, that's not true. I have lit my pipe many times, but that hardly qualifies as starting a fire. I had better get the things from the barn."

"No, we'll go together. It will be easier to manage all of the things that way, anyway."

"Capital!"

CHAPTER THIRTY-THREE

"Elizabeth, is there anything that you are not capable of doing? You drive a motor-car, you are a superb nurse, you are an efficient secretary, you prepare remarkable picnic lunches--thankfully in abundant quantity for unforeseen emergencies like this--and now you build roaring fireplace fires with all the finesse of Baden-Powell's boy scouts."

"Thank you, Avery. Remember, my father was a Gamekeeper and Master of the Hounds. Even daughters learn how to take care of themselves in the countryside and woods in such a family.

"Here, help me move this old bed frame over here closer to the fireplace and out of this drafty corner. It looks as though all this old feather-tick mattress on it needs is a little fluffing up. You should be very comfortable on it.

"I found a ticking rolled up in that hamper that I can spread for myself, over here by the fire. With the four blankets we have, we can both have one to lie on, and another to cover with. We should be quite comfortable if we have to spend the night here. I, for one, shall enjoy myself, as it will take me back to some very happy times when I was just a girl." While Elizabeth was talking they finished moving the bed and other furniture to suit her.

Assuring himself that his services were momentarily not required, Avery made certain that the door was properly secured against the storm and checked the windows for leaks and fastening. Peering out in the direction of the old barn, even with the late afternoon light, he was unable to see much beyond the edge of the porch because of the violence of the storm.

Returning to the chair at the fireplace he shook his head as he remarked, "This storm is becoming dreadful. The lightning is as bad as I have ever seen."

Elizabeth looked up from the feather-tick mattress that she was plumping out, and after watching the flashes and displays through the window for a moment, nodded in agreement. "With that tree down in the lane, I won't be able to get the car out past it until someone comes along and helps us clear it out of the way. It is a good thing that you suggested we bring additional flash lanterns, blankets, and food."

"I thought that the motor-car would break down. I had no idea that we would be marooned by a storm of this nature. Upon my word, I do not think that I have ever seen such violence in a storm since I was in school in Canada.

"I think we have the leaks all taken care of, the fire is taking the chill off of the room, and there is plenty of water for tea, and enough food in the basket to last a brigade for a fortnight."

"Good, then if everything is settled down, and we appear to be here for the rest of the storm, if not the night, it's time for you to get out of those sopping wet clothes--"

"I'm not sure that would be proper of me."

"--and wrap yourself in one of these heavy blankets while your clothes dry by the fireplace." Elizabeth continued, ignoring Avery's protest. "Here, you can change behind the blanket we hung up to hold the warmth in this end of the room. Use two of these horse blanket pins you found in the old barn to keep it around your shoulders."

"But, what will you do? You are as wet as I am, you know."

"After you have changed, and I have hung your clothes to dry, I will change mine and use the other blanket."

Bundled up in the heavy army blanket, Avery sat in the massive old oak chair, smoke lazily curling from the clay pipe he was enjoying that had belonged to Elizabeth's father, as he drowsily eyed his entire wardrobe hanging along the wire above the fireplace, while he waited for Elizabeth to complete her change on the other side of the blanket room-divider.

His uniform; trousers, shirt and jacket, along with his bill-cap still dripped slightly; his socks, undershirt and under-drawers while still wet, were drying quite well, and his shoes would easily be dry within a few hours.

While his feet and legs protruded somewhat embarrassingly from below the blanket, he was becoming used to the idea of it all. The blanket no longer seemed rough or exposing, and he found himself quite peacefully relaxed. Stretching his six-foot frame, he settled his 180 pounds back into the great chair and listened to the comfortable little humming sounds that Elizabeth was making from time to time as she prepared to change out of her wet clothes.

Though Elizabeth was shivering and wet, through and through, she still felt quite warm inside. Before withdrawing to the other side of the curtain to take off her wet clothes, she had removed her jacket and made certain that it, along with all of Avery's clothing, was properly hung over the wire that they had found and stretched across the room above the fireplace so that while the clothes would dry, the heat that they would need for their own comfort would not be blocked.

Seating herself on the little footstool, she unlaced and pulled off her wet shoes, and carried them over to the curtain's edge. As she unbuttoned the top of her skirt, slid it down over her hips, and unbuttoned and took off her military blouse, she saw the flashes of the lightning reflected on the walls in the late afternoon near-darkness. By the time the thunder rolls had caught up with their flashes, she had pulled off her slip, loosened and dropped off her brassiere, stepped out of her underpants, and stood unclothed as she dried herself before preparing to wrap herself in the blanket.

Considering her full five-foot, seven-inch height, she regarded herself in an entirely different light than she had ever before. The wisp of smoke that drifted up from the pipe of her father and the indulgence of the man on the other side of the blanket across the room, reminded her that her whole world had changed since she had met Avery Martin.

From nearly their first moments; when they had huddled beside one another under the umbrellas on the Channel beach, and when he later held her closely in the damp and confining cave along the foot of the cliffs and had laid upon her in a clumsy effort to protect and warm her from the cold--in turn producing a new awareness and sensuous release in both of them that they were both grateful for and embarrassed by--through the months of professional contact and admiration that had built for him in her, to the excitement of this very afternoon when she blurted out to Avery her love for him, she felt an ever greater and compelling need to be possessed by this man.

And he, while not yet expressing his feelings to her in words of love, did hold her to him, and kiss her with such tenderness, while embracing her with such firmness, and exciting her with the very pulse throb and heat of his body, and his attention and alertness to her emotions and clamoring needs, that, she rather than experience discomfort in her nudity, but a curtain's distance separating her from this man, was satiated with even more desire, as well as a new pride and power in herself and her body.

At her height, nine 'stones' weight, or slightly over one hundred twenty-five pounds was not a problem, medical or otherwise. Her body, while slightly lanky, was acceptably proportioned, and while not as fully and classically formed as Sally's, Elizabeth, now that she considered it, felt reason to have pride in herself. Her shoulders were squarely set, her arms were slender and with just a suggestion of wiriness and muscle, as were her legs. Her stomach, quite flat, showed the sleekness and smooth muscling of the rest of her body.

Her breasts, while not noticeably large or overly developed, nevertheless, unencumbered by clothing, appeared as though sculptured in Grecian classic style, culminating in apices of soft, rose-like-pink nipples, that, as she dried and regarded them, stood firm and erect in sharp reminder of her continuing excitement of the day.

Finishing her drying, she pulled the towel across her back, briskly rubbed down each of her legs and the inside of her thighs, gingerly patting at the spray of soft auburn at their convergence, and wrapped the blanket around her shoulders, pinning it across her breasts and again, just below her navel.

Gathering her clothes together in order to hang them, along with Avery's, to dry by the fire, she resolutely took down the blanket that separated the portion of the room that held the fireplace and great oak chairs from the table, footstool, and featherbed, and-- her purposes well in mind, confidently stepped over into Avery's world.

CHAPTER THIRTY-FOUR

"Avery? Be a dear and help me arrange these things along the line so that they will be sure to dry." Elizabeth said as she dropped her clothes in the vacant oak chair. "My goodness but this old fireplace is doing a magnificent job! This room has become warm as toast in no time at all. Come now. With this blanket around me, I can't seem to reach up high enough to get my things over this line."

Putting the pipe aside, Avery cautiously stood, and making sure that the blanket still served to cover him, as Elizabeth handed her clothing to him, took each piece--the stocking, undergarments, skirt and blouse, and carefully and disingenuously arranged them on the line beside his. Reflecting to himself that he seemed to be less nervous about the task at hand than he thought he would be, he turned to see what more she had for him to do, only to find that Elizabeth had moved so close to him that as he moved, and brought his arms around for the task he finally perceived, she, indeed had stepped into their circle.

"Oh, I beg your pardon, Elizabeth." Avery exclaimed as he started to step back, only to find that he was unable to because

Elizabeth had taken a firm hold on his blanket and was clearly preventing his retreat, as she said,

"No, Avery, you have no need to do any such thing. I am here in the circle of your arms by my own design. It is I who should beg your pardon, except that I have no intention whatsoever of doing so. I have arrived at a conclusion for myself, and though, I confess, it is most brazen by any standards, I intend to see it through."

Elizabeth crept closer into Avery's arms, and felt him begin to tremble and then relax as she, now gaining further confidence, went on, "Dear Avery, hold me closer--like you did this afternoon on the hummock. I need to feel your closeness, your warmth, and your agreement if not your encouragement, as I try to tell you what is in my heart. Hold me Avery."

Avery drew Elizabeth closer to him, and began to realize that he, too, found powerful comfort in her nearness. He felt her bare feet touch his as he moved for a more comfortable stance for their embrace. Then as she leaned her head on his chest, he felt the curve of her thigh nestle between his, and the point of her hip gently press into his lower stomach. Elizabeth's hands no longer held the blanket at his sides, but were clasped firmly together where they had found each other beneath the blanket and behind his back, drawing them ever closer to one another. Avery followed her lead and held her in his full embrace, while allowing himself to savor her nearness.

For a time they stood in a silent, yet searching embrace. Occasionally Avery felt Elizabeth's lips form a kiss through the blanket to his chest, and he pressed his lips into her hair in return.

Presently Elizabeth began to speak in so soft a voice that Avery felt as though her words were in his mind and heart rather than through the air and world about them. "Avery, I love you. I have waited all of my life for someone to say I love you to. I am so happy today--tonight--because I have finally found someone that I can love, and can feel comfortable saying 'I Love You' to. I think--from the first day I saw you--when I reported in at Essex there was something about you that spoke to me above all the hubbub that told me that you were special. I found myself making excuses to bring papers to your office, and then when I was assigned as your assistant, I didn't know what to do. Up until then I had made excuses to come to see you, and once I was part of your office I had to make excuses to not come in to see you. I wanted to touch you. When we were in surgery, I dropped instruments all over the place. Every time you touched me, even through the surgical gloves, I trembled. All I could think of was touching you back. If you remember, I asked that you allow me to be the floating nurse. I had to! I couldn't go on wanting to touch you and dropping instruments every time you came near me, much less touched me. I was so happy to be with you, but I was miserable, too. I was so attracted to you but you didn't even know I was alive. You were quite proper. You thanked me for my good work. You made favorable comments in my service record, you even expressed admiration for my variety of talents, but you never once notice whom I was or how much I thought of you.

"When Sally came to our station and was assigned to your staff, and I saw how beautiful she was, I was sure that whatever chance I ever had of your noticing me would be taken away by her. But you didn't notice her, either. I don't know if it ever made any difference to her, but I felt sorry for her, and for you too because you couldn't see anyone or anything except your practice and your pipes and tobacco. I guess I made an effort to become Sally's friend, not because I thought she was in need of a friend because she was by herself over here, but because I felt something in common with her. You had not noticed her except for her professional talents, either. There was another reason, too. I thought that if you could be indifferent to someone as lovely as she was, then it wasn't just me, and maybe there would be some chance--some way that I could find to earn your attention. She gave me hope.

"Avery, even then I had to fight with myself. I had spent my entire life in training to serve others. I had never been allowed much time to think about the things that might serve my hopes and desires—my needs, if you will. My satisfaction and happiness--and there was a good deal of it--came from doing a good job and from the acceptance of others. But, nowhere did I ever see anything or anyone that I could love--until I saw you. I don't know why, but when I first saw you, I knew I had to someday tell you that I felt for you. I had to put myself squarely in front of you, and if you walked right over me and never knew I was there, I had to take that chance. I had to tell you that I wanted you to at least notice me. I had to have you hold me and kiss me like you did this afternoon. I had to have you hear me say that I love you, and that I want to be with you and a part of you in any way you want me. I want to hear you say you love me, but if you don't and can't say you love me, then

I can understand and still will be happy with whatever you have for me. I want to be held by you. I want to be possessed by you.

"Standing here, close to you, feeling your body only a blanket's thickness away from me, feeling your heart beating and your blood pulsing as mine wildly tries to keep pace with my hopes and the lightning that seems to be flashing inside of me as well as outside of this cottage, I have this need, this prayer to have you want me as much as I want you. I had prayed that I would find a love, but as the years added on I began to lose faith that I would have the time left to find someone. The war came along and I was sure that signaled the end of any chance, but then you came along.

"Avery, I love you so very, very much. I want to be yours in whatever way you find you can have me. I will be your mistress, I will be anything you want, but most of all I want to be your lover and you mine, if only just once."

Elizabeth, now silent, turned her head away, and seemed to have lost all of her strength as she almost clung to Avery for support. Avery slowly nodded his head as he looked down at Elizabeth, and then turning her face up to his, he pressed a kiss on her forehead as he said,

"Elizabeth--my dear--I have always been a very shy person, timid by most people's standards. In my youth I was never comfortable in the company of people. My own sister Gwen terrified me. She was so full of energy, so anxious to try everything that came along. I never learned to drive a motorcar because from the very first, either father drove our machine, or Gwen, from the age of 12, was behind the wheel, and I never challenged her. I merely closed my eyes when her driving became more than I could bear.

"I found that books were good friends; they did not argue with you, nor make fun of your 'quaint' ways. I never attended a public school in my life. As a lad there was our governess who saw to my lessons and encouraged me to become a student of medicine. After that there were the private schools, and by then I was assured of a life of isolation and contemplation. No, my dearest lady, I had long since given up any shred of a notion that I could possibly be of interest to anyone, much less that I would ever find myself as I do now.

Avery held Elizabeth ever closer, as though trying to draw encouragement from her nearness and the exciting warmth that he felt from her wherever their bodies were in contact, as he went on, "I want, so very much, the very same things that you do, Elizabeth. I want to be close to you, to hold you, to have you hold me, and to feel the excitement of one another in every way possible, but I am, at the same time, terrified. I don't know what to do. I feel your closeness. I want to feel you even closer, but I find myself so inadequate.

"But there is one thing that I am sure that I can say. I Love you Elizabeth. I must have loved you ever since I saw you running across the beach to me with those two umbrellas in your hands. I loved you when we were in the cave together, and I had the first feelings of my life about what it was like to hold a lovely lady you in my arms. I felt warmth in my loins that I repressed as sinful when I held you close for what at the outset was to protect you from the rain and cold, but what turned out to be a moment of delicious sensation, for which I later chastised myself.

"I tried to make some sort of amends by offering you a transfer, and when you refused me, and offered to sacrifice your career instead, I loved you even more, and yet, I was confounded and unable to admit to my feeling, nor was I able to express my regard for you. I have admired you all these many months and have wistfully wondered how I could find a way to unlock the decades of restraint that held me so tightly. There were many times that I found myself aching to share a personal word with you, but unable to bridge the gap that I had always found between me and the world that I longed for--and now more particularly, you. Oh, my darling Elizabeth, I not only love you, I need you with a desperation that has been churning inside of me for all too long. I need your love, I need your tenderness, I need your understanding, because now I find that all else means so very much more with you. I wish to have you as much as you wish me to. I shall try to be and do what you expect of me, for knowing you care for and love me, as I find that I do you, is most overwhelming. Elizabeth, let us help and share each other."

As though guided by one common sense, they withdrew from their embrace, and as Avery first undid one and then the other of the two pins holding Elizabeth's blanket about her, she in turn undid his and untied the cord that held his garment about him. For a moment they stood, now stripped of their covering, touching and holding to one another by just the tips of their fingers. While evening darkness has surrounded the now cozy woodcutter's cottage, they found the fire provided not only the warmth they needed, but also a delicious and soft light to add to the pleasure of the moment.

But for a time they saw nothing of the room about them, nor were they concerned with their bodies. What they did see by the soft glow of the fire was each other's loving eyes and radiant smile. And then without any sense of it they slowly blended into each other's arms and held one another closely.

After a time, Avery lowered his arm, sweeping Elizabeth up as she put her arms around his neck and kissed him first on the neck, then the cheek, and then fully on the lips. They clung to each other as he turned and lowered her onto the featherbed and, leaving her only to gather the blankets, he laid down beside her and again taking her in his arms, they kissed with all the accumulated emotions of two lifetimes of denial.

Avery could feel things that he had never dreamed of, much less considered the existence of. He felt the pressure of Elizabeth's lips, but he also felt their warm, and even more exciting, tremble. He could feel her hands as she held his face while she kissed him. Her breath, like little warm jets of air, drifted across his face and her tongue flicked in and out of her mouth, wetting her lips, and caressing his as he drew away from her for only the moment it took to catch his breath. He was entranced by her, and yet it went on.

He felt her arms and hands move about him, now on his shoulders, now pressed against chest, yet not holding him from her. He could feel strange, indefinable warmth from her breasts as she lay in his embrace, and he realized that he had felt this same sensation earlier, even through her covering blanket, and before that through her uniform as they stood in the rain. (He was fascinated by the sensation, and when he later called it to Elizabeth's attention, she, while somewhat embarrassed by his questioning on the subject, was at a total loss for an explanation, although concurring in his enjoyment of the phenomenon.)

As Avery revealed in his newfound experiences, Elizabeth was far from left out. She, too, was thrilled by Avery's new confidence and ardent kisses. She felt a charge of excitement each time he moved his lips, and while his mustache initially provided some distraction, its softness seemed to offer an added caress as time went on.

She had earlier discovered, as he swept her up in his arms, and lightly lowered her onto the bed, that he had strength beyond his appearance, and that there was a sort of inbred grace of action about him, for he showed no awkwardness in his movements, and the moment that he left her to gather their covers was no more than the time it took for her to catch her breath from the excitement that surrounded her.

His arms held her with a new authority, a new strength of body and purpose that she had hoped for, even though he had earlier appeared fearful and hesitant in his declarations. As he had taken her in his arms and first held her close, moving his entire body close to her, and then carefully taking her face in his hands and gently telling her that he loved her, followed by a long and deeply searching kiss, she relaxed all reservations of whether or not she had made the right decision to put herself squarely in the path of Avery Martin.

She knew, regardless of the outcome, that she had made the right move. That her life would never again be the same, and that if never again were she to share this man as she now did, and knew she was about to, her life would have been worthwhile and she would have given, received, and shared something that would always be beyond her mortal dreams.

Truly, as she felt his confidence and physical ardor become conspicuously more in its presence, she also felt a glow come about her, and her entire body tingled in anticipation and readiness for their next expressions of love. As Elizabeth nestled herself below the body of Avery, she took his head in both her hands and opening her eyes wide she looked as though to indelibly write every feature of this man, who was about to become her champion, her prince of the night, their mutual guide from each of their virginities; the exotic companion to her visualized ecstasy, into all of the corners of her brain, body and soul. Then she, opening her thighs in anticipation, felt the rapture of his pressure and then soothing initial entry, and with that she pulled him to her and pressing her trembling lips to him, let loose of all of the pent up love within her and opened her mouth and all of herself to him, as her tongue darted across and caressed his lips, while he in turn, discovering his excitement had reached its zenith, sought out the exotic comfort that had been denied throughout his life, and thrust as deeply within her as possible as she in turn enveloped him.

How long they clung to each other; how long and in what manner they embraced, kissed, and made love seemed rather remote. The storm had slackened outside; the moon and stars had appeared above, and yet they were oblivious to anything other than each other.

Elizabeth would always remember the thrill of the moment of realization that her love for Avery was being consummated. She would never tire of reliving how, as he held her in his arms and kissed her, she had found herself first supporting his body on hers as she savored the presence of him. How he laid upon her breasts; how his stomach pressed on her; and how his legs held her down between them, and how she first became aware of the warmth and hardness of his erection and the excitement it caused in her as she felt it as it pressed and throbbing against and then enamoring deep within her. She remembered that she had tried to control her responses, trying to be almost passive, but her excitement won out and she fervently threw her arms around him and squirmed free of his restraining thighs and enveloping him as completely as possible, drew herself close to him. And Avery, responding to Elizabeth's actions and encouragement, engorged himself, yet with tenderness and gentleness consummated the apogee of their love.

Something about the manner in which they became aware of one another and arrived at this evening must have spilled over into their lovemaking, because while there was initial eagerness and passion, there was no anxiety. There was the mutual sensation that their entire lives had been spent in preparation for these moments. As Avery, from time to time, watched Elizabeth by the soft light of the fire, he found her expression was wreathed either in smiles, or in the pleasure of realization. He marveled at how lovely she was. How, while she was in his arms, while they were locked in this embrace of mutual giving and receiving she showed him all of the expressions, the extremes from angelic to erotic, and how he found that he feasted on all she offered and what he saw.

He found himself in disbelief that anything so exciting and exhilarating could have possibly have happened to him. Without a doubt, he was certain that he was the most fortunate, the luckiest, and the happiest man alive. He certainly was totally involved and in love in every way, he could imagine, and as the thoughts ran through his mind, he gently kissed the nipples and then the smiling lips of his love that now nestled in his arms.

Feeling the touch of Avery's lips on hers, Elizabeth sleepily opened one eye to look again on her lover and returning his kiss, snuggled closer to his warm and comforting body, and seeking out his genital of love and grasping it as though it were a jewel of security, fell asleep with thoughts of how pleased she was that this dear man had possessed her, and how great the gift of his love had come to be in her life and dreams of the future.

As for Avery--as he, too, drifted off to sleep--while he was sure that he would still look forward to a good pipe of tobacco, and medical case histories would still be his choice of reading, here was no question that his first delight, choice, and intent henceforth would be in the company and arms of Elizabeth Nickles, soon to be--if he had anything to say about it--Martin.

CHAPTER THIRTY-FIVE

"Harry...?"

"Uh-huh."

"Let's stop and sit down for a little while. I think you're pushing yourself too much."

"Oh, I'm all right."

"You haven't been out of a hospital in over six months. You're not exactly ready for a twenty-mile hike--"

"This isn't any twenty miles."

"--Or a hill climb, and that's what this sure is. Come on, if you aren't tired out, I am. Here's a nice grassy spot that's out of the wind. Just for a few minutes, to catch our breath."

"Okay. We're about at the top of this darn hill anyway. Wait a minute while I spread out these ponchos for us to sit on. There. How's that?"

"It couldn't be better. This is really warm and cozy. Couldn't you just sit here forever and forget there ever was a war out there?

"Yeah, Mrs. Worsham sure knows the places to send you to."

"Harry?"

"Uh-huh." Harry replied.

"You really care about Mrs. Worsham, don't you?"

"Uh-huh, she's just like a mother to me. As a matter of fact, I hate to say it, but I never felt that close to my own mother back home. I guess I really love Mrs. Worsham, too."

"What does 'too' mean?"

"Simple. It means I love somebody else--too."

"Oh," Sally said.

"Just, Oh? Nothing else?"

"I can't think of anything else."

"You're really tuned in today. Geeze." Harry complained.

"Oh. Who do I think you love? Is that it?"

"Uh-huh, you know who?"

"I think so." Sally said.

"Who?"

"Your sister!"

"No! Well, yes, of course, but that don't count. Somebody else beside that."

"Oh."

"Hell's fire, we're back there again."

"Harry, don't get excited. I'm teasing you. I know who it is you love."

"Well, tell me then. Inching to the farthest edge of the spread ponchos, Sally grinned at Harry as she answered. "Yourself."

Pretending to ignore her answer, Harry continued, "And who, Miss smart aleck, do you love?" Sensing Harry's pretense,

Sally impishly replied, "Not anyone around here, that's for sure."

"We'll see about that, Harry said as he spun around, grabbing Sally by the shoulders, and wrestling her to the grass. Holding her in his arms as much as he could, while still controlling her struggles, he pinned her beneath him. With the most ominous and throaty growl he could fashion without laughing, he looked hard into her face and said,

"Now, you either tell me who it is you love or I will, ravish you, starting with your lips. I shall kiss you again and again until you become mindless; until you beg, until you throw yourself upon my good nature, begging for mercy. So, confess wench!"

Picking up on her part of the charade, Sally fiercely struggled, and, in mock seriousness, protested. "I shall confess--for today--that it is you who commands my love. And I shall not oppose you further, provided you pledge me your love in return. You sound more like Half-baked to me. But, I do love you, Harry."

"That sure took long enough. I don't know if it was worth all the bother I...Oof, hey those are my personal ribs you're punching in! I love you! I love you, too! Anything! Don't hit. Rest up for a minute!"

"Harry?"

"What now? It isn't even a half minute yet."

"Are you ever going to kiss me, or are you going to just sit on top of me like a dumb rock and waste these moments asking dumber and dumber questions?"

Finally recognizing the new readiness in her voice, and now seeing the loving softness in her eyes, Harry drew her even closer, and tenderly kissed Sally with the gentle passion reserved for lovers that have found in each other the attainment of their dreams, and readiness to search out more of each other.

As though on cue, hardly had they settled into their embrace, the ear splitting crack of the lightning bolt splitting the tree to the ground, less than 50 yards up the hill, and the torrent of rain that followed put aside all thoughts they had of continuing exploration and passion for each other.

Grabbing their ponchos and other belongings, they ran pell-mell down the hill through the suddenly swirling wind, driving rain, and crashing lighting; to the Inn. By the time they arrived they were both as completely drenched as though they had swam the brook, which had now grown to a raging river from the cloudburst, and had over-run the footbridge as they were crossing it.

Once within the safety of the Inn, they looked back at the angry black skies that continued to claw, wreath and swirl about the hummock where they had been. They agreed that they were lucky to be alive, and that the next best thing was a hot bath and shower.

Dorothy Worsham had been pacing the floor of the public veranda of her Spotted Dog Inn. She had been concerned for the weather when the two young American service persons had blithely headed off to the 'Swarthmore Commons' hummock. She had given them the best of her mild warnings to keep an eye to the weather, but it was to no avail. Off they had gone, and hadn't she been right, what with the awful blackness mounting itself right in the face of where they proceeded to adventure.

"Lord, good sense is not a virtue of the young, nor is the willingness of the acceptance of it. Well, I shall have to be watching along with you, over them, so it appears."

She must have wiped that teacup twenty times when the lightning struck, and only by the will of the Lord, Himself, was she able to catch it on the third 'tip' into the air. She blessed herself as it was part of the very special set that her Stanley had given her as a wedding present those many, many years ago. She only brought the set out on the most very special of occasions. "Glory be, to have lost it at this very special occasion."

"Where are those young ones?" she said aloud to herself for what seemed to her to be the twentieth time. And then she saw them straining to cross against the now knee deep rushing current that had overrun and was threatening the existence of the footbridge.

Seeing that they had managed to cross, she ran to the linen closet and returned nearly obscured by an armload of cashmere robes for her charges, which she thrust upon them as then burst headlong into the public room of the Inn.

"Thanks to the Good Lord for the safety of the both of you."

Gasping for breath, the out of condition Harry, simply nodded. Sally, hugging Mrs. Worsham, breathlessly gasped, "My goodness, this is worse than the storms we have in the Rocky Mountains, back home. At least they don't exactly come so suddenly out of a clear blue sky, or out of nowhere. But you did warn us, didn't you Mrs. Worsham?"

"Aye, that I did, and it's 'Mum' to you as well, my girl. Remember? Now, I'll not have you in those wet uniforms of yours one second longer. You can dress yourselves each up to suit the finest of convention in my fine cashmere wool robes, and I will hang your clothes to dry. By the time you have your supper, and your friends return, you will be back as you were. Now each of your rooms are ready. And they all climbed the stairs and walked out onto the second floor veranda.

"Harry, as you are the tall one, and the end room had the bed for the long gentlemen, you'll be in there. The next room happens to be the finest lady's room in the Inn, and I thought you would like to have it for your Sally, lass. The other two rooms; the next lady's and the last gents, fell by lot to your Miss Elizabeth and Dr. Martin, when they return.

There is plenty of hot water, soap, and soft towels in each of the bathing rooms, so I suggest that you get yourselves busy so as to not take a chill or a cold. I should not like to have you take a memory of that sort from your stay at the "Old Spotted Dog. Scat, now!"

Deciding to enjoy the exquisite comfort of the cashmere robes for the evening rather than try to put back on their not quite dry uniforms, Harry and Sally dined alone with Mum Worsham that evening. They had been concerned that Avery and Elizabeth had not returned from their sojourn, but after deep consideration between the three of them, they decided that Avery and Elizabeth were going to places that both of them knew very well, and that with the intensity of the storm which had moved off in the direction of their travel, it was very likely that they simply could not get back that evening.

Sally, with an impish grin, privately said to Harry, "This turn of events will not bother Elizabeth in the least, and it might very well be good for Avery. Spending an evening at an Inn without the insulation of the entire British army, or a patient and a nurse, might finally help thaw out Avery."

The storm had long since abated, and the sun had slid behind the hills in the west, and the nightly rumbling of the German bombers, the whomping of their loads of death, and the chatter of the defiant anti-aircraft guns crept up from the skies to the south. Yet, Harrow, seemed to be at peace with the world as Harry walked out into the darkness of the second floor veranda.

"Harry, is that you?"

"Sally?"

"Yes, I just wanted to make sure. We can't start up any more episodes like back on the Brazil, can we?"

"Good God, No! Where are you? It's as dark here as it was back there. Should I hold out my hand?"

"Want to get it bit?"

"Geeze, no! Where the devil are you, Sally? It just isn't safe around you in the dark, girl."

Sally snickered, and because she was behind Harry and could make out his faint outline against the near total darkness, quickly stepped forward and tightly wrapped her arms around him, announced, "Here! Gottcha!"

Harry's senses came wildly alive. One moment he was contemplating the skies, the next with complete calm wondering at the location of Sally. Seconds later, at the touch and pressure of Sally's body against his back, he became explosively charged.

He whirled about in her arms, and almost hungrily swept her into his arms and sensually enjoying the closeness of their bodies through the cashmere robes they each wore, he kissed her with a longing and lovingness that left Sally quite breathless. He held her tightly to him. He took a subconscious inventory of the beauty of the moment and the points of their contacts. He felt her lush thighs one by one beside his and her pulsating abdomen now pressing against his. Her breasts were firm against his chest, and her arms were now tightly entwined around his neck. It suddenly came to him that he was barely the aggressor in this moment of frenzy.

"Dear God, Sally, I love you. I need you like everything I have ever thought of in my entire life. You have become everything to me. I want to hold you in my arms forever! Please never, never leave me."

Sally freed her arms enough to pull open the robe across Harry's chest. She turned her face to press her cheek on it, and then after a moment gently and then feverishly began to kiss Harry across his chest. After a moment as she moved her body, opening her robe, and somehow seeming to spread and roll her hips so that their bodies were standing engaged with one another as closely as possible, Sally softly began to speak.

"Harry, my precious man, my dear sweet man. If you truly want and need me as you say you do, then you need to know that you are the fulfillment of my lifetime of dreams. We have found each other under the most unusual and difficult circumstances and we have already built a bond that is outside of a physical relationship. You filled my heart with joy when you found it in your heart to come all the way back from the withdrawn man that I first met you as, to the loving, sweet, human person that now holds me so tenderly. Yes, Harry, I want and need you as much as you need me. You complete my life, Harry.

"My dear father always told me that there was a right man for me out here somewhere, and I believed him then. I really never saw the 'anyone' that came close to being 'right one.' And then you came along. And even with all of your hurt and anger, something reached out to me and told me to be patient. Be patient. And now there is no one else but you, because I know that there is no one else for you but me.

"Please Harry, hold my hand; with the one that has the scars of our first meeting, and hold me to you. Oh yes, Harry, I do so love and want you."

Harry gently took Sally's hand as she had asked, and after holding her tightly for a few moments more, led her to his room, where they much like Avery and Elizabeth, spoke more of and consummated their love for one another.

When Harry awoke shortly after dawn the next morning, he gazed in joyful rapture at the still sleeping, faintly smiling, goddess that still lay beside him. As their foursome were the only guests at the Inn, and Sally was laying partially across their robes, Harry took a chance and without dressing, quietly and quickly slipped out the bedroom and down the veranda in the altogether to discover that neither Avery's or Elizabeth's beds had been slept in, nor had their luggage been moved in the slightest. Deciding that they most certainly had not returned last night, he smilingly returned to his room and his love. Harry also discovered that there was an unlocked connecting door between the room assigned to him and the room assigned to Sally. He was sure that this would be good to know.

Slipping back into bed beside Sally, and still not arousing her, he lay for the longest time simply awestruck at her simplicity, her beauty, and her meaning to him. How had he ever gone this far in life without her in his life? And then contemplating that he really ought to put some on nightclothes, he too drifted off to sleep.

Harry was sure this was the most unusual dream possible. He was dreaming that there was a very tiny Indian dragging a couple of teepee poles down his stomach and slowly back and forth across his groin area. It was becoming most disconcerting, if not maddening. He was beginning to squirm about and ready to slap it away when he heard a snicker. Opening an eye, he saw Sally gently dragging two soda straws down his stomach, and looking beyond that, discovered a most embarrassing but intense consequence.. "Oh my God! Sally!"

"Well, what are you going to do with that thing? It seems like a shame to waste it, doesn't it?

Sally skittered away from Harry, and looking back at him as much as dared him to follow her lead.

"God, girl, you are wanton! You are insatiable! Are you serious?"

"Yes, yes, yes!"

"You started out a virgin last night…"

"Yes, but now I'm not, and you did it! And you and I have got a lot of catching up to do."

"Geese, you know what you really are?"

"What?"

"Absolutely, unmatchable, wonderful. God, I love and need you, Sally!"

"Good, keep thinking it, keep saying it, and keep doing it. Harry! Are we going to use that thing, or what?"

Harry rolled over on top of Sally and for the first time, now in the clearing daylight saw her unclad body, and how exquisitely beautiful and well proportioned she was. Her face was as if it had been molded by Varga or Petty for the greatest of the beauties of the magazines of the 1930s and 40s. Her shoulders, arms, thighs, and body in general were as though sculptured by Michelangelo, and her breasts not only thrilled him as he gently caressed them, but his eyes grew large in wonder of them, at how their nipples strained up to his touch.

He pressed his hand on her stomach and it had the feel and tone of a finely tuned and drawn instrument, and then on her vulva where she gasped and rose to him as she had done the night before. As he parted her legs to prepare to enter her, she brought her body up to his and this time not waiting for him to thrust into her, did instead reach up and grasp onto and sheath his now hardened and eager member. She reached her arms and legs around his hips and winding them about him as tightly as she could, thrusting hard to him while pulling him to her with all of her physical might.

Reflections

He could feel that he had reached near the depth of her and that she was enthralled with the sensation. She began to make sounds that seemed to spill forth from the depth of her groin, and manage their way up through her body and out of her lovely lips into his awaiting ears. She gyrated, thrust, and ground him into her, and he in turn ascended and thrust as deeply into her as her pelvis cage would allow. He felt the full engorgement of her clitis this time, and she, experiencing it for the first time too, became even more violent in her lovemaking.

They gyrated, they impaled, they held, and finally Harry felt the flow begin and then she sensed his unbelievable new sensation, heat, and rapid engorgement. And somehow even more encouraged, matching his flow and ejaculation with an addition tightening of her entire uterus wall, and a massive evaluative flow of her own, Sally produced a water flood of vaginal fluids just as Harry burst forth all of the semen that was welled within his body. They had experience the absolute ultimate culmination of their physical love. And they lay exhausted and overjoyed in each other's arms and fluids for what seemed to be the rest of the morning. Actually, it was only until they became rested and mutually sought each other to find out if they could duplicate this feat...which they nearly did a numerous times over the next day and a half.

Their lovemaking was sweet, gentle, and violent at time, but always with exotic romantic consideration for each other. Harry's prime concern was that Sally should have the most exotic of experiences and recollections. Sally's need was that Harry should never lack in fulfillment of his lust or his passion, and that she should discover each and every way of satisfying and discharging that need along with her own. Time and again, they lay fulfilled and exhausted beside each other; Harry drained, and Sally enriched. Time and again they satisfied the renewed desire to begin anew. With each enrapture, their bond grew tighter and more enduring.

By the time Avery and Elizabeth returned, late on the third day of their stay, Harry and Sally had completed an absolute commitment to each other, and Harry had proposed immediate marriage, which Sally had accepted. Immediate marriage in the military service, meant 'at the convenience of the service' which could take as long as six months in some cases.

Avery had also proposed marriage, and the absolutely giddy Elizabeth had experienced swirling rapture as she accepted. However, Avery's and Elizabeth's situation would be even more difficult, and as the British wartime service had a strict rule against married members serving with or subordinate to one another, their wedding would have to be in secret, and they would have to go on being Major Martin and Lieutenant Nickles until after the war, or until the unlikely chance that the regulation would change.

When they finally all did get back together again, and Elizabeth and Sally had a moment together, Elizabeth simply could not keep her pride in the prowess of Major Martin to herself.

"Now Sally, if you tell of this I will never speak to you for the rest of my life, and I will put poison in your breakfast tea, but I must tell you how proud I am! We are to be secretly married! I am so excited, and Major Martin is very enthusiastic about the idea, and wants to have the ceremony preformed as soon as we can find a vicar who will secretly do so. We want you and Captain Morgan to be the witnesses, of course.

"But there is so much more, Sally. Major Martin, Avery, is a stout one in ever so many a ways! You know of course that he is so precise in his manner and erect in his, Ohhhh….. I mean he is an upstanding man among men. I know Sally, my face is as crimson as the Union Jack, but I simply do not care!

"You simple cannot believe the measure of inexplicable excitement that that man creates within me! Not even three days we were at the woodcutters cabin, and he was out and about learning at chopping at the wood, and bustling about, and mind you he found time for nine times for us together!

"Nine times we had at it, and the ninth was as good, if not better than the first! Nine times in less than three days, after thirty-seven years of never times! I do declare, he kept me on my backside to the point where I am the happiest woman in Yorkshire. No, make that the whole of the British Isles. Of course, I did give him a bit of encouragement…..About nine times".

CHAPTER THIRTY-SIX

"Well, I see that I have the lot of you together again at last. And it does me heart good to see your four happy faces around me, once again. I'll be having your breakfast muffins and tea ready for you in but a twinkle." Mrs. Worsham simply beamed.

She had been concerned about the absence of Avery and Elizabeth for the past nearly three days, but she had consoled herself that they were both of grand English stock and could well fair for themselves in fair or foul weather. That they were alone together was of no concern to her, any more than the presence of Harry and Sally by themselves on the upper floor of her Inn. She could well see for herself that there was a grand harmony among them.

"And when do you expect that my grand visit from you all will be ending?" she went on to say.

"I expect that we shall have to return to Harrow tomorrow. Avery replied "Although I certainly wish we could stay here another fortnight. Certainly, this is a blessed spot. I expect that we can schedule a day or two each of the next weeks, however."

And the next day they all packed into the motorcar and returned to Harrow.

CHAPTER THIRTY-SEVEN

BACK AT HARROW, THE THERAPY sessions for Harry became more intense. While the four did return to Mrs. Worsham and her Spotted Dog Inn for the next two weekends, Harry was subjected to testing and stress evaluation by not only Avery's team, but by a team from Colonel Middleton's headquarters. Avery and Elizabeth slipped away and found a vicar that would perform a secret marriage for them. The next day, with Harry and Sally in tow as witnesses, they returned and were duly joined. Elizabeth was beside herself with the realization that she was now actually the wife and partner in all manners of speaking with the man of her dreams. That she was in fact, though it be secret for the balance of the war, Mrs. Avery Edward Martin.

The next week Harry received a visit from Colonel Middleton, himself. The Colonel spent some time satisfying himself that Harry was fit to return to duty, and after conferring with Avery at length concurred with Avery's conclusion that Harry was, indeed, adjusted and ready to return to duty. Finding a private room, he and his adjutant, Major McFarland, called Harry in for a close examination of the last moments of the evacuation flight that had gone so very sour.

"Let's get down to business, Captain Morgan" the Colonel said. "Can you help us shed further light on the last moments of the evacuation from Lybia? Major McFarland and I have conflicting reports from the aircrew on what occurred. How did it go so wrong at the last minute? The plan was known to only those of you on the flight and beyond that, a totally trustworthy group at M-5 and OSS. And with all of that shroud of secrecy, the Germans were, for all practical purposes, waiting for us.

"The only thing they did not compromise was the locations of the flight beepers, which thankfully went off at the right times and led our bomber flights to their targets at the invasion. There had to be a 'mole' in your group, but we are not completely sure that we have been able to dig him out because while two others of your group survived along with you, only you were conscious during the entire evacuation, and at the end. Keesling and Paul have been unable to shed any light on the last moments of the flight, nor have the flight crew. We are in hopes that now that you have recovered from your trauma, you can fill us in as to where the 'fly was in the ointment.'

At First, Harry was not at all pleased to be drawn back and involved in this investigation. He had no desire to re-live the moments of that flight, but he began to realize that his input was critical. Upon consideration, he began to hope that re-living it would find him some justification for the feelings that he still shied away from in respect to the incident.

"Colonel", Harry squirmed uncomfortably in the chair that had been provided for him. "For a long time I have done everything I possibly could to forget that flight and how it turned out. I have felt responsible for the deaths that occurred when we tried to get out of there. Janish, Abher, and Monier are gone and probably dead, and I still feel that I could have saved them if I had really tried."

"You don't know that for a certainty, Captain, but go on." The Colonel replied. "I want to hear from you how you recall the time from when you found you were discovered and the shelling started falling around the plane."

"Well, somehow the Germans got word that we were in the area, and they sent a patrol out which intercepted us at the last minute. The landing was just as Colonel Barnaby planned it. We met the operative, Captain Abher, who was on the ground. We separated and did our respective jobs, and we were getting ready to assemble and wait for the people that had gone in and were returning with the operatives from Bengasi, when all of a sudden the plan fell apart. I agree, somehow, they had to know that we were there.

"And now, we are quite certain that they did, Captain." Major McFarland interjected. "We had a deeply imbedded 'mole' in the group, which is bad enough. The big problem is that he was also quite completely trained and aware of unknown to us aspects of our field 'mode of operendi.' And we now know that he is actively functioning against us from the continent."

"How do we know that? Everyone that didn't get out died!" Harry asked.

Major McFarland continued, "Because it now appears that no one died in that evacuation. The three men that we had written off as lost in action actually survived without substantial injury, and one took the others into custody and turned them over to the Germans."

"I can't believe it!" Harry exclaimed. "Do we know who the 'mole' is now? Not Abher; he was an American officer on the boat with me from the states, and Monier? He was supposed to be our man on the ground. Janish? Janish had nothing but hate for the Germans. He said they murdered half of his family, and I thought you had verification of that. I can't believe it was any of them, but if there was a 'mole' there is no one else. So, which one?"

"Janish or Monier?"

"Janish? Why would he help the Germans after what they did to him?" Harry asked.

"Because they still held his mother and sister captive in concentration camps deep in Germany, and gave him every reason to believe that they would die by slow torture unless he worked for them to undermine us."

"Good God! But it could make sense. But when he was blown out of the plane, we thought he was killed. I was with him right up until the shell blew him out after he pulled Keesling into the plane.

"On the other hand, Monier also was left on the ground, and we know a lot more about Janish", Major McFarland suggested.

The Colonel asked, "You say that you and Janish armed our signaling devices and other equipment? I had been inclined to believe that he could have been the "mole. But your impressions of the last moments break down our prior extrapolations and assumptions. When Monier left the rest of you to hide the minibus he could easily have left a signal for the Germans. He easily could have used an activator to send a single note message for which we now know that the Germans had a receiver in each of their sensitive points. We have since changed the frequencies of our signal transmitters so that has been corrected, but both Monier and Janish still knows our codes and can assist the German high command in deciphering them.

"So, we need to either get them out of there or kill one or both of them. Each is too dangerous. To that end, we have a plan, and we believe that you can be of great value in pulling it off. I have talked at length with Major Martin and he believes that you are totally medically clear to return to duty and what little I am able to tell him of this plan appears to him to be within your capabilities."

"Wow, Colonel, you really cover a lot of ground."

"We have to Morgan, we don't have much time. We have to get this done before there is any chance for an invasion of the continent because either of them will be able to cypher everything we do. To that end, we have a plan that will bring Abher, Monier, and not only Janish out but will get his mother and sister from the camp that they are now in. We have learned that they have been relocated into Holland in keeping with Janish's requests. That much our agents have been able to learn."

"How did we get on top of all of this, Colonel?"

"We got lucky. Captain Abher, as you know him, was sprung from the German Guards, by the French underground, and he is now working as an operative again. He managed to get all of the intelligence that I have just shared with you through the underground network and out to us. We had no idea what had happened to any of them until we heard from Abher."

"Our plan is to have Keesling, and Paul who are both fully recovered and are now 'on station', with you, go into Holland and meet Abher who will work with you in getting the two women out of the camp and into the pickup area where they will be grabbed up by RAF air people.

"We think we know where Monier is in Holland; keeping tabs on Janish. Then you will find both of them and either kill them or get them out, too. We prefer that you get them out so we can interrogate them and find out as much as we can about what the Germans have really learned about us and the British M-5."

"Sure is an ambitious plan, Sir."

"Are you up to it, Morgan? We think you are and as you are the only one we have on station that really knows all of the participants, and was conscious throughout the botched pickup, while Keesling will lead the mission, you are the logical person to lead the logistics of this mission. Keesling and Paul will be with you, and Abher will join you. You will have to really think on your feet so that we can pull it off. We think it is doable, and frankly, we have to do it to protect the Invasion schedule. So, what do you think, Captain? Are you up to it?"

"Yes, I sure am. It will give me a chance to vindicate myself in my own eyes as well. Yes, I want to be in on it. There is one thing; can I get permission to get married when I return? My recovery nurse and I have fallen in love and we wish to be married. However, I would rather have this Holland business behind me before I tie the knot. Okay, Sir?"

"Yes, I am also aware of the progress you have made in your personal life, the Colonel said, "and I concur, and will sign the forms when I return to the office this evening. In the meanwhile, I expect your released from the Hospital shortly. We will start the intensive training with you, Keesling, and Paul within a week of your return; the language acquisition program will start before you leave here, and you should expect that we will be taking you in to the Holland shores on a submarine within ten days following your additional weeks of preparation and training. Of course, you will be restricted to our training facility once you leave here. Oh yes, you may tell your intended that I will see that her request papers are completed as well."

"Thank you, sir. We will name our First after you."

"Oh, sure….."

CHAPTER THIRTY-EIGHT

"I SAY, ELIZABETH WILL YOU mind coming in here for a moment? Avery called as he read through the mail that had had accumulated over the weekend. "I have a bit of administrative work for you."

"Yes Avery...I beg your pardon, Major. What is it that seems to be beyond your means?"

"It seems that we have another memo from Colonel Hawthorne wondering if Captain Archer will soon be available to return to her regular station here at Harrow. Also, I have a directive address to Captain Archer issuing her permission to be married. I fancy that she will be pleased to hear about that."

"Oh, Avery, she will be beside herself with pleasure, I can assure you. Remember how pleased I was when we became married, even though it has to be a secret until this bloody war is over. I must call her and bring her in so that she can share this good fortune with both of us. I won't be but a minute."

Avery looked about in dismay because as usual Elizabeth had gone into the next stage of things before he ever got a chance to finish the last comment or activity. He was about to say that he had received orders for the two of them to return to

Great Wakering to resume his responsibilities in behalf of the British troops that soon would be returning from the pending invasion. As a Neurosurgeon his services would be indispensable, and for all of her flightiness, Elizabeth was a crackerjack surgical nurse and aid, as well as his secret wife for the duration.

Avery had come to miss the male companionship that had developed between him and Harry Morgan, but like a true soldier he realized that this bloody war effort came first and their duty stood above all things.

On the other hand, he was pleased and satisfied that he had returned what had been brought to him as an emotionally based, blind, irrational, unresponsive, and irresponsible American soldier, and a fortnight or so ago had returned him to his OSS unit, completely fit to assume any responsibility that his training would confronted him with.

Yes, he was pleased with the work that had been done with and in behalf of Captain Harry Morgan. And now it seemed as though things were going to come full circle for Harry and Sally Archer with their both having received permission for marriage. As Harry was in training and preparing for a mission, it would have to be upon his return from his next assignment. Yes, Avery was pleased.

———

"Elizabeth said you had something I would be pleased to hear and to have, Major?" Sally had poked her head around the corner of the doorway and was grinning at Avery.

"Yes, by Jove, I am sure you will be pleased with at least half of what I have to discuss with you. Come in and sit down, if you please. I have a document from your Col. Hawthorn granting you permission to marry, and…

"Oh, how simply wonderful. I have certainly been waiting for that. I knew that Harry's CO had issued him one and we were sure that his Colonel Middleton could convince my Colonel Hawthorn to sign a permit for me. I will have to send Harry a note tonight about this. I hope it catches up with him, wherever they have him training now."

"Ah, yes, and there is more that I have to talk to you about. It appears that our little team is being broken up as Elizabeth and I are to be posted back to Great Wakering, and your Colonel has asked that you rejoin your American Unit at their facility here in Harrow. And yes, I have noticed one further item; you have not had a single day of Leave since you arrived in England except the weekend with my sister Gwen. The time that we were all together here and at Mrs. Worsham's Spotted Dog Inn has really been duty time for you, regardless of how you contrived to use it.

"Therefore, I am having Elizabeth prepare a seven day leave for you, and as you have reported that you had such a smashing good time with my sister in London, I suggest that you go back there again. Unfortunately, Gwen is not at her flat in London as she is now serving at a rehabilitation hospital at Brighton. But even though she is not there I shall give you my key to her flat and you can use it while you are there. I shall send a note to her through channels that you will be using it, although because of the nature of her assignment I doubt that she will be able to return to London while you are there. Nonetheless, you should have great time watching the Changing of the Guard, going to Piccadilly, Nelson's Square, and the Albert and Victoria Museum."

A highly amused Elizabeth was sitting at her desk just outside of the door reflecting that Sally would probably find a few other places to poke around in to liven her seven days. Leaning back so that she could see through the doorway, she asked, "Major, shall I prepare the leave papers to start tomorrow?"

"Ah yes, please do, we do not want to waste a day of her entertainment."

As Sally rode the train to Waterloo Station she reflected that she was making this trip with a far brighter outlook than she had the last time she had been on one of these British contraptions. Even the weather looked brighter, and as she came closer to London she could see the sun peeking out over the meadows to her right.

It was just becoming dusk as she found her way to Gwen Martin's flat, and using Avery's key let herself in, hung out a fresh uniform, and dropped her kit-bag in the bedroom.

There was no question about her next choice of action as she hastened to Gwen's arousingly luxurious bathroom and quickly undressed, leaving her clothes in a pile on a cushioned chair, and as she intended to change to a fresh uniform when she finished her bath, she remove the Captain's bars from both lapels of her shirt and along with her dog tags placed them on the large bath towel on the makeup table near the tub.

Filing the tub she tested the water and finding its temperature most agreeable stepped into the tub and total immersed herself as she had done so many months ago at her First visit. She felt that she could stay there forever if she only did not have to breathe.

The German Henkel Bomber had slipped by the coast watchers and RAF protective screen and was making good time for Coventry where the British munition factories were located, but suddenly one of its two engines failed and the other shortly thereafter began 'missing'. With the prospects of not even arriving at his target, much less returning to the continent, the pilot decided to abort the mission and attempt to return to his base in Belgium. He gave instructions to his navigator to plot a return course. Never having done this the navigator swung the plane around to the south rather than to the north. This brought the plane on a course above London and it was promptly shot down by the British anti-aircraft batteries. While the crew safely bailed out, the plane, although on autopilot, spiraled down with a fully armed bomb load into the back of the building that contained Gwen's flat.

The impact explosion completely destroyed the three story building and created an immense fire which the fire crews savagely fought a losing battle to keep from spreading to buildings across the street and adjacently. It appeared to them that either there was no one who had survived, or not at home in the building, or that they had been vaporized by the explosion.

But Sally had 'been at home'. Being totally immersed in the water of the tub she had been saved from the initial heat and concussion of the explosion, however she had been knocked unconscious from its pressure. Fortunately she was saved from drowning by the fact that the tub had been fractured and the water had run out.

When she came to her senses she found herself totally nude on the floor of what remained of the room, amid all of the shattered tub and glass walls. She reached about in the near darkness and found the fire scorched bath towel which she threw about herself, and finding nothing else to hold it in place, she painfully grabbed one of her now fire-scorched Captain's bars and used it as a makeshift pin to hold the towel about her. Pushing her way through the broken glass and burning frame of the building, she finally reached the street where she collapsed.

Down at the under street 'Highland Hart Pub', Piper Sgt. Ivan McIntyre was having one last pint before he headed back to Scotland and his regiment. Suddenly the building shook as though it would fall in upon him as it nearly had so many months ago. Thinking that London was no place for a fighting man, he hastily gulped down the remains of his pint and clambered up to the street where he saw that the buildings down the block were engulfed in flames and that there might be need for his strength to help pull survivors from the wreckage. As he hurried in that direction he stumbled across the body of a nearly unclad woman, and after rolling her over to check for vital signs he recognized her as the friend of a lass who he knew as Gwen who had patronized the pub earlier when he had been there, and who he believed to be named Allie.

Picking her up in his arms he started toward the aid station but finding that he was entirely cut off in that direction by the conflagration and explosions, he decided to take her to his nearby billet where he tried to revive her.

After some time she began to come around and he tried to comfort her, saying "Here now lass, you're to be all right now. It's Allie, your name?

The girl looked up at him, wide eyed but with blank expression and said. "I don't know. I do not know who I am, where I am, or how I got here. Who are you?"

In over twenty-five years of service to the King, Sgt. McIntyre had never been confronted with this sort of a situation. "Can I take you to your people, lass?"

"I don't know who my people are or where they are. Do I know you "

"Do you know a lass named Gwen?"

"No, I do not know that name at all; I don't know anything or anyone except maybe you. Who are you?

"Piper Sgt. Ivan McInyre."

"No, I don't think I know you or ever saw you before."

Sgt. McIntyre walked across the small room and sitting in the chair scratched his head while gazing at the near holocaust up the street. He was due to leave for his regiment in Scotland in that evening. Standing up he looked out of the window and seeing all of the devastation about the area he came to the only conclusion that he felt was worthy. Somehow he would find clothing for this lass and he would take her to

Scotland and leave her with his wife, Matilda, until he could find a better situation for her. Turning her loose here without her knowing who she was or where she was, was simply out of the question.

So, shortly after dusk, with Sally, now known to even herself as Allie, he climbed aboard the Flying Scotsman train for Edinburgh and his wife. Sally not knowing who she was, but confident in the company of the Sargent. clung to him and to the tarnished Captain's bar that remained the only connection that she had from before the fire and of her prior life. Her memory of all else was simply gone.

And there she lived as Allie McIntyre for the next 25 or more years as the adopted daughter of Ivan and Matilda McIntyre. When she delivered a son some eight months later they gave him the name of McIntyre as well.

"That was a bugger of a bomb that Jerry dropped here, Eh?"

"Hell mate, he dropped the whole blinkin' airplane in with it. We is lucky that this whole end of London didn't go up."

"Aye. How many poor blokes have you had to throw in the meat wagon? I pulled out two what once was women."

"Six, Harvey. And I hear that them Jerrys jumped clear and are toasting their tootsies at one of our fancy camps for them. 'It don't seem right that they can do our folks this way."

"Mortie, lookie here! Here's a set of dog tags for an American-- and a Captain's bar, too. 'Scorched to a bloomin' crisp! They was for a female! The tags say one named Archer,

Sally Ann Archer. We gotta be sure to turn them in to the Fire Marshall so he can turn them in to the American Graves Registration bunch."

"She must have been visiting here at the wrong time. Must have been one of them two females we drug out that was burned so bad we couldn't tell much more than they wasn't blokes."

"S'pect so. God Damn them Jerrys, anyway."

"You're sure as hell right about that, Mortie."

CHAPTER THIRTY-NINE

A‍L KEESLING SQUIRMED AROUND BUT found it all but impossible to make himself comfortable. "Dammit Harry, this Limey sub is as wet and cold as a leaky icebox!"

He, Harry, and Jen Paul were crammed into the confining area of the conning tower of the submarine in preparation for their undercover landing on the Holland shoreline. The conning tower, a small watertight compartment within the submarine's fin, equipped with instruments and controls and from which the periscope was used to direct the boat and launch torpedo attacks, left little or no room for the three men plus the four frogmen that would take them to the beach.

"It beats that 'swim to shore' we had at Portsmouth, in the training for this operation." Paul remarked.

"Yeah, and a lot more." Harry thought. When he reported back to Maude Glen, he figured that they would only have a 'refresher' at Maude Glen, but instead they went through the entire training program once again. A night infiltration, overcoming people who were supposed to be German security soldiers, retraining on Morse and secret code, and even a night jump along with the 'swim to shore.' In a way he was glad to be on the sub, cold or not, and on the way to the 'job at hand.'

After all, once he got back he was promised a leave so that he and Sally could get married.

"Okay, lads. The skipper says it's about time for 'over the side' with the lot of you. The Conning Tower commander said. "The frogmen and the raft to take you in are ready, and all we have to do is make sure that we are not spotted when we break surface for you. Mind you now, this has to be quick. The skipper don't want us to be a blooming target out here."

Within minutes Harry could feel the sub angle upwards and then he heard the commotion of the rafts being unlashed. The next thing he knew the three of them were on the deck of the sub and easing down the ladder to the assault rafts.

"Mind you now lads, the rafts are all loaded with your 'stuff'; and all you have to do is please drop down into the rafts and not into the drink." One of the frogmen said.

No sooner than the warning had been given, Al Keesling slipped crawling down the ladder and all but fell into the bitter cold North Channel waters.

"Easy lad, you're not a blooming halibut, you know. Just relax and we will have you in and then you can tie yourself to the slats. One of the frogmen joked as he pulled Al into the rubber raft. "I fancy that you yanks just ain't made for sea duty."

After the frogmen had secured Harry, Al, Jen, and the supplies that they would need once they reach the shore, they cut them loose from the submarine, which quickly submersed out of sight below the surface of the water.

Directing their attention to the shoreline some thousand yards away, they began to paddle as well as ride the crest of the waves on the in-going tide. About the time they had reached a point where they could hear the surf sounding on the beach, they observed a tiny flashing light, which they headed towards.

The landing on the beach was uneventful. The rubber raft slid up on a fortunately unoccupied and unguarded section of the beach and moments later the trio were met by the Dutch resistance fighters who gathered up the supplies and munitions that had been sent in, and hustled them off to a nearly demolished but deserted pillbox in a nearby heavily wooded area.

Moments later the frogmen swam the raft back out through the breakers to the waiting sub which broke water just long enough for the raft to be lashed to the rigging and then submerged to wait for what they all hoped would be a signal of success from the team. At that point the plan was for them to resurface and the frogmen would take the rafts in to bring the team and their quarry back to the sub for a rapid return to England, via Perth, Scotland.

Once they were inside, Harry questioned, "Weren't we supposed to meet Abher when we got here?"

In the shadows at the end of a small table, a hooded figure, raised his head and said, "You are as right as rain, Harry, and here I am. I'm glad to see that you recovered from North Africa and Colonel Middleton has you back with the team again. I knew about Al and Jen being back online again but I didn't know for sure what your status was. I'm glad you're here because I think it will help us clear up some questions that we still have.

"To begin with, getting Janish's mother and sister out of here is probably going to be simpler than we thought. They had been allowed to return to the mother's home in Delft. The control on them seems to be primarily that they are checked off each day when they report to work at the pottery factory that Field Marshal Goring is so interested in. They seem to be exquisite artists and had been given some privileges because of that.

"We have been in contact with them through the underground and they are ready to leave at a moment's notice, so we have projected to pick them up tomorrow night by RAF airlift. They will not be missed until the following morning at the earliest, and by then we will have them safely in England.

"Janish and Monier are another matter. I am not aware of the latest evaluation of their status since I have been unable to communicate directly with Colonel Middleton since he has completed his evaluation with you, Harry. How about a quick fill-in?"

"After talking with Colonel Middleton and Major McFarland I am even more convinced that Janish is clean and that Monier is the Red Herring. After all, didn't Monier turn you over to the Germans?"

"Not exactly. Janish, Monier and I were picked up by that German Patrol when your pickup plane left, and from the next day on we never saw one another. I was lucky, and when my prison patrol truck was strafed by American fighters and rolled over and killed the driver and guard I managed to get away and got picked up by the Free French who have protected me ever since, and even smuggled me up here.

"As to Janish, the underground tells me that he is being held at a German checkpoint on the outskirts of Delft, and they are attempting to use him to break our codes by putting pressure on him and/or his mother and sister.

We know that Monier is at another location in nearby Goda, and seems to be 'held' by the Germans, but we are not certain what his status is. The Dutch underground believes he is a 'Quisling informer' and that he is playing both sides against each other. They also have information from the French underground that leads them to believe that he was planted by the Germans into the Free French of North Africa as an informant.

The only solution to this problem, based on the information you have given me, and what little I have been able to get from OSS in England is that we either kill both of them or get both of them out of here to England because there is no question with the upcoming invasion they can breach our security and our codes because there simply is not time enough to change everything because of these two.

"So, with the assistance of the Dutch underground we are prepared to raid both holding areas and bring the two of them out or kill them, whichever seems to be the most practical solution at the moment.

"Harry, you and Jen were the closest to Janish so we are depending upon you to go with the underground unit that goes to where he is being held, and based on your judgment either bring him out or kill him.

"Al, you and I, along with another Dutch underground unit will go to the location where we know that Monier is, and either bring him out alive if possible or kill him. We simply can't take a chance on having our codes and securities breached this close to the invasion."

Harry, Al, and Jen took a collective deep breath and looked at one another with the realization that they were being asked to make a judgment, and based on that judgment to kill another person. On the other hand, it was evident to them that they all realized the gravity of the situation and the needs for decisive action.

Fritz Steen, the leader of the underground for this area, took over and explained the finer details of the two-pronged action. Fritz would be in the group that went with Harry and Jen to evaluate and retrieve Janish. His knowledge of the village and building that Janish was being held in would be invaluable; however, he made it clear that the decision to either bring him out or kill him was not one that he would make. Jen also affirmed that he would not make the decision whether or not to kill Janish. That would be left up to Harry.

Fritz went on to say that overcoming the guards and securing the village and route to the air pickup site had been practiced and that it should present no problem.

Eli Loonsten was in charge of the resistance group that would be working with Abher and Al Keesling. He said their task would be somewhat more difficult than Harry and Jen's. Monier was in a larger village than Janish, and there would be the possibility of a 'firefight' in order to take the German block house where Monier was known to be. However, he had no qualms about the operation and expressed complete confidence that everything would come off as planned, and that both of the 'targets' would be taken and delivered for the pick-up the following night.

Once the planning and logistics had been completed the entire group either turned in for some much-needed sleep, or disbanded until the next evening.

CHAPTER FORTY

"Harry, jen, al, time to rise and shine." Captain Abher announced. It's nearly midnight and the underground will have the two women here any minute. We may need to help with the rigging for the pickup. The planes are due in exactly 15 minutes after midnight. By then we have to have the frames up and the harnesses set up so that when they come down with their hooks they can scoop both passengers up at once.

Moments later two hooded figures were brought into the old pillbox and introduced as Ella and Gudrun VanKeelen; Janish's mother and sister. While both of them spoke halting English, Fritz Steen explained in Dutch what was expected of them and what was the procedure that would be followed.

With that they set out for the pickup station and found that the other underground members had already set up the pickup framework and set out and lighted the target line lights, and all the women had to do was step into the rigging and wait for the planes.

Moments later the two transports, under RAF fighter coverage, circled and swooped down and the 'packages' were scooped up and on their way across the Channel and to the safety of England.

As quickly as it had been set up the rigging and guide lights were disassembled and extinguished and buried in the underbrush nearby. Three hours later a coded signal was received that the women were safely in Perth, Scotland.

"Well boys, now comes the sticky part. Abher said. "We have to be ready to snatch or kill both of the targets tomorrow night and there will be no chances for a second go at it. You might as well face it; there will be either some dead Germans or some dead Americans and Dutch. Let's be damn sure it isn't us."

"In the meanwhile, let's get some sleep because we won't be getting any tomorrow. Our underground friends are going to fade back into their natural places, but they will be there when we need them tomorrow. The 'krauts' will put two and two together pretty fast, and when they find that the VanKeelen women do not show up for work tomorrow they will come looking. The neighbors will tell them that they went to visit another fictional sister in Arnhem which should let us get through the day, but we will have to hit our two targets tomorrow night without fail. There will be no moon so we will have the advantage of total darkness."

True to their word, as Harry and Jen started to check out their equipment Eli Loonsten and three other resistance fighters appeared at the hiding place, and moments later Fritz Steen appeared with three friends. It was decided that Eli's group would go with Abher and Al, and Fritz Steen's group would go with Harry and Jen.

Fritz had brought a horse drawn cart filled with hay and manure, as had Eli. These would be used to hide the assault teams under the hay so that they could move into the town areas, as it was normal for farmers to bring their animals and carts into the villages at any hour of the evening.

Harry and Jen, along with two Dutch crawled under the hay while the third member of the Dutch team led the horse. The same arrangements were made for Abher and Al.

After about thirty minutes of jostling along Harry heard Fritz Steen whisper, "We pretty near there now. You be ready to crawl out from there and we rush the place. Yes?"

And a few minutes later Harry heard, "Out, now. We here and we go in for Janish. Yes?"

Harry slipped out of the back of the hayrack and along with Jen and the two Dutch crept up to the side of a building where he could clearly see Janish through the window. There was no question, he was a prisoner. He was handcuffed and chained to the wall. While they were considering the best way to free Janish a truck pulled up to the front of the building and containers of food were taken in. After the truck left the two guards set the food on the table and then unchained Janish from the wall and brought him to the table where it appeared they intended to re-chain him.

Harry and Jen looked at each other and silently agreed that this was the opportunity they had been looking for and now was the moment to strike. Bursting through the door Jen killed the two guards while Harry was pushing a very willing Janish out of the door when a door they had not seen opened and another guard with a Lugar pistol emerged.

Harry shot at him and missed, and the guard fired a burst at Harry striking his steel helmet with one of the bullets which ricocheted before Harry, with a second burst from his Thompson machine gun, killed him. Harry grabbed up the Lugar from the floor and stuffed it into his assault gear pocket in case of the need for another weapon. As Harry turned to run out of the door to follow the Dutch fighters and Janish, he stumbled over the body of one of the Dutch underground resistance fighters. He began to lift the man to drag him out when he saw that his eyes were blank and that he was dead. There was a ragged bullet hole in his forehead.

Harry suddenly realized that the shot that had hit his helmet had shrapnelized and ricocheted into the skull of the young man and killed him. Harry stood there, frozen in his tracks. Jen came back into the building and dragged Harry out and to the hayrack which was slowly moving out of town.

Harry was sick with the realization that if he had not missed or been so slow in reacting the young man would still be alive. All the way back to the pillbox he retched and shook with the realization.

When they got to the pillbox both Jen and the now freed Janish tried to console him. Thirty minutes later when Abher and Al Keesling came back with the report that Monier had sided with the Germans for protection and that they and their group had killed him and six German guards with no significant injury or any loss of lives, Harry was still beside himself. He felt that he was a piranha to his own kind.

Finally Abher grabbed him by the shoulders and shaking him, said "God Damn it Harry, get hold of yourself, man.

People die in this God Damn war. Be sorry for the man but you still have to go on. Now shape up."

"Yah, Harry. The now un-shackled and freed Janish said while he grabbed Harry in a bear-hug. "That feller knew what he was up against. We Dutch all knew that we could be killed by the Germans for just crossing the street the wrong way at the wrong time. His name will live on and we will all remember Hans for his bravery. It was not your fault. It was just his time."

With that Janish leapt up and, giving Abher a lusty bear hug, planted a kiss on each cheek as he said, "You make my heart happy forever, Captain.

"Okay! But enough for now. We have to get out of here you know, so we better start moving right now. Are all of us ready? Good! Let's head for the beach. I am going to send the signal to the sub to be ready to pick us up in forty-five minutes. That should give us time to get there and be in the surf waiting for the frogmen and their raft. I will be going with you this time as my job is done here until the invasion. The underground unit has created a diversion commotion which you can hear going on now as a cover for our movement." Abher said.

As they moved out of the pillbox and toward the beach they could hear the explosions of the undergrounds mischief and to their relief saw the beach completely void of patrols which had responded to the blowing of a minor dyke by the underground.

Reaching the beach the group waded out into the surf and within moments were greeted by the British frogmen with two rafts which they quickly paddled and pushed out to the waiting sub.

At one point a large spotlight from the shore swept across and momentarily focused on them, however, seconds later the sub's deck gun fired three rounds and extinguished the light and the threat to them. Within five more minutes the entire party was securely inside the sub which quickly submerged and sped on its way to its base at Perth, Scotland.

CHAPTER FORTY-ONE

―――――――

Once a round of hot tea and coffee had been passed around Al said, "Well it looks like we pulled it off, didn't we? We got Janish and his family out and now we have to figure out what we know and where we go from here, Eh?"

Janish looked up and addressing the group and the OSS and M-5 officers, said, "I think it time you listen to what I have to say, okay? We need to talk about what that Monier tried to do and what I found out about him and the 'krauts' and what they want to do.

Janish went on. "Them Krauts think that there will be an invasion, that is for sure. They think that it will come up around Dieppe where the Englishers tried a raid one time, and where they bragged they chased them off. They think maybe, too, that it will come here on the Dutch coast because we got such a good underground to help with the invasion. They brag they got over a million man army sitting in Belgium to go either way and the Hitler says he knows that anything else that looks like an invasion is just a make believe to pull them out of place.

"Now for that Monier! He was a spy!"

Al interrupted, "You really know that for sure? You weren't being held at the same place. How could you know what he did?"

'Hah! That's what them krauts wanted me and you to think. But the woman that makes the food for krauts and once in a while goes to where he is says he sits around with the SS and every question they ask he tries to answer and then explain what I tell them, which is foolishness and they don't believe that either.

"One time they brought him here to where they had me chained up and chained him up like me. Then he acted like he was a friend, but from the questions he was asking I could see that all he wanted was information about the OSS and M-5 operations. You could tell he did not know anything from the inside and he wanted me to tell him about us. I didn't do it, but I told him if they would bring my mama and sister from the concentration camp in Germany and let them go back to work at the Delft factory, I would tell him things."

"When they showed me that mama and Gudren was back in our house, then I told them a whole bunch of foolishness. I made up that we had a million men in the OSS and Rangers and that they were going to land in Amsterdam and Hamburg and Berlin all at one time.

"I know that Monier was a spy for sure because after they took him away from me, here, then they come and pounded on me and then with their stories that they knew so much, and it was the same as I made up so he had to tell them. He was a spy alright. What you call a 'mole', not so Captain?"

The M-5 officer nodded and after conferring with the senior OSS officer said, "Janish, you have passed the test and as Monier is dead, this chapter is closed. We are not going to send you in again until we are well into Holland with considerable armed forces, but consider yourself back on the team. We should be getting into Perth in a few hours and you can consider yourself on duty again, but inactive and free to relax. All suspicion is removed from you."

"The rest of you on this mission are returned to your OSS command and will be given a 7 day leave to London."

"You know what I'm gonna do, don't you Al?" Harry said.

"No! Go on a seven day drunk with me and Abher and Paul?"

"Hell, No! Get Married! I got the prettiest girl in the Army Nurse Corp waiting for me at the hospital in Harrow. I'm going to get married."

Once Harry, Jen Paul, Janish, Al Keesling, and Captain Abher, had a good night's sleep and had been through primary debriefing they were all returned to their primary training station, Maude Glen. When they arrived the orderly advised Harry that Colonel Middleton wanted to see him.

"You wished to see me, Colonel?" Harry asked as he entered the Colonel's office.

"Yes, my boy. Take a chair. I have some information for you that will unfortunately be quite disquieting, I am sure."

"Oh? What can that be Colonel? The mission went okay, didn't it? We all got back in one piece and Captain Aker and you are satisfied that Monier, who is now dead, was the one that had tipped the Germans off to our mission in North Africa. I would have thought you would be pleased at this point"

"As far as the mission and the work you men did on your raid, it could not have been better. I am completely satisfied with the outcome. Moving forward in his chair, the Colonel assumed what appeared to Harry to be a more personal attitude, as he began.

"Harry, this is something that involves you and your aspirations, and I am distressed to have to bring this to you".

"What, Sir?"

"I really don't know any other way to tell this to you other than straight off the cuff; we have it, with confirmation, that your intended bride, Captain Sally Archer has been killed during an air raid while visiting in London."

A speechless Harry slumped back into the chair as the Colonel continued.

"Her former commanding officer, Major Martin, who was your attending physician during your rehab, had given her a seven day leave before she was to return to Colonel Hawthorn's American nursing group. Captain Archer chose to go to London to use Major Martin' sister's vacant flat, and while she was there it was directly hit by a German plane that had been shot down with a fully activated bomb load aboard. It totally disintegrated the building and all that was found were five totally burned and unidentifiable corpses, two of which were women, and Captain Archer's dog tags and one set of her Captain's bars.

"When Captain Archer did not return to her American Nursing unit at Harrow, her commanding officer, Colonel

Hawthorn totally dismissing the notion of her having deserted, contacted Major Martin who in turn contacted his sister who made a quick trip to London from her station in Brighton.

"Miss Martin found that her flat and building had been totally destroyed and when they checked the timing of Captain Archer's arrival at London and the plane's crash they matched. Then Miss Martin checked with the Fire Brigade and they advised her of the finding of the corpses and Captain Archer's dog tags and Captain's bar, and that the effects had been turned over to American Grave's registration. She went there and all of what I have told you has been documented and her effects left there. I am sorry, so very sorry for you, my boy. Is there anything we here can do for you?"

For the longest time Harry was beyond acceptance and unable to speak. Finally he said, "Yes Sir. I would like a Leave to go to London and see the information at Grave's Registration for myself if you can arrange it."

"Of course, I believe that we can immediately place you on detached duty, and I will arrange your Leave of seven days at once. You have my and the entire staff's condolences. I hope you will be able to find a way through this because Major McFarland and I believe you have a grand future in our organization.

"Though this is of little consolation at this point, paperwork is going through to promote you to the rank of Major. Your service to OSS and M-5 has been most valuable and this promotion is totally in keeping."

A devastated Harry, stood, saluted his commanding officer and all but stumbling retreated to the outer office to wait while his Leave papers were being drawn up.

"Is this the American Graves Registration Office?" Harry asked.

"Yep, what can I do for you Major?"

"My name is Major Harry Morgan and I have been referred here to see about the effects of a Captain Sally Archer, CRNA that you may have here."

"Let me check, we haven't many yet. 'Course that unfortunately is going to change after the invasion comes off, ain't it?

"Archer, Sally Ann, Captain. Yes this is all we have, sir. One fire-scorched Captain's bar and a chain with her two dog tags on it. The fire brigade people confirmed to us that one of the two unidentifiable corpses completely match her sex and size. They told us that it was an unquestionable identification and that she has been buried in a common grave in Canterbury. Sorry Major, that is all we have."

Harry stood, leaning on the counter, blindly staring at, for all the world, at all that was left of Sally.

The desk phone behind the Corporal-clerk rang, who excused himself to turn around to answer it. While he was attending to the phone call Harry picked up the tags and bars and tearfully pressed them to his face and lips. 'God, he thought was this all there was of Sally for him?' He could not leave all of her behind. He had to have something of her for himself. As the clerk was still busying himself with the phone call, Harry stuffed the scorched Captain's bar into his blouse pocket and blindly ran from the building.

How far Harry walked that afternoon, evening, and night is debatable. He walked from the Registration office, often bumping into other pedestrians and more than once he was restrained from walking into traffic by an English 'Bobbie'. When he finally became aware of himself he found a bench in St James Park and simply sat, and sat, and sat. His mind could not or would not comprehend that Sally was gone.

Finally it came to him that he must find a way to ease the anguish and pain that he was suffering, and that way was to volunteer for whatever missions would enable him to die as well. He knew that he could not take his own life, but maybe God would find a way through such service to take his life for him. Harry caught the next train back to Maude Glen and Colonel Middleton.

"Colonel, I have been to London and seen for myself that Captain Archer is truly gone. This is devastating for me and I need to ask for a duty that will extend me to the point where I can go on from this loss."

"Oh? Colonel Middleton asked, "And what might that be?"

"I understand that a special Ranger assault group is being put together for the up-coming invasion, and I wish to volunteer to be a member of that group. I think that I am steeled

Reflections

enough to handle it, and I am certain that I will no longer shirk duty when I see it.

"And to be perfectly truthful, Harry lied, "I have resolved my issues and losses and am anxious to get on with what life has in store for me. How about it Colonel?"

"Well! Yes we are considering placing a very select number of our OSS personnel in the forefront of the invasion forces, and yes, they will be part of a first surge Ranger group designed to scale the cliffs yet to be designated, and yes, you do have all of the training, but I still have reservation about you, Major. I will see how you do in the next week here, and will give my decision thereafter."

"Major Morgan, I have decided to accept your volunteering for Ranger duty. You and Major Keesling, who has also volunteered, will be transferred to a station designated as X-9 for specialized training. It seems as though the Ranger folks do not think we know how to climb a rope ladder or scale a cliff. At any rate, they assure you that this will be a physical test for both of you. But, I think you two will show them that we know how to prepare. I have talked to Major Keesling earlier, and he is now packing for the jitney over to X-9, so with my best wishes, you need to be on your way."

"Thank you Sir." Harry snapped off brisk salute, turned on his heel, and left for what he anticipated to be the beginning of the final adventure and end of this life on this earth.

CHAPTER FORTY-TWO

It seemed to harry that of late he was spending all of his life in English mini-submarines. When he and Al arrived at Station X-9 they discovered that it was really a warehouse on one of the piers at Bournemouth, and their advanced training consisted of climbing up and down rope and pole ladders inside of the building. Additionally, they were instructed in quick departure from mini-subs and given a short course in frogman training. Neither enjoyed that, although the frog suits were insulated, the south channel waters were still both salty and bitter cold.

Once they had cleared the training program each were assigned to a different Ranger battalion as part of an initial assault team.

And now it was the evening of departure, except that due to a storm in the channel, the date for the assault was set back and Harry had to remain underwater for another twenty-four hours to wait to see how the weather conditions would change.

Finally the boat commander announced "Okay, Mates", over the intercom. "We have a go for it, so we will be moving in so that the 'sappers' can go over the side to cut loose the mines and underwater wire so you can have a nice Piccadilly London Strand to march right up to them there cliffs you have to crawl up like you was a bunch of blooming monkeys. Get your kits together because we will be up to surface in about fifteen minutes."

The bombardment from the combined offshore fleet's heavy guns had been raining down on the Normandy coast for nearly six hours when Harry, along with about fifty other Rangers, slid over the side of the sub. Harry was surprised to find that he was quite buoyant in the salt water, and with the flipper feet, as the English called them, was able to quite silently move in toward shore. His entire group reached the shore undetected and were about to run for the cliffs when one of the frogmen reminded them that they would have to wait until the 'sappers' had cleared a mine free path for them. This took another anguishing thirty minutes when all of them felt that certainly the Germans on the cliffs above would begin firing upon them. But the heavy navel guns had the German defenders cowering in their bunkers or attempting to return the fire of the fleet.

Finally the path was cleared to the base of the cliff and Harry's group made a mad scramble for its protection only to find that the German's were rolling grenades over the edges upon them. Nevertheless, the climbing poles were assembled and with a minimum of casualties a small section of the cliff above was secured from which the rope ladders were dropped and the balance of the 'fighting fifty' as they called themselves, were able to scale and secure the entire section of nearly one hundred yards of access.

In the process of the securing and defended the rope setters Harry grabbed a German machine pistol with a belt of cartridges and hunted out and shot nearly twenty German defenders and brought in an additional forty that surrendered to him. He knew no fear, only a deeply rooted anger. All he could see before him was that the Germans had taken Sally from him and as long as he lasted, he would take as many of them with him as he could. Those that he had killed had offered varying resistance and those that surrendered to him threw down their arms and in some instances plead for their lives. He felt no mercy, only the need for retribution.

As Harry returned with his prisoners he met an advanced part of an Infantry Battalion who relieved him of his chargers, and also gave him some rations and whose non-com medic discovered that he had received a bullet wound in his lower leg, and gave him a chance to settle down and relax somewhat. His efforts were noted and he was rewarded with a Silver Star and a field promotion to Lieutenant Colonel. by the Regimental Commander.

Harry was returned to England for a fourteen-day rehabilitation leave after which he was posted to Station X-9 s an advanced tactics training officer. This occupied the next 90 days of his tour of duty until he because so agitated for action that Colonel Middleton reposted him to active service as a special observer from Aachen to the Rhine in the area across from of Dusseldorf and Cologne, where he came in contact with the 294th Forward Observation Battalion, and more particularly Sgt. Norman Cone and Corporals Lew Collat, Gus Kelly, Mel Ossoff, and Austin Shepard. Each of these non-commissioned officers were advanced observers who operated at great personal risk, with and beyond the infantry front lines in successful efforts to seek out German munition concentrations, heavy guns, and rockets sites, as well as troop concentrations and enabled Harry to seek out, pinpoint, and target a German 'Big Bertha' railroad gun that had been ravishing Allied troop and Military concentrations at will.

Harry was highly attracted to these highly dangerous areas and sites and spent much time with these outposts. While the outposts were bypassed and over-run by German troops, they were never occupied in direct battle as Harry was on the D-day onslaught at Normandy.

Harry moved on with the 294th in the crossing of the Rhine, and later up through Castle and Brunswick to the crossing of the Elbe and led a group that supported a Scottish brigade which rushed through Schwerin on to Rostoff and Lubeck to thwart a Russian effort to strip the harbor of it shipping before the British-American troops could secure it.

The Unit was instrumental in the liberation of the Ludwigslust and Wobbelin Slave Labor and Concentration Camps near the Hagenow Concentration Camp where the physical evidence of the sheer brutality and misery further embittered Harry. After these actions Harry was promoted to full Colonel and received his third and fourth battle star and an oak leaf cluster on his purple heart.

And now the War in Europe was over and Harry was confronted with what he should do next. Of course, there was still the war in the Pacific, and he could take out his anguish on the Japs as well as the Germans. After all, it was this war which had found him his greatest joy, and it had also taken that joy away from him. It didn't matter if it was German or Japanese. It was still the war and he was going to get over there. Even though he had points and decorations which would allow him to retire from the service at his discretion, he was still at war with those that that had hurt him.

It did not take Harry long to get himself on one of the first transports headed back to the states, and after the mandatory 30 day furlough with the retirement option, he intended to head straight for the west coast and the 'next' war.

He had learned that his mother had passed on during his absence, and that he would have to stop at Troy to see Lawyer Vance to close out estate issues, but as soon as that was done he would continue on to the Ports of Embarkation on the West Coast.

CHAPTER FORTY-THREE

The Homecoming

"Gladys! Are you sure that all of this damn foolishness that we're going to over Morgan is worth it? The closer it gets, the more I wonder what sense there is to it!"

"William David Bender, don't you dare back down on me now! After all, let's not forget who got the bright idea to turn this into a circus. I'm not the one that said we can use this against the union push. All I ever said was that it would make it a lot easier to get the people back to the company if they saw Morgan and all his medals getting back into place again, now that the war is over."

"I know, but what if he decides he doesn't want to come back to town? Just because he agreed to that meeting with old lawyer Vance that you trumped up about his mother's things don't mean that he won't go somewhere else. That whole business you women got worked out at the train station with `Cully' Whipple giving him the key to the city, and...."

"Now, W. D., stop worrying about the mayor. If he can't make a five line speech and pin that key and ribbon on him, then you can do it."

"And that's another thing, Gladys, I don't like giving him, or for that matter, anybody, a damn job with a promotion, in front of that many witnesses."

"Look, W. D., you've never had any trouble with promises or witnesses before. One thing that always impressed me about you was that you could turn that tongue of yours around a phrase so well that not one person I ever saw--except me, of course--ever knew that all that cake you had been sharing for all these years was no more than the stale crumbs you were shaking out to the wind...."

"So why change, then? If it worked before...."

"Because it's a whole new breed that's coming back. You need them in our factory, and you need one of theirs to use to handle them. Do you think for one minute that what worked for us when we gave them a quarter an hour and made them happy, because they never got even as far as Fort Wayne except on the company excursion bus, will work with people that have been all the way to London and Paris, and even Australia?"

"Good God, man, if you want to control them you are going to have to show them something! You can believe for a fact that now that the war is over the unions are going after them. They'll show them something! You can count on that much!"

"Yes, Gladys, we used that patriotic, no strike, all for the war effort angle pretty well, didn't we?"

"Of course we did, but that's over with the war. If you want to run your plant the way you did before the war, you are going to have to use "him" to do it for you."

"I suppose you're right, mother, but I just can't hardly stomach him! So he got lucky and got some medals, and they gave him all sorts of promotions; that still don't make him one of our kind! Why, even now I don't know what ever possessed me to let you talk me into letting him take Irene out before he went overseas. I'll tell you one thing, he needn't think about doing any more of that, now!"

Gladys smiled at W. D., and getting up, began to clear the breakfast dishes that they had been talking over as she continued the conversation- to herself.

"W. D., I do love you, but there are times when you can't see what's going on right under your nose. But, I guess that's just as well. If you knew that he not only took Irene out, but right on our back porch couch took her virtue, you'd never sleep again until you had destroyed him--when it makes so much more sense to "gut" him a little bit at a time by using him to control the other people, and making him love the power so much that we can exterminate him by taking it from him when he thinks it's all his for the keeping.

"I'd even give him Irene, just to enjoy watching him dissolve when we take her away from him again. From what she told me, he took her here three or four times here, and then he saw her at Smith and he took her another three or four times, there. I still can't believe that he didn't talk her into that purge she said she use, and I'm surprised that it didn't kill her. No, his time has just about come, but in more ways than one!"

"Cully! Will you quit shining your shoes on your pant legs! And let me tie that tie right for you. You look like a man who's expecting his first baby, and you with nine. Shame on you. Brace Up!"

"Well, Mrs. Bender, if this was another baby I wouldn't be nervous. I got lots of experience all the way round with babies, but I ain't never made a speech in front of people before. There just never been no call for it since I got to be mayor. Why there ain't nobody ever run against me in the twenty-five years since I got appointed to fill out the term when old Calvin Wanschnieder run off after the Harding scandal. They was too busy looking for the lost tax money to think about speeches, and that suited me just fine because I never had to worry about having to make no promises or keeping any, neither."

"No, I just naturally don't take to speeches, and I just never was much shined up to what you call the prestige part of this job. I expect I'm what you call a working mayor."

Gladys found it was all she could do to keep from rolling her eyes right out of the top of her head, and covering her suppressed grin with her hand, she returned, "All right Cully, you look just fine now. Leave that tie alone and go down and see if Professor Dietzson has the City Band all collected and tell them to go into the freight house, quick, and practice playing 'The Stars and Stripes Forever,' 'For He's a Jolly Good Fellow,' and 'Back Home Again in Indiana.' Oh, you tell him that if he misses my cue for 'Hail, Hail, the Gangs all Here,' I promise him I will absolutely cancel the company donation to the band picnic for the rest of his life! When I shake Colonel Morgan's hand, the band plays for all they are worth, regardless of if Mr. Bender is speaking or what's going on!"

"Yes, Ma'am, consider it done!"

"Mother?"

"What do you want, Irene?"

"What do I get to do?"

"You give him the bouquet of carnations."

"Wouldn't it be more exciting if I give him a kiss, too?"

"With your father watching? Do you want him to have a stroke?"

"Why not?"

"Why not your father should have a stroke??"

"No! Why not a kiss? We're engaged!"

"*Were engaged!* And your father never knew about that, either. I had the devil's own time with him getting him to think that ring was a dime store friendship ring. I still think he got it in a dime store, anyway."

"Well, I still think I ought to get to kiss him. You can bet that Mary-Lynn Farley tries to kiss him, and she never even went out with him; anyway, not the way I did!"

"Look, young lady, I haven't got the time to settle with you now. We are right here in front of everybody on this station platform, the train with your "hero" will be here any minute, your father is ready to bolt, run, and chuck the whole idea, and you want to really start something by acting up and kissing! Didn't you get into enough trouble with what started out with just kissing on our back porch? I just wish I had come down to let the cat out a half hour earlier and you wouldn't have gotten yourself mixed up with these crazy notions."

"Mother, I just want to kiss him. It's not what you think. I can kiss a hero and not get that way about him. Besides, we were engaged and that ought to mean something. It wasn't like we didn't make promises."

"Look, drop it! There were no promises, just mistakes!"

"MOTHER!"

"All right, hush! Kiss him then, but only on the cheek, and if I shake my head, absolutely not! I will not have your father lose his temper over you and that Morgan on this day. I will not have your father made a fool of because of your foolishness!"

"Yes, mother."

"Gladys! What are you and Irene prattling about? Now where did the mayor go? What happened to him? Why do I let you talk me into these idiotic things?"

"Colonel, better wake up now. Troy's just a short piece around the bend. You got, maybe two, three minutes before we pull in, and it ain't but a two minute stop once we get there."

Harry, shaking the hand from his shoulder and the sleep from his brain, looked past the conductor and through the windows across the train car to see the smoke stacks of the Bender Company march into sight.

"Take the platform at the front of the car, Colonel. `Brings you right on the station platform. Besides, I ain't gonna open the back one."

As he waited for the conductor to open the door of the car, Harry noticed that the City Band was trying to get into some sort of formation and order on the end of the platform, and that there were a lot of people standing around the station platform as though they were waiting for someone.

It had been over three years since he had been in town and while the community didn't look much different, the people did. They didn't have the marks of the brutality and inhumanity of their fellow man that he had seen all over Europe, but there was that same look of hope and expectancy that he had seen everywhere since the end of the war. It was as though the air was full of freedom and the people were full of the hope of finding a way to share in it. And yet, they were still the same, and some would miss all of it, most would never change, only wonder.

Morgan was pretty sure that he had seen Cully Whipple, but then he recalled that he had never seen Cully out of his grocery clerk's apron before, so he couldn't be sure. He had no doubt that he had seen old man Bender, nervously standing behind Whipple, and Mrs. Bender beside him seemed to be standing guard over both of them.

His first awareness of Irene was really the jerking about of the enormous bouquet of carnations that she held. For a moment he felt the urge to go back into the coach and ride on to the next stop, but then he remembered that he had heard that Bob Bender had gone into the Air Force and was a pilot on a bomber in the Pacific. He decided that this welcoming was certainly for Bob, and he would be able to slip unnoticed from the train.

Stepping from the train, he began to move down the platform and away from the crowd, but as he did so, eager hands reached out and turning him around, marshaled him to the front of the nervously shaking Cully Whipple, who while clawing at his tie was doing his utmost to respond to the restive 'harrumphs' of Old Man Bender and the prodding of a skittish Mrs. Bender.

"Well, Colonel Morgan, sir," Cully Whipple began, "Colonel, we here in Troy welcome you back and on account of you being a hero in the war, I gets to give you the key to this here city. `Course, there ain't nothin' here worth locking up, but all the same, this here is the first key we ever give to anybody, and that says something for what people hereabouts think about you. There it is! And, very truly yours!"

His speech and moment of mixed anxiety and glory completed, Cully jumped back from an utterly perplexed Harry and as he slid around behind Mr. Bender he congratulated himself on having had the good fortune and nerve to get through all of it. He was particularly proud of how he had finished the speech; just like the end of some of the fine letters that he had seen Mr. Marchowsky down at the grocery store get from the big suppliers in Terre Haute, and Indianapolis. "Why, they couldn't hardly do any better than that!" he smiled to himself.

Suddenly remembering that he hadn't finished all that he needed to say after all, he peered around Mr. Bender and blurted out, "Oh, I clean near forgot; Mr. Bender, here, wants to say some more nice things about you. Ain't, that right?"

Trying to suppress an exasperated glare in the direction of Cully and repress the urge to never again speak or listen to his wife, W. D. Bender moved forward, beginning, "Harrumph! Yes, Harry, my boy, or now I should say, Colonel. I speak for all of the fine and grateful citizens of Troy when I clasp your hand in mine and tell you 'Well Done'.

"When I clasp your hand in mine, it takes me to a time many years ago when I held in very much the same manner the same hand of a fair youth of one of our cherished employees--oh that she could have lived to share this finest hour with us--and pressed into those dear and trusting fingers his very first coin, and as an unselfish and loving elder spoke words of counsel, of frugality, and of loyalty to such an innocent and trusting youth.

"Oh, words cannot be found that can express my joy at seeing that you have taken those paternal admonitions and used them as your staff and guide to lead your country's forces to glorious victories, and having done so, now lay down your sword and stand ready and eager to beat it into plowshares, and have returned to your succor to resume your former tasks and place in life.

"Ah, such is what true and loyal Americans are made from. But, there is more. Much more! We have not let you, nor any of our other sons and daughters suffer the slings and darts of our cruel enemies, and thereby risk all without preparing for you an added measure of reward. We do not ask you to forget your brothers and sisters that have fallen and to close your eyes to the great American dream of freedom from persecution and want, nor to the great victories that you have sacrificed for.

"We stand in the vanguard of your attendance and four square in the lead to shower you, and all like you, with the fruits of your victory. You shall not need others to speak for you nor to take up your cause, because your cause as young returning working men and women shall be our cause. The doors to our industry and the paths to our hearts shall ever be wide to you and yours. Your concern shall be ours, we shall be as of one pulse, for we shall look to you as our children and shall counsel you as we do our very own.

"Our hearts are full, and as a token of our great pride and intention, I pin this medal honoring you in behalf of your returning brothers and sisters as the First Son of the city of Troy, and with these beautiful carnations donated from Mrs. Ivan Mellot's flower shop on Caswell Street, which you are about to receive, we tell you how proud we are of you.

"As for the Bender Company, I am proud to tell you that not only is your old job waiting for you; we have a new and important position for you as……….."

"I have to shake your hand, Colonel Morgan! We are all so proud of you….." Gladys' interruption was completely blown away, as was almost everything else on the platform by the explosion of the City Band's rendition of `Hail, Hail, The Gang's All Here`,…except for the three slide-trombone players who were reading and blazing away at Morton Hertell's music that he had forgotten to change from the `Stars and Stripes Forever.

In the confusion, Irene slid past her otherwise watchful mother and father and stretching up on her tiptoes, crushed the carnations into Harry's hands, herself into his arms, and wetly sliding her lips across his cheek to his mouth and then to his ear, as she just loudly enough whispered through the commotion, "If you remember what we did on our back porch, I do too."

Quickly drawing back, she searched Harry's unbelieving face for a sign of recognition or concurrence, and finding none that she could identify, self-consciously fell back into the crowd of well-wishers who were now pressing in on Harry. A smug Gladys looked across the throng at her husband, daring him to deny that this was not an absolute success. They had more than the tools of success; she was certain that they now held the weapon of control and the key to their empire.

A wretchedly disconsolate Harry's reaction was, "Drivel!" He had learned enough to know when he was being used, and if that was the game, he would stick around for a few hands. He felt the emptiness being filled with anger and then the anger and hate came in full measure again, like foam of acid. God, it even felt good!

It was like there was a purpose for his life again. He had never felt this enthused since before he lost his beloved Sally, and for a time it puzzled him that he could have such feelings for destroying, and that it was so much like and almost as thrilling as the enthusiasm he had for loving and wanting Sally.

While it had puzzled him at first, it later caused him concern, and finally it began to worry him until he found that he was questioning his sanity for a time, but then one warm summer Saturday afternoon as he sat hidden among the willows, alongside the lake, the answers came to him.

He had earlier found that he had to find a place where he could shut the world away from his mind. He performed his job at the Company in a pristine manner and without compassion or regard, held to the line that produced the most benefit and production for the effort involved. He had been given his job back, but within a few weeks of his return, he was called in by Mr. Breitweizer and told that he had been advanced to production assistant, and consistent with the new technology that was all the rage since the war, his responsibility would be for the expeditious movement and quality control of the factory. It would also be his job to keep an eye out for unrest among the people, as, while wages would be increased whenever and wherever possible, the Company would have to move with caution. He would be expected to use his position and prestige as a returned war hero to show the people the advantages of being patient and compliant.

Harry fully acknowledged to himself that he found great satisfaction in the power that he found himself holding over the people in the plant as well as the degree to which he was able to isolate the Benders and their management from the people.

It was not long before he found that it would take very little for him to control the emotions as well as the minds of the workforce. They had come to look to him as the answer to the questions that he had seen in the eyes at the train station, and he reveled in how he was able to play at manipulations with them. He knew he had them, and knowing that, he put them aside and no longer `played' for them. His subconscious began to tell him that it was time to prepare for bigger game.

He had taken a room at the old Blackhawk Hotel and while he ate most of his meals at one of the small corner tables in the dining room, he spent little time in the lobby, and when the weather was good, tried to stay out of the oppressiveness of his tasteless room.

He had rediscovered the hidden fishing spot of his childhood, out behind the heavy willows near the stone lake bridge. Without question, this was the place where he felt the most comfortable and was able to work at piecing his life together again.

He always took a pole and some bait with him, but the bottom of his tackle box was filled with two loaded pistols and a mangled Captain's bar. Many afternoons were spent without ever un-reeling the lines or baiting and casting out of the hook. For the most part, his time was spent looking out across the water, occasionally cleaning or loading and unloading first one and then the other of the pistols, but always holding or looking at the bar that was the only bridge to the lost happiness of his entire life.

Harry often thought that it was strange that he could not cry or even feel emotion welling up in his throat. There were times that he thought something that might have passed for a prayer to help him to feel for what he could not.

For the most part, he merely sat motionless, staring at where the water met the sky, hoping for something to put meaning and purpose into his life again as it had for such a few short months, which now seemed so very far away in England, and so very long ago.

CHAPTER FORTY-FOUR

It was a day that he was glad was Saturday. He had worked at the plant until the customary noon closing time, and then stopped by the Hotel, and had the cook put him up a couple of sandwiches and a thermos of coffee. He went up to his room and got his tackle box and the telescoping casting rod with his new reel, and headed out along the willow road to his `fishing spot.'

As he was about to break through the heavy willows along the side of the road to find his favorite fishing and meditation place along the bank, he became aware of a drunken Charlie Harris staggering up the road closely followed by a blue Chrysler convertible roaring wildly around the bend of the gravel road and hitting Charlie with its front fender knocking him into the ditch, and then totally veering out of control and nearly hitting the now diving Harry. The car continued on showering him with gravel and dirt and running over his tackle box and the prized rod as it finally crashing into the end buttress of the massive stone bridge, where it overturned, throwing its occupant, Mr. Bender, into the lake water where he, striking his head on a submerged rock, lay motionless.

Harry paid no attention to Mr. Bender. His concern was for his tackle box and its precious contents. As he searched for his scattered tackle box he came upon Charlie Harris in the ditch and told him he had better get out of the area before the police arrived. Beyond that his attention was directed to clambering back onto the roadway and surveying the mangled remains of his fishing rod and reel and looking for the scattered contents of his tackle box. The few pieces of tackle and artificial bait were scattered all along the road, and his two pistols were still jammed into the remains of the tackle box, but his cherished Captain's bar was nowhere to be found.

Harry methodically walked back and forth along the road, and when he could not find the bar, he began to nervously crawl along the road on his hands and knees—all the time ignoring the condition of Mr. Bender, until after the better part of a quarter hour when he happened to see a faint glimmer down in the ditch alongside the brackish water and mud.

Scrambling down to the glimmer, Harry found it to be his precious Captain's bar, and carefully cupping it in his hands, made his way to his place along the water's edge. After carefully wiping the dirt, but not the marks of the burns from his treasured Captain's bar, he tenderly pressed it to his cheek, and the tears that had never come since that day his heart was broken in that June that once seemed so long ago began and coursed down his cheeks as though they would never stop.

But, eventually they did, and when they stopped it was as though Harry had been drained of all that had made him responsive; that had made him able to love and to be loved. He remembered the joy with which he had looked at the world and the happiness that had filled him to the point of bursting his heart...and he knew it all stemmed from Sally, and he felt not just anguish, but robbed, gutted, and as dry inside as a forgotten slaughterhouse carcass.

He felt pure venom envelope him, and as it grew so did his enjoyment of it. There was a purpose about it. It gave him the need to live, just the way loving Sally had. It filled the void of the loss of Sally the way no other thing had. If the Bender families were 'using' him enough to almost hate him, he would show them what hate was. He would not only use them; he would destroy them. It was apparent that Mr. Bender was already gone through the accident. No never mind. He had been trained and honed by a war to a fine edge in the skill of hate. He had been taught to kill, and if it took that, he was still unemotionally capable. The war and the German's who had been responsible for the loss of Sally were a lot less personal about it than the Benders were, and he had taken some measure of satisfaction in killing those that had been remotely responsible for his losing his lovely Sally.

It would be very simple to transfer and concentrate his hate and vent his anger and aggressions against the Benders. The Benders would learn that he would never be used again by them, or by anyone else.

He would destroy their hold on him, the people of the community and the Bender Company, He would undermine them, and he would confront and destroy them. If he had to, he would take Irene from them and use her against them. If it was their purpose to conspire together against him, he would beat them and crush them into dust or even death at their own game.

As Harry gathered his belongings and clambered back onto the road he decided he had better report the accident and the apparent drowning of Mr. Bender to Police Chief Sweeney in Troy. By then Charlie Harris was nowhere in sight and Harry presumed that he had taken his advice and made himself scarce. He wondered how badly Charlie was hurt as a result of being hit by Mr. Bender's car, but when he got to the police station and reported the accident noting that Mr. Bender had lost control of his car and crashing into the stone buttress of the bridge, he made no mention of Charlie Harris. His only comments were that Mr. Bender came very close to hitting him before he crashed.

Harry was asked to ride out to the scene of the accident with Chief Sweeney and the city ambulance where it was confirmed that Mr. Bender had probably died, instantly of a fractured skull with further complications caused by being immersed in the lake.

As the Bender Company was the principal employer of the city of Troy this information as it moved through the city threw it into a near panic, however Gladys Bender, Mr. Bender's widow stepped into the breach and assured the community nothing would change after the mourning period. Mr. Breitweizer would continue as general manager and she would step in as president and chairman of the board on an interim basis.

CHAPTER FORTY-FIVE

Seizing upon the opportunity, Harry called upon Gladys and the Bender family to express his condolences, and to his surprise found a very appreciative Gladys, and sons Bob and Joe. Beyond that he was deeply surprised with the attention that Irene lavished upon him.

Even though he felt inwardly awkward he accepted the position of pallbearer for Mr. Bender and as such gathered with the family after the internment services. Again, Irene continued to show him unusual attention.

About a week later Mr. Breitweizer called him into his office where he found Gladys Bender as well. Gladys stated that she was going to make some changes in the company as a result of her husband's demise, however they would be on a temporary or 'let's see how they work out basis'. She announced that she was advancing Harry to the position of the Assistant to General Manager Breitweizer inasmuch as Mr. Breitweizer expected to be retiring within the next three or four years and it would be an opportunity to see if Harry could perform the job.

It also gave Harry and added opportunity to visit the Bender home for otherwise business purposes; however while he was there he noted that Irene still centered her attention upon him.

It did not take long for Harry to convince Irene that it would be a very good idea for the two of them to elope to Crown Point Indiana which had no marriage waiting period, and where they could just walk into any chapel and be married as long as they had a blood test.

This action on Harry's part and agreement on Irene's part completely upset Gladys and the rest of the Bender family but they held their peace as they agreed that the impulsive and volatile Irene would soon tire of the moody Harry. And as they predicted for one reason or another, this occurred.

However, while the marriage spawned barren, because of Harry's prime desire was to have a tie to the company, Irene's desires in respected to Harry were much most physical. Harry had no physical interest in her whatsoever because he still carried the image of Sally in his heart and in his eyes.

Finally, after about six months of inattention Irene stopped Harry before he bolted out the door for work and said, "We are going to talk this morning, and right now! Sit down at this kitchen table. Do you realize that you have not touched me in over three months? I get better look from the caddies of the country club. I am not going to put up with this Harry! We are either going to live like ordinary people or we are going to have a divorce! Which is?"

Harry hunched forward in his chair, put both elbows on the table and looking across said, "Irene, you just don't interest me that much. If you really want to know the truth, I married you in order to secure my job at the company, and I am not going to agree to a divorce so forget it!"

"What about all that jumping around on my folk's back porch and out at Smith College in Massachusetts when you were in the Army? Didn't that mean anything either?"

"All I can tell you Irene that was then and this is now. I have been through one war and one hell of a lot and things have changed and they can't change back! You can do what you damn please with your personal life—I really don't give a damn, but no divorce." And with that Harry turned on his heel and headed out the door to work.

About an hour later Gladys came by and Irene poured out her heart to her. Gladys sat and calmly listened and then told Irene to do exactly what Harry said. Go about her personal life and do not be concerned with what he thought about it anyway. Spend more time at the country club, take an outside job if she was that bored, join a couple of bridge clubs, even some social groups. Find a life of her own. There would come a day when they would have Harry boxed in and the two of them could call all the shots.

CHAPTER FORTY-SIX

THE WAR WAS OVER NOW and the young men and women that had survived their service were returning. Many were going to other locations but many were returning to their hometowns and seizing opportunities which had been created as a result of the war.

One of the young men that return to Troy was Lieutenant Commander Bob Harkness who had become somewhat of a war hero in the South Pacific by downing 16 Japanese aircraft. But Bob had had enough of war and was returning home with hopes of establishing a business in his old hometown. His father, Carl Harkness, was delighted to have Bob return because he had been nurturing a family insurance agency for the past five years hoping that Bob would return and take charge of it. It was a natural acquisition. Bob stepped in and after a few months training with the national company and adjusters, took off like a cannonball. His father had been successful, but Bob wrote a whole new chapter, in fact it became necessary to add personnel to the here-to-for one-man office in order to cover the added business that was being acquired.

While Bob's return was after Harry and Irene's elopement, even then he was so busy organizing his new company that he did not really have time to catch up on the local happenings around the town. He was not aware of the fact that Irene had been married until he happened to run into her at the country club one afternoon. Over couple of cocktails two old high school sweethearts brought themselves up to date, and the very frank Irene poured her broken heart out to Bob. She said her marriage to Harry had become a failure. She said she needed a job, a place where she could get out of the house some parts of the day.

Bob had never lost his infatuation for Irene and remembering that he needed to increase his office staff offered her an afternoon half-day position as receptionist and evening trainee for agent. He said it wouldn't pay much, but at least it would fill her requirements. Privately, he was excited to be in her presence again.

That evening Irene, with some trepidation, told Harry that she had taken a part-time job as a receptionist with some evening work in an insurance agency to give her something to do. His response was a grunt and just be sure to give me the phone number. He didn't even ask the name of the company.

When Irene started at Bob Harkness's office she found that it was somewhat of a shambles. There were three interview offices and a private back-office-room which had a hotplate, sink, coffeepot, and all the other necessities such as a restroom and a left over from Bob's dad's time there – a very nicely upholstered futon and reclining chair. Everything was in some disarray and she spent the first week alternately dusting and sneezing, but by the end of that time the office had taken on a sparkling appearance.

When Dad, Carl Harkness, dropped in to see how things were going he thought he was in the wrong office but at the same time was obviously immensely pleased with what he saw. Apparently the clientele were too because Bob's business literally exploded and he quickly became the outstanding insurance agency for that section of the state.

After about a week or so and things had settled down, Bob and Irene found themselves alone in the office in the early evening as a result of an appointment which had been canceled by an insured.

They were about to close things up early and leave for the evening when Bob asked Irene if she would like to finish off the coffee before they left. Irene very willingly agreed, and as they were getting the sugar, coffee, and cream together they came into moderate physical contact with one another, and it became enhancing.

Rather than sitting at opposite sides of the little coffee table in the service room they had sat side-by-side on the futon and in pouring the cream and adding the sugar they physically came in contact with one another – and they were quite aware of it.

"How long is this going to go on Irene? Bob asked "You know what we're doing don't you, and what this could be leading up to?"

"Yes. A very direct Irene answered. "This is where I should have been in the first place. I let my infatuations get away with me and it has cost me an awful lot and I don't know what to do about it, but that's why I'm here, because maybe we can do something about it on our own –if you want to.

"I don't know about you Bob, but I know that I need you and need you in every way. With the exception of two or three foolish instances back at the beginning of the war and one after the war, you will find me the same person that I was when we used to fool around in the rumble seat of your dad's old Buick. I am married in name only and I can't live on that way. Harry will not even touch me. Harry and I might as well live ten miles apart, 24 hours a day—certainly at night. Harry will not give me a divorce, nor has he given me any grounds for one.

"Mother says she believes she can come up with a plan where she can break my marriage but it will take a bit of time. My question to you Bob is; do you care for me, and do you care for me enough to let me have a part of you even though I am married to another man?

All of the time that Irene had been pouring out the details of her heart Bob had been sitting back in admiration of her and what she was going through. He had not considered that he would be asked to be a party to this contrivance, but now that it had been thrust upon him; did he really care for Irene? Did he care what Harry thought? Did he want to be involved with Irene? Suddenly he realized that he would have to make a decision and be prompt about it.

Answer 1, Yes, Answer 2 No, and Answer 3, he most assuredly wanted to hold Irene close to him because there was no question in his mind that they were in tune with one another, even more than before the war.

Bob silently took the coffee cup from Irene's hand and placed it and his on the table before the futon they were seated on, and wrapping her in his arms and kissed her deeply. Irene in turn almost weeping in gratitude wrapped her arms and body around Bob and kissed him and snuggled in as closely to him as she possibly could.

As the office was locked, and the room had no exterior windows there was no opportunity for anyone to witness the joy they found in each other. The room was most comfortably heated, finding a coverlet, in but a moment they had spread open the futon and searched through and shed each other's clothes and lay closely coupled in one another's arms, even more so than they had ever thought of in the prewar days in the backseat of dad Harkness's car.

What sexual experiences Irene had were with Harry. They had been on the aggressive if not savage side whereas Bob Harkness was the epitome of gentility. His every touch, his every caress, his every motion, his every intrusion with tongue or otherwise was as though it was the caress of a feather if not a gentle drift of a breeze. They lay together, immobile at times, undulating at others, compensating at still others as though they had been lovers from time immemorial. Their enjoyment was complete.

Bob and Irene discovered that their bodies fit one another. He was able to kiss her deeply at the same time that he could feel her breasts, firm against his chest, as he penetrated her as well. She was able to wrap her legs about his thighs, clamp down on him, and force her ample breasts up into his chest area as well as fully engage all of his sensuous parts. His penetration brought her an unexpected ecstasy such as she had never known of, much less expected. She tightly engaged and clutching him with all she had. Irene had never known such ecstasy. Bob had never known such unbridled response.

In their enjoyment, they found that when Irene chose to be on top she could still maintain the multiple areas of contact, and derive the multiple orgasms along with Bob. All in all, their sexual experience far exceeded anything either had anticipated or expected.

As Irene's hours of employment were late in the day and after regular working hours this allowed for this kind of repeated relationship without any suspicion.

Harry generally ate his evening meals with some of the men of plant or at the Hotel, and as in the past, it was a very normal course for Irene to have to eat her evening meals and spend her evenings alone as Harry would be back at the plant anyway, so everything was working just fine – for now.

CHAPTER FORTY-SEVEN

THE YEARS PASSED AND BEFORE anyone realized it nearly two decades had passed. Harry was content with working at the company and paid little or no attention to Irene who maintained an intense relationship with Bob Harkness. She had broached the subject of divorce from time to time but he flatly denied any interest whatsoever. She was his wife and that was the way it was going to stay. He flatly told her that he was giving her no cause or grounds for divorce, and whatever she did was her own business and as far as he was concerned he intended to continue to ignore what he heard of it, if he heard anything at all.

Since Mr. Breitweizer had retired and Harry had been appointed Executive Vice President and General Manager in control of the company his control approached complete and even with his sensitivity to his involvement in the death of Mr. Bender, his control of Charlie Harris and his wife, Ann, by and large gave him autocratic control.

As he lay across the desk mulling over what his next choice of action should be he heard the voice of Gladys Bender outside of his office door saying, "I do not care what he is or what he says, Ann, I am **still** President and Chairman of the Board of this company and Mr. Morgan will not lock doors in **my** company that I want open! So Ann, please unlock the door or I shall have to get a maintenance man to knock it down because I intend to speak to Mr. Morgan, **now**."

Within but a few moments the door was unlocked and Gladys Bender strode into the office and took a chair across from Harry. With her deliberate manner she again smoothed otherwise invisible wrinkles from her dress and said, "Did Irene advise you that I wanted a conference with you? And have you started making arrangements for getting young Alan office space, and the lake cottage set up for Cyd and him until such time as they can find proper housing?"

"Yes, Harry responded, "We called Charlie Harris and he is cleaning out the lake cottage today and it should be ready by this evening. I also understand you want to heavily involve this young man into the management of the company. Is that correct? Haven't I done a good enough job for you over the past twenty-some years? I also understand that you are withdrawing the voting proxies that I had been voting over the past years and that I will have nothing to say at the board of directors meeting. Is that also correct?"

"Yes, Harry you are right on all scores. I will be voting my stock as well as Irene's for the present time, and now that Alan is here I wish to have you train him to take over the company."

"Just like that! Harry retorted. "And what about me and all the years that I put in here? Don't they mean something? Am I just out on my ear?"

"No, Harry, you will be given the option to sign a separation clause which among other things will provide you with what I believe will be a very substantial and comfortable income and future. Regardless, that is the way it is going to be now!"

"Well, it will take a lot more than that to get rid of me. Remember, for all practical purposes I am the only one who knows how this plant runs, and how to run it. No! It's not going to be that easy."

Gladys calmly returned Harry's emotional retort with silence as she opened her purse, and with her gloved hand concealing what she took out until the last minute, said to Harry, "By the way have you ever seen anything that looks like this?"

Harry was thunderstruck! Gladys had placed before him the exact match to the burned Captain's bar which he had coveted these many years since the war in the memory of his beloved Sally.

"Where in the world did you get that? It is the match for the one here in my hand that I've had ever since the war. How could you have found it?"

Gladys laid down the matching Captain's bar and folded her hands across her lap and quietly said to Harry, "Harry, I'll make a bargain with you. When you sign the documents I have for you I will tell you where I acquired that burned Captain's bar and beyond that I will probably further shock you beyond belief once you sign the documents and Ann notarizes them.

"I will tell you at this point; beyond leaving the company you must grant Irene an immediate divorce, which I think you'll be more than anxious to do once I complete the information to you."

"Are you telling me that you know where this Captain's bar came from?"

"At this point, I am not telling you anything, Harry. That I have the Captain's bar should allow you to surmise that there is much more to be divulged at the proper time. All you have to do is sign these documents. But up until then, nothing."

Taking the Captain's bar which was on his desk and the one which Gladys had set beside it, he studied them closely and realized that they were a pair; a match to the one that he had seen and snatched at Graves Registration in London so many, many years ago, Harry said, "Yes, they are a match how did you ever come to find the second one?"

"Sign the documents, Harry."

"Yes, I'll sign the papers." He hastily signed the documents that Gladys set before him; the last two showing only the signature line. One was the total acceptance for a divorce from Irene with no conditions, and the last was a document giving Harry a paid leave of absence of one year after which he would return to the W D Bender Company as President of the W D Bender Company. Then looking to Gladys, he said, "Please where did you find that Captain's bar?"

Gladys leaned back in the chair and said "Harry you are going to have to take this slow and easy because I could hardly believe it when I saw it, myself, but I found this Captain's bar in the jewelry case of young Alan McIntyre. I remembered having seen a similar military ornament in your case behind your desk, and I asked Alan where he got the bar and he said it was all his mother had from what she believed might have been her military service. He said she had no recollection of her service and only having been adopted by Piper Sgt. Ivan McIntyre and his wife, Matilda, and having grown up in Edinburgh Scotland, where he was born and grew up, and lacking one of her own, she took the name of Allie McIntyre, and gave him the name of Alan McIntyre. He said she really did not recall any of her life prior to a massive fire in London. He said she had no identification, only the Captain's bar.

"So, Harry, it appears to me that Alan McIntyre may very well be your son, you will be further pleased to know that his mother—your Sally--still lives--in Scotland. Once you are free of Irene and have completed the training of young Alan I suggest you might direct your attention toward Scotland for your own reasons.

But for now, his attention was set in a new direction. He was already inwardly making plans for the arrival of Alan McIntyre's mother. His beloved Sally.

EPILOGUE

CHAPTER FORTY-EIGHT

AFTER SLIDING THE SIGNED DOCUMENTS across the desk to Gladys, Harry incredulously asked Gladys, "How in the world did you come upon this and tie it all together? I have known Alan for nearly a year over the past two summers that he interned here, and I knew he came from Scotland, but I thought he just had a war-widowed mother. I would never have dreamed that she could have been an American. Are you really sure this is all true, Gladys?"

"I'm practically one hundred percent sure, Harry. From the conversations we have had and what he told me about his mother and this Captain's bar and the match that it has for yours, there is just no room left for speculation. His mother Allie is really your intended Sally that you have spoken of to Irene."

As Harry came to grips with the overall situation he said to Gladys, "You should be in this chair I am in and I should be sitting in the chair you are in. We are really sitting in the wrong chairs you know."

As he got up to switch chairs with Gladys she shook her head and said, "Harry, that is still your chair as long as you are training young Alan. You are still Executive Vice President and General Manager until such time as you believe he is capable. I sincerely believe that your now anxiousness to complete the divorce proceedings with Irene and then to make provisions for your Sally to either come here or for you to go to Edinburgh to get her will serve all of our purposes. However, in your absence I will be taking over this office and it will only be used for board meetings and my own particular purposes. Alan will not use this office in the foreseeable future.

"I think your biggest job at this point in time is trying to figure out how to recognize and deal with the fact that you have a 25-year-old son that you never knew you had before, and frankly to this point does not know that you are his father, either. I have left that up to you, however I will help you wherever I can."

Harry shook his head as he said, "Yeah, this day has certainly gone from one extreme to another without anyone really knowing what's coming up next. Is Alan coming in today? His office space that I had arranged on a temporary basis will be available by tomorrow."

"Harry, I doubt that he will be in for the next couple of days what with getting settled into the lake cottage. What I think would be a good idea would be if you went out to the cottage this evening as sort of a welcoming committee of one, and I will drift in about them and between the two of us we will break upon him your relationships and his need for attentive training so that you can have the appropriate time go to Scotland to bring his mother here."

"Gladys I think you have it right on target. I'll meet you out there about 7 o'clock this evening."

To all's surprise the shock of the evening never occurred. When Harry and Gladys broached the subject of Harry being Alan's father, Alan remarked that when he had worked there before he had seen the burned Captain's bar in Harry's trophy case, and was curious that it so closely matched the one that his mother had given to him before he left to go to school in the United States. However, he had felt that it was improper to question it, but still wondered where it came from. He readily accepted that it had been his mother's other bar and that Harry was his father.

"After all, after 25 years, Alan remarked, "it's pretty nice to find out you have a father somewhere on this earth and particularly someone you know, trust, and respect. I think the biggest job is to get my mother to realize her name is Sally and not Allie and also not McIntyre, although she was always pretty sure it wasn't McIntyre; she just didn't know what it was, and for that matter we still had no idea what it was until you just told me that it was Sally Ann Archer, and that she was from Colorado and that her father was Vic Archer, a high country rancher. This should make an interesting investigation for all of us."

Alan proved to be an apt student and as much as Harry threw his way he seemed to always be willing and able to take on more. Harry brought Charlie Harris in as an assistant to Alan as a positive move and along with Ann Harris, Harry's executive secretary in the outer office they proved to be a remarkable and now happy, team.

Charlie, now free of the pressures that Harry had exerted upon both him and Ann, was coming into his own and rapidly became a top-notch expediter and troubleshooter as well.

Ann was rapidly becoming a complete executive secretary, and looked forward to coming to work each morning because she now felt part of a vibrant organization and because she saw a remarkable social change in Mr. Morgan.

As to Mr. Morgan, his demeanor change was astounding. He and Irene had divorced within two weeks and he took a comfortable room at the hotel. His attitude changed and his willingness to cooperate and work for the general good was self-evident.

Shortly after the divorce Irene and Bob Harkness started being seen together in public and then within a few weeks announce their engagement to be married. They, too, slipped off to Crown Point, Indiana for a hasty marriage ceremony on the way to their honeymoon at Yellowstone Park.

Generally speaking, the Bender Company was running at top efficiency again and Harry was doing his best to restrict his involvement to consultation.

One Thursday afternoon Alan came into the area Harry was using for an office and asked him, "I had a wire from my mother today and she wonders when you're going to come to visit? Or is she going to come here to visit us? How did you like that?

Harry looked up with a big grin and said, "How do you feel about you and I meeting her at the airport in Indianapolis on the day of her choosing as soon as she can work it out? I have been anxious to figure out how to make this step but I think your mother has made it for us. 'Want to go to Indy?"

"I sure do!"

So the following Thursday Cyd, Alan, and a most nervous and anxious Harry were waiting at the Virgin Airline gates.

Alan had suggested that Cyd and he would stay out of sight so that his mother would not see him, and that they would wait to see if Harry recognized her or if by some miracle she would recognize Harry as she debarked from the plane.

As it turned out Harry, standing quite apart from the others, was the first to see a lady of about 5'4" with beautiful auburn hair and just a touch of gray come in from the gate area. In that instance he knew that he was reunited with his Sally. . . And then it struck him; what if she should not recognize him or ever know him? That could be as heartbreaking as all the years they had not been together.

As he slowly walked over to be within her field of vision and glanced at her she saw him and said, "You seem to know me, don't you? Are you with my son Alan? Am I supposed to know you? And yet, somehow I think I do know you". She took Harry's hands and looking at them said, "My, this left hand has really been scarred, hasn't it? Like someone dug their teeth into it a long time ago. Were you in the war? Is that where this happened?"

Harry said, "We can talk about that later on. Yes, we should know one another. We have a lot of ground to cover and I think the fact that we are even together after all of these twenty some years says a lot for how successful we will be in building a life between each other once again. I can tell you Sally that I have missed you every day of my life and I will spend the rest of my life making up for our separation.

"I know you believe your name to be Allie however it is Sally, Sally Archer, and that you come from Colorado and that your father was a high country rancher at the time that you went into service as a U.S. Army nurse, First Lieutenant, and were a Captain when last I saw you. I think this is a good start and I think we can build on this and before long you'll be back feeling as well as you ever have."

CHAPTER FORTY-NINE

A MONTH OR SO HAD passed by and Harry and Sally had found that more than enough common ground had returned and they got married. Harry was ecstatic. Harry loved hanging around the house, and was just getting used to not having anything to do other than helping Sally recall her time in England when the phone rang. It was Irene.

"Are you still at the company, or has Alan taken over completely now?"

"No, I'm out and haven't been down there in a couple of weeks. Why?"

"It's Gladys. She is in no shape to make the big decisions and to run the place as Chairman and GM and she is too proud to admit it, and besides, we have a client out in Frazier, Colorado that really needs to be serviced and I was wondering if you could drop down there and see if you could help Mom out. After all, she had been your 'Ace in the hole' for nearly twenty years."

"Thanks for the tip; I'll see what she will let me do. The trip to Colorado will be useful to us as it may help Sally recall more of her memory if we can see some of the country she grew up in"

Reflections

And that afternoon Harry dropped into Gladys' office asking if there was anything he could do while he and Sally were in Colorado trying to find her father's ranch—which of course was reverse psychology.

Gladys suggested that they might find the time to call on the client in Frazier, Colorado, and that if they could do so the trip could be written off as a company expense. All product information and arrangements were worked out in the next few days, and in the meanwhile Harry made a few production suggestion suggestions that eased the problems that Gladys and Alan were facing. On the following Friday Harry and Sally caught a sleeper out of Indianapolis via Chicago and Denver to Grand Junction, Colorado where they rented a car.

As Sally rode through the mountains she found herself recognizing innumerable features, and once the business at Frazer had been successfully concluded, they decided to drive back to Denver via Rocky Mountain National Park, to catch the train home.

So far nothing really tied in, but as they drove into flatlands west of Granby, preparing to go through Rocky Mountain National Park, Sally exclaimed, "Stop the car, Harry! I know where I am. Drive out toward Hot Sulphur Springs and Kremling. I am sure this is the western range area where my dad used to range cattle. Let's ask around town to see what we can find out."

As they drove along nearly every curve and hillcrest opened a portion of Sally's past for her. Yes, this was where she had grown up around, and now she remembered they had moved in to 'town' before she had entered service, and she was sure it was Granby.

Once they had returned to Granby they went to the police Station and asked if anyone had ever heard of Victor Archer and the Chief responded by saying, "I sure have. He's just about 15 miles down US-14 going east, but he has been a damn recluse ever since his daughter got killed in the war.

But then taking a closer look at Sally and Harry he said, "Jesus Christ, you are Vic's daughter, ain't you. We thought you was dead all these twenty some years. I am going to drive you out to Vic's, myself, because I don't know if he will believe his own eyes. My God how he pined for you, girl! If he ain't at the new ranch he'll be at his places up on Twin Sister's Mountain the other side of Estes Park, and you couldn't find that if you was standing on it. I'll just call in a Deputy and close up here and see that this gets done right."

The Chief insisted that they stop for some hot chocolate and a barbeque at the visitor's center along the drive on Trail Ridge Road through the Park. As for Harry, he was astounded by the hundreds of Elk that he saw along the way through the Park, and even in the Village of Estes Park. These eight hundred pound plus creatures wandered aimlessly about with little regard for people, golfers on the two city golf courses, automobiles, or other animals.

As it was getting late in the day it was fortunate that it was summer and the sun didn't go down until nearly 9:30 p.m. as it was almost 8:30 when they turned off onto Fish Creek Road preparing to climb up to Vic Archer's Cabin off of Little Valley Road.

"By Golly, he damn well better be home and not snorting around somewhere after all we are a'doin getting you all together." The Chief remarked as they pulled into the drive.

"Hey, Vic! Lookie here what I got for here for you. Come on out, you old bear. The Chief turned around with a grin, "You gotta treat him like he was a Bull Elk or a Boar Bear or he don't pay no attention."

A voice came growling down from the deck above starting out, "Jesus, Calvin Oakes, ain't you got nothing better to do than to come clear across the park to bother the hell out of me? Now who you got with you to pester me with?

"Oh, MY God! It's my Girl! I done give her up for gone these twenty some years and now here she is with you and this feller. Get yer asses up here where I can be sure what I'm seeing and where I can get a hold and a hug on her. Sally! Sally, I can't believe it! We all give you up for dead better than twenty years ago when I got this letter from the government with your dog tags in it, and now here you is in my arms. He gave Sally a mighty bear hug and then punched Chief Calvin on the arm saying, "Where in hell did you find her? "

"Vic, I didn't find her. This here feller here brought her in to my office a' looking for you. He claims he is her husband and the story what they got to tell is one you just ain't gonna believe. Now get yer shirt changed and we're all going down to 'The Other Side Restaurant' to have Scott Weibermeier fix us up something to eat, and after that you got room enough for the three of us up here, 'cuz I want to hear the whole of the story and I'm staying overnight and even as long as it takes."

And the telling of the story took all of that evening and the next day, and the next evening, and well into the next day. By its end Sally had pieced together and recovered enough of her memory so she could completely revive her past, and understand the love she had for Harry. After the Chief happily left to go back to Granby, Sally and Harry stayed on with Vic Archer for another month, and each year retuned for long summer vacations in the mountains.

True to his word and agreement with Gladys, Harry returned to Troy and assumed the position of President of the W D Bender Company and completed the training of Alan McIntyre. Within the next few years, with Harry's enthusiastic participation, Harry found complete comfort in retiring and resigning all positions with the W D Bender Company, and accepted an appointment as a Director of the Board and Vice Chairman of the Board. Alan McIntyre took over as President and General Manager. Joe happily remained on his Arizona golf courses, Bob final got his Star a Brigadier General in the Air Force; both of them remained Directors. Gladys retained her position as Chairman of the Board. Once these details had been taken care of, the two of them, Sally and Harry Morgan happily retired to one of the mountain cabins of Vic Archer.

Oh, yes, they did return to England to visit Dr. Avery and Mrs. (Elizabeth Nichols) Martin, his sister Gwen, along with 'Mum' Worsham and Al Keesling who was by then managing 'The Old Spotted Dog Inn'.

But that is another story in itself.

Made in the USA
San Bernardino, CA
09 April 2015